Shape the Future

Lindsay Woodward

ISBN: 978-1-9995855-3-2

For Edna, Roy and Martin
I'll never forget the past

ONE

A horrible sense of dread prickled at my skin as the six words that had just been uttered echoed through my mind. I didn't know what to think.

How had it all gone so wrong? The day had started out really well.

'I bet you've already worked out how many seconds it is,' Scott had said to me that morning as he fiddled with the knot in his tie, determined to perfect it.

'Don't be silly,' I replied, glancing at the clock next to me. It was five twenty-seven in the morning and my head hadn't been able to resist working through the sums.

'You're doing the maths now, aren't you,' he said, grinning at me, flashing his stunning white teeth.

'No,' I giggled.

'How many?'

'I don't know.'

'How many?' He moved over to the bed where I was still snuggled up.

'I don't know.'

'Tell me,' he said, running his hands under the covers, tickling me.

I squealed with laughter. 'It depends what time you'll be

back!'

He tickled me some more.

'After work sometime,' he laughed.

'That's vague.'

'I won't stop until you tell me,' he said before he blew a raspberry on my stomach.

It took me a second to catch my breath, I was laughing so much.

'I haven't worked it out.'

'We both know you have,' he said, now working down to my feet.

'Not my feet! Not my feet!'

'How many?'

'Okay, okay! About four hundred and seventy-five thousand, two hundred seconds,' I said through my giggles.

'I knew it!' he said, backing away from his tickling. He sat on the bed and kissed me. 'My little nerd.'

'Don't call me that!'

'I love you being a nerd. I wouldn't have you any other way.' He kissed me again and my smile broadened. 'So I'll see you in about four... hundred thousand million... whatever you just said, seconds.'

'About four hundred and seventy-five thousand, two hundred seconds.'

'Or five days to everyone else.'

'I'll definitely see you on Wednesday?' I asked as my smile slipped.

'Definitely. Nothing is going to stop me coming back to you. Now get back to sleep.' He kissed me one more time and stood up. 'I love you.'

'Love you too. Travel safely.'

'Will do.'

His infectious smile was the last thing I saw as I pretended to catch his goodbye kisses.

The silence quickly settled around me and that's when I always felt the sadness creep in. It had only been a few minutes and tears were already stinging at my eyes.

It was just five days this time. I'd see him again before I knew it. I took a deep breath and snapped into my positive thinking mode. I told myself that this moment was the longest time until I saw Scott again and every minute that passed from then on was a minute closer to me seeing him. It would get easier, just as it always did.

I rolled over as the first tear escaped. There was nothing I could do about it. It was so hard. He was the first man I'd ever met that I actually wanted to spend all my time with, yet I barely got to see him.

I wanted to tell myself how lucky I was to spend any time with him at all and focus on the many positives that came with being his girlfriend. But when we weren't together I missed him so much it made it impossible to feel upbeat about anything.

I had to pull myself together. It wasn't healthy that a man was affecting me so much.

Even if he was the most amazing man on the planet.

I didn't even know I'd fallen back to sleep, but suddenly my alarm was playing its irritating melody and it was time for me to face the day. I pressed the button to halt the noise and I sat up. It was Friday. I had to be grateful for that.

As I did every morning, I took a second to think of all the things that I had to look forward to that day. I had no clue that in just a few hours my world was going to come crashing down around me. Instead I scanned through the twelve hours ahead of me to remind myself if anything exciting was in store.

I smiled as I recalled that I was seeing Freya at lunchtime. And I had no meetings, so that was something to look forward to as well. I always preferred days where I could bury my head in my computer, uninterrupted.

I followed my normal morning routine of cornflakes and a quick shower, before throwing whatever clothes I could easily find on and straightening my dark blonde shoulder-length hair. By eight o'clock I was ready for action and I departed from my little one bedroom flat in Greenwich.

Life for me was full of routine. Well it had been until Scott had come into my life. Before he'd sent me into a whirlwind, a typical week was going to work, going home, watching telly (normally something sci-fi related) and occasionally visiting the gym. Then at the weekend I'd mix in socialising with friends or going back to Bedford to see my family. I came from a close-knit family and I'd make the trip home as often as I could.

Life with Scott was totally different, though. When he was around we'd do a whole array of fun and interesting things. In the week we'd go out for meals, go to the pub, see a show or go sightseeing, and then if we were blessed with a weekend together he'd take me out of London to breathe in fresh country air. I loved London, but there was nothing like an escape to the country.

It was as if I were black and white Chloe when he wasn't around and then a rainbow of excitement when he was with me.

True to form, at that moment I was very much in black and white Chloe mode. The dark clouds of loneliness, self-pity and dread were definitely hovering directly above me as I made the short walk to the DLR. I joined the train to Canary Wharf, heading to my place of work. I was a Data Analyst for a major financial company. It wasn't the most glamorous of jobs but I happened to be really good at it.

As a kid no one grows up wanting to be a Data Analyst, I'm sure. I wanted to be a Science Teacher just like my mother, until I did my A levels. It was then that I found I had a passion for numbers and I developed the ambition to become an Accountant. However, after completing a degree in Economics at the University of York, I decided that Accountants spend far too much time dealing with people and I changed my mind.

I'd always been far more content sitting in the background doing the clever stuff. I'd never wanted any of the glory. And that's exactly the job I ended up with. I processed information, hidden away at my desk, and I handed it over to the people who did all the talking. It was like the job was made for me.

I arrived at my stop and stepped off the DLR. I was caught in the middle of a swarm of business people heading towards the heart of Canary Wharf. It wasn't far to my building, though, and within ten minutes I'd made it through the horde and up to the fourth floor where my large but unimportant desk sat.

I flicked my computer on, got myself comfortable, and began another data heavy day.

I needed the break by midday. I'd barely moved except for one cup of coffee and a nip to the toilet. But I'd managed to get through the vast majority of the report I'd been working on - which I'd assumed would take me all day - so I felt having a slightly longer lunch might be warranted.

I grabbed my bag and headed to a little bar near the River Thames where Freya had booked a table.

Freya was my best friend and had been since my first week at university. We were so close we'd even moved to London together, although the geography of our jobs meant we weren't able to live together anymore.

That Friday she'd got the day off. Another friend of hers from university, whom I vaguely knew, was coming down to stay with her. They were off to a birthday party at the weekend for someone else that I didn't really know, but Freya always made sure she fitted me in. She was very thoughtful like that.

I stepped in the bar and saw Freya waving at me wildly from the back. I did a little wave in return and I headed in her direction.

'Hi!' Freya said, hugging me tightly as I joined her and her friend. 'How are you? You look great! Is that a new jacket?'

Freya always had to find something complimentary to say. It *was* a new jacket as it happened, but that wasn't the point. She'd find a way to flatter you if you were wearing a bin bag.

'Hi Chloe,' her friend said and I instantly panicked. I knew I'd met her on a few occasions but I couldn't for the life of me remember her name. It was someone from Freya's Sociology course but that's all I could recall. I could feel my cheeks burning as I just stared at her in silence. My ability to talk myself out of situations was very poor. I was a planner; my spontaneous side was non-existent.

'Hi. How are you?' I finally said in return, not only now embarrassed by my lack of memory, but also for the awkward length of time it took me to reply.

'Me and Ange were just talking about the last time we were all together,' Freya said, coming to my rescue. I actually sighed as I took my seat. Her name was Angela. Crisis averted. Thank goodness.

'When was that?' I asked.

'At Kimberley's wedding,' Angela said.

'You were at Kimberley's wedding?' I asked with surprise.

'Yeah, Kimberley's my cousin. Did you not know?'

'No.'

'Chloe was a little distracted at the wedding,' Freya smirked.

'Really?' Angela said, raising an eyebrow.

I couldn't help the smile that broke free as I remembered the night of that wedding. It had been the best night of my life.

'That's the night she met Scott,' Freya informed Angela.

'I need details,' Angela said.

I shook my head. I hated talking about myself.

'What can I get for you lovely ladies?' the waiter said, appearing at the side of our table.

'The duck wrap for me,' I said without even so much as glancing at the menu. I'd wanted it to look like I knew the local eateries and I was a regular, so I'd popped down to review the menu the day before. The truth was I never went out for lunch. Lunchtimes for me normally consisted of a sandwich in the canteen with one of my sci-fi books. I didn't really have any friends at work. In fact, I didn't like many people I worked with at all.

They were all young, eager and hungry for success. They'd smile to each other's faces and then stab each other in the back at the first opportunity that might elevate their status. From day one I'd instantly clocked the fake smiles and pretend friendships and I'd wanted nothing to do with it. I was much happier fading into the wallpaper.

I was good at my job. I knew I was. But I also knew that by not partaking in the game of two-facedness and sucking up, I'd never have a chance of reaching my career potential. It wasn't me, though. I could never "play the game".

I just took comfort in the fact that I got to walk home each day with my head held high. I don't think many of my colleagues could have said the same.

I'd never shared with Freya how bad my working life was. She was a fighter and I knew she'd just encourage me to stand my ground, which was never going to happen. Scott, on the other hand, had understood. It was like he'd known how unhappy I was before I'd even told him. He was the only person I'd ever met that I could truly open up to.

After a bad day, he'd just give me a hug and let me rant. He'd listen without lecturing me on what I needed to do to sort it out. I was never going to sort it out. I'd made my peace with being stuck in a cycle of putting up with it during the day and moaning about it when I got home. That was my life. It was nice to have someone who accepted me just the way I was.

'I'll have the duck wrap too,' Angela said.

'I'll go for the burger,' Freya, the stick insect said.

'Perfect, thank you ladies.'

'How's it going, then?' Freya asked with a beaming grin as the waiter left us. 'You still all loved up?'

'Was he a guest at the wedding?' Angela asked. I could

see her mentally working through the guest list.

I shook my head. 'No, he was working at the hotel.'

'He lives in York?' Angela asked with astonishment, as if long distance relationships were utter madness. The wedding had been in York as that's where Kimberley (another friend from university) lived, so it was a reasonable assumption, but I didn't think it warranted quite that reaction.

'No,' I replied and then I hesitated, realising how much I wish he did just live in York. 'Actually he lives all over the place. He travels a lot for work. He's a hotel consultant. He travels the world visiting lots of different hotels, helping them to improve.'

'Wow,' she replied, still with that edge that told me she thought I was mad for dating someone so out of reach.

'Things are still good though, aren't they?' Freya asked. 'It must be hard with him travelling all the time.'

It had been six months since I'd first met Scott and in that time I hadn't seen him for more than about three days in a row. We could go for two or three weeks without seeing each other, and when he travelled abroad I wouldn't hear from him either. He had such a busy schedule that he didn't even have time to message me.

It had never bothered me, though.

Okay, that wasn't true. Every time he left I felt my heart crack a little.

Scott was the most passionate, exciting and life-affirming person I'd ever met. He made me feel energised and every moment with him was truly wonderful. But that only made the gaping hole he left when he was travelling even larger.

It was one small act of fate six months before that had brought us together.

After the Wedding Breakfast had finished, there had been a huge queue for the ladies toilet at the hotel. Earlier that day I'd spotted a disabled toilet down one of the corridors off reception and I knew other people had been using it, so I made my way there, hoping the queue would be shorter.

To my pleasant surprise there was no one waiting for it at all. It was engaged but at least I was next in line.

I stood patiently outside ready for my turn when I heard a slightly off-key voice singing *Yellow Submarine* from within. It was a cocky and confident man, I could tell, and I instantly knew that whoever he was I really liked him. There was something about him and his singing that exhilarated me.

As the door opened and he stepped out I think my jaw might actually have dropped open. He was gorgeous. He was tall with dark blond hair and twinkling brown eyes, and the second he saw me his face seemed to light up in return.

'Do you like The Beatles?' he asked me. He had a grin that grasped his eyes.

I shrugged, scanning my brain for any Beatles song that I could think of. 'Only eight days a week.' I don't know where it came from, but I couldn't have been happier with my answer.

He laughed. 'I love it!'

He took me in his arms and danced with me up and down the corridor. I don't think I'd ever felt so thrilled.

After a final twirl, he kissed me on the cheek and walked away, flashing his enchanting smile at me one more time. It took me a few moments to compose myself.

Thankfully, that wasn't the last I saw of him. Not an hour later he caught up with me outside as I was grabbing some fresh air, and then before I knew it we were kissing passionately, deep within the sculptured grounds of the hotel.

I had never had a one night stand and it was most unlike me to invite a man into my room without me knowing him very well first. But there was something about Scott that intoxicated me, and I could see quite clearly he felt exactly the same way in return.

He had to get up early the next morning to sort out the breakfast staff, but we swapped numbers and texted solidly for the next couple of days, before he came to see me in London.

'Earth to Chloe.' I glanced at Freya who was waiting expectantly for me to answer her question.

'It's going really well,' I replied, blushing again. I'm sure I never used to daydream before I met Scott. 'We're taking things slowly. A day at a time.' It was a conscious lie. I was very aware of how I actually wanted to give up my job, marry Scott and follow him all over the world. There was nothing slow about our desperate passion for one another. But I couldn't admit that to Freya. I hated admitting it to myself. It was far too overwhelming. Every time I started to think about how I'd met what I could only describe as my soulmate, it would bring tears to my eyes. It devastated me how delicate the whole relationship was. He didn't even have a proper address. He lived from his suitcase in hotels across the world. He was far from a stable man.

But we loved each other. Surely that would make it work eventually? It was all I could cling on to and anything else was blanked from my mind.

'Sounds sensible,' Freya nodded. 'I suppose just enjoy it for now and see where it goes. Don't put your heart too much into it. I don't want to see you get hurt. These long distance things rarely work out.'

I smiled and nodded as if I was feeling very casual about the whole thing, but her words struck me sharply like a knife cutting into my heart.

'Do you have a picture?' Angela asked.

'Erm, yeah,' I nodded, as if I might be able to find one somewhere, not letting on that I'd got about five hundred. As I didn't get to see Scott very often, I made sure I took pictures at every opportunity.

I grabbed my phone from my bag and quickly flicked through to find a really good one.

'Here,' I said, finding one of him in a park taken a couple of weeks before at our weekend away in Canterbury. He was dressed smartly in jeans and a black jumper, standing next to a swan. He'd been pretending to have a philosophical debate with the swan and I'd been in stitches.

Angela took my phone from me to get a better look. She instantly turned pale.

'Is everything all right?' I asked.

'He's your boyfriend?' she checked with trepidation.

'Yes,' I replied as my heart started to thump.

'Oh.' She placed the phone down on the table.

'What is it?' Freya asked.

'Nothing. He looks nice.'

'Ange!' Freya nudged. 'There's something the matter. You have to tell us.'

'It's just... Well... I know him. I've met him loads of times.'

'You've met Scott?' I asked.

'I'm so sorry, Chloe,' Angela said. Something about her tone made my mouth go dry.

'You met him at the wedding?' I asked, trying to find some logic.

She stared at me saying nothing and I couldn't breathe.

'You must have met him at the wedding,' Freya encouraged. 'At the hotel.'

Angela shook her head. 'He doesn't work in hotels. He's not a hotel consultant. He works in sales. Computers or something like that.'

I didn't know how to respond. It seemed ridiculous. Why would he lie?

'And he's dating my cousin Donna.'

TWO

There they were. Those six words.

I didn't know what to do with myself. It was like my brain had shut down and all I was aware of was a mounting ache in the pit of my stomach.

'No, you must have that wrong. Are you sure?' Freya said, freeing the words that I should have been saying myself.

'It definitely looks like him,' Angela replied. 'And his name's Scott.'

'It's possible you've made a mistake, though?' Freya nudged.

Angela opened her mouth but nothing came out. She looked down at my phone again; at the picture of Scott grinning inanely next to that stupid swan.

She shook her head. 'It's definitely him. I'm so sorry.'

It was then that the sickening horror ripped through me. I had to use all of my strength just to stop myself from crying.

'I know he's with her this weekend,' Angela said, quite softly. 'It's Donna's birthday. He's definitely there. You could go up to Harrogate and see for yourself.'

I wanted to sink into the earth and disappear. Scott was

in Newcastle, not Harrogate. He'd said he was going to Newcastle to help a hotel up there. He couldn't be in Harrogate.

'Who's having the burger?' the waiter asked, carrying two plates of food. Freya took charge and made sure we all got our meals but I couldn't do anything. All I could do was stare at the table and hope that I might wake up. It couldn't be true. This couldn't be happening. Scott was my soulmate. He couldn't be cheating on me.

My duck wrap appeared before me and I wanted to throw up.

'Is that why he was at the wedding?' I muttered. I had to know something more.

'What do you mean?' Angela replied.

'Was he her plus one or something?'

Angela shook her head as her face crumpled. 'That's where they met.'

'He met her at the wedding?' I almost shouted. My brain darted through the events of that night. 'But I was with him all night. Like *all* night.' I was speaking with unusual force. I was so desperate to find any way that she could be wrong.

Angela shook her head. 'When I said they met at the wedding... It's... They met at breakfast the next morning.'

'No, but...' I was thumped in the chest with a severe blow. This time it really hurt.

'Did you come down for breakfast?' Freya asked. I could see her trying to recall what had happened the next morning.

I shook my head. My eyes were stinging so badly now. The tears were there, teetering on the edge. 'No. I was tired. I overslept.'

The truth was far too painful to utter. After our lustful night together, Scott had insisted that he was going to look after me. He arranged for me to have breakfast in bed. It was all paid for and taken care of, I just had to wait for its arrival.

Had he really been getting me out the way so he could chat up another woman? Who would plan for that? It was absurd. It was cruel.

It was also not like him at all. I'd never thought of him as anything other than sincere. Could he really be living a double life? Could he really be that heartless?

'Why was he at the hotel?' I asked, desperate for something to make sense.

'He was staying at the hotel for work,' Angela replied very carefully. 'He lives in Darlington but travels all over for his job. Like I said, in sales. They met over the scrambled eggs or something like that. He's a bit of a charmer, isn't he.'

'But he doesn't have a northern accent!' I argued back, as if this proved absolutely that Angela was wrong about everything.

'He's not from Darlington. I think Donna said he's from Bedford, or somewhere down south.'

I took a deep breath to control myself. That was where I was from. I grew up in Bedford. It was where all my family lived. Why would he say Bedford? He'd told me he'd moved around a lot as a kid. He'd never said a word about Bedford.

He'd clearly told me loads of crap.

I pushed my untouched food away. My stomach was doing somersaults and all I could focus on was not crying.

'I have to get back to work,' I said with a quivering lip.

'Are you going to be all right?' Freya asked. 'I'm so sorry, Chlo. You need to speak to him. Promise me you'll speak to him. I'm sure there's a reasonable explanation. Maybe he's got a twin?'

All I could manage was a nod. I stood up and Freya jumped to her feet. She hugged me warmly. I could have done without it to be honest. It just made me want to cry even more.

'Nice to see you again,' I said to Angela who was looking up at me with deep pity.

'You too.'

'Call me soon,' Freya said. I tried to smile and then I left as quickly as I could.

The first thing I did as I stepped outside was text my

boss to say a migraine had developed over lunch and I was heading straight home. I rarely called in sick so I knew there wouldn't be too many questions.

A couple of uncontrollable tears escaped as I made my way back on the DLR to Greenwich, but I somehow managed to mainly keep it together.

The second I got home, I headed straight to my bed and I cried into my pillow in a way that I'd never cried before. I had never felt so sad, hurt and helpless.

Hours passed and I did nothing but sob and drink wine in an attempt to numb the deep, agonising heartbreak.

By five o'clock, I'd changed into my pyjamas and I was sitting up in bed. It had started to go dark outside on what had been an unusually warm mid-October day. I hadn't turned the lights on in the flat. It was just me, my red wine, a box of tissues and nothingness.

It had dawned on me during my heartfelt sob that it wasn't as clear cut as Scott was cheating on me. I was actually his bit on the side. We weren't even in a proper relationship.

I'd been dating Scott – if you could call it that – for six months but he'd not met any of my friends or family. He'd always insisted that we spend the little time we had together getting to know each other, just the two of us. However, with this new excruciating hindsight, I could see that what he'd actually been doing was avoiding meeting anyone that I was connected to.

I'd convinced myself that it was sweet of him to not want to share a minute of our time with anyone else, but in reality he'd just been using me as his fling.

Had he intended to use me from the start? Or had I put him off when we first slept together that night at the hotel in York?

Was I really that bad in bed? Or maybe I was really good in bed but he didn't like my personality?

But then that didn't make any sense either. We didn't get much time together, but the time we did spend together was varied. We would go out and see places. We'd spend hours awake just talking and getting to know each other. We had incredible sexual chemistry, I can't deny it, but it was just one part of what made us work.

I gulped down more of my wine as I reminded myself that we weren't working. Nothing was working.

The room lit up as a notification flashed on my phone. I glanced over expecting it to be yet another text from Freya checking up on me or my mum asking another question about how her latest app should work.

I nearly spilt my wine all over me as I saw it was a text from Scott. I swiftly placed my glass down on my bedside table as I picked up my phone. My hands were shaking and my heart was beating so loudly it was almost echoing around the tiny, sparsely furnished room.

How's your day been Pepper Pot? It's been warm up north today but the temperature's dropped now. Wish you were here so we could snuggle up together. There's a crackling fire by me but it's nowhere near as enticing without you. Love you. xxxxxxxxx

The tears were racing down my face before I'd even got to *Pot*. He'd started calling me "Pepper Pot" after we'd spent a rather drunken hot and stormy evening together in the summer listening to *Sgt. Pepper's Lonely Heart Club Band*. I'd known the odd song from The Beatles, but Scott was a mega fan. He knew so much about them and when he talked about the band it made me feel like I was living back in the sixties and enjoying them for the first time with everyone else.

I don't know how he ended up being such a huge fan. He never liked to talk about his past. He'd told me he was orphaned and had no family whatsoever, and as he travelled so much friends had apparently been hard to keep.

What a load of crap he'd fed me. It seemed so obvious as I sat there with my wine, but at the time I'd felt sorry for him and I'd believed every word he'd said.

What was I supposed to do with that message? How could he say he wanted to snuggle up with me when he was with his girlfriend? His actual girlfriend that he shared a life with. A girlfriend where he'd met her friends and family.

I read the message again and again and slowly I started to calm down. There was nothing in his words that suggested he was lying. There was just nothing to give me any doubt that he loved me.

My brain snapped into gear.

I had no evidence. All I had was Angela's word and there could be a hundred reasons as to why she was lying or she'd got it all wrong. I'd just taken her word for it. I hadn't got any evidence.

I had to study the facts.

For a fleeting second I considered travelling up to Harrogate. I'd have to wait until the morning when I was sober, but I could do it. I could get the train from Kings Cross, like the first one that left in the morning. Then I could see for myself.

I gulped down more of my wine as my heart started to throb at the idea of it. It could give me the answers I needed. But it could also backfire badly.

I calculated that there could be only two possible outcomes: 1) I'd catch him with this Donna and be stuck utterly heartbroken in a place where I knew no one else, miles from home, and I wouldn't know what to do, or 2) Angela had got it all wrong and I'd have travelled all the way up north to find out that I don't trust the man I love, who I very much did trust twelve hours before.

I sighed. Freya was right. I just needed to ask him.

But what if he lied? He would hardly be likely to tell me the truth all of a sudden after creating such a web of lies.

But maybe I'd be able to tell something from his response. What, I had no clue, but something maybe?

I placed my wine down again and I studied my phone. All I had to do was ask him. Tell him what Angela had said and ask him what was going on.

Wish I was with you too. I've had a very long and hard day so having an early night. Speak soon. x

I'd typed it and had pressed send before I could even think about it. It was all I could do. If I was going to get any answers from him then it had to be in person. Text honesty was never going to work.

Besides, there was a very small part of me that was worried he might just never show up again if he found out that I knew the truth. I at least wanted to see him one more time.

The next few days were agonising. Scott had sent me numerous texts, and he was growing increasingly worried by my short responses. We normally waffled on to each other for ages, but all I could tell him was that I wasn't feeling very well and having regular early nights.

It was almost the truth.

I'd watched back to back chick flicks through most of the weekend thanks to Amazon Prime, the majority of which I'd never seen before. I'd always been more of a sci-fi sort of girl.

I'd introduced Scott to many of my favourite sci-fi films. He wasn't really a big film lover, but he'd always been very willing to spend hours viewing back to back movies with me. Another reason why chick flicks had been far more appealing. We never watched chick flicks together.

After surviving the weekend, Monday and Tuesday had then both dragged on, and I'd been unusually unproductive at work. Not one of my colleagues had noticed my sad silence. Although, to be fair, I barely spoke on a good day. I was the quiet, solid worker who avoided attention like the plague and no one expected anything more from me.

By the time Wednesday finally came around, I couldn't have been feeling lower.

Scott had texted me before I'd even left for work to say

he'd be at my house no later than seven pm and he was going to look after me as I hadn't seemed myself. His concern just made me even more confused and sad. Everything he did told me that he loved me except for the fact that he had a secret girlfriend in Harrogate. Although she wasn't the secret one, I was.

The more I thought about his behaviour through that Wednesday, the angrier I became. As it grew ever closer to the moment that I'd actually have to face him and find out what the hell was going on, my rage was increasingly replacing the sorrow.

It was good. I needed to feel that way. I needed to shout at him and make him see how much he'd hurt me.

I buried my head in my work that day and left bang on half past five. I got home with ease and I sat in my living room in silence, waiting for his arrival. It was all I could think about. Soon I was to get my answers. It was time for the truth.

At ten to seven I heard the buzzer go. This was it. I stood up, shaking, and I walked over to let him in.

THREE

'Pepper Pot, are you okay?' Scott said the second he saw me. He placed his suitcase down and stroked my cheek gently. The concern was evident in his eyes. He was genuinely worried about me.

I stayed silent. I didn't know what to say.

'You haven't seemed yourself at all. I've been really worried about you. It sounds like you're suffering from exhaustion. You're not depressed are you?'

He waited for my answer but all I could do was stare at him blankly.

He kissed me tenderly on the lips and then wrapped his warm arms around me. Every problem I had normally melted away when I was in his embrace, but this time it was different. It was making my head spin.

Since Angela had broken the bad news, I'd progressively built up Scott in my head as evil. I had it that he was clearly a two-timing bastard with about as much depth as a puddle. But if that was really the case then why could I feel his love for me? It surely wasn't possible for anyone to fake such concern. It wasn't just evident on his face, but in his arms, his tone, his touch. It all felt so real.

I backed away from him and headed towards the living

room in my tiny but modern one bedroom flat. I didn't know what to do with myself, and I was well aware that I was still yet to say a single word to him. But how could I phrase the question 'are you really cheating on me?' after a hug like that?

'Pepper, what is it?' he asked, following me. 'Please talk to me. You know you can talk to me.'

I sighed as I sat down on my sofa, feeling the weight of my misery upon me. He was right: we did always talk about everything. Although the ratio of our voices being heard was normally eighty percent him and twenty percent me, I still always knew that he was ready to listen.

I liked him talking. Before I'd met him I'd always preferred peace and quiet and I'd always hated talking about myself. But everything was different with Scott. I automatically opened up to him in a way I'd never been able to before, and occasionally he'd sit down quietly and watch the telly with me. We complemented each other perfectly.

So why did he have to go and mess it up!

'You look awful,' he said. 'Is it work? Friends? Family? What is it, Pepps?'

I couldn't look at him.

'Right, first things first, I'm getting you a glass of wine. You look like you could do with a glass of wine.' He disappeared off and returned a moment later with his suitcase. He unzipped it and pulled out a bottle of red wine that he'd wrapped up in his jeans for protection.

'Why did you need your jeans if you were away on business?' I asked, as if I'd laid the perfect trap for him.

He looked across at me, confused. 'I don't work twenty-four hours a day.' He paused for thought. 'Do you mean you'd like me to leave clothes here? Is that what this is about?'

I couldn't find any words to respond. It was the last thing I'd expected him to say. A flash of serious contemplation crossed his face before he said very quietly, 'I'd love to do that.'

I stood up with frustration. That suggested a more serious commitment. Why would he say that if I was only a fling?

I needed to ask him. I needed to ask him! But I was terrified of the answer. I was also terrified that he'd lie to me. I was terrified of every possible outcome as absolutely nothing good could come from that one simple question.

I grabbed the wine from his hand and stomped off into the kitchen.

'Have I done something to upset you?' he asked, following me into my immaculate kitchen.

I unscrewed the top and grabbed two wine glasses from my cupboard.

'What makes you say that?' I replied.

'I don't know, perhaps the fact that you've barely said a word to me via text or in person since I left here last Friday. It's more than you're just feeling ill, isn't it. I can see that quite clearly.'

I stared down at the kitchen surface. I had to ask him, but the words just wouldn't form. It was too hard. It could mean the end of the best few months of my life and the whole idea gutted me.

If only I had some evidence. At least then I could have a proper conversation with him. At least then I would know whether he was lying to me or not.

I suddenly sneezed. I always did when I was tired. It was like my body's way of waking me up or something. I glared at Scott, challenging him not to laugh. He always said I sounded like a horse when I sneezed, and it had been a running joke between us. I will admit my sneezes were a bit peculiar, but now was not the time for a laugh. If he made fun of me like normal, I knew I would either slap him or cry. His jest was always good hearted, but things were too delicate for him to be his regular, jovial self.

I could see his lips begin to curl into a smirk, when his phone rang. He grabbed it from his trouser pocket. 'Sorry, Pepps, work call.'

He nipped off into the living room and my jealousy raged. It was Donna, I was sure of it. I quickly sloshed the wine into the glasses and then dashed into the living room to join him.

'No, it's... I'm really busy at the minute,' he said. He saw me and smiled awkwardly. He was listening intently to whoever was speaking to him. Did he really look awkward or was I just imagining it? This was hell.

'I've got to go... I know... You know. You know I do,' he continued. 'I'm catching the flight first thing tomorrow. No, Heathrow... No, that's ridiculous. Look, I've got to go. Fine. Bye. Yes. Bye.'

He hung up and sighed. 'Sorry,' he said. 'This hotel I was with today are a bit needy. There's so much more work to do, but... If I had my way things would be very different, believe me.'

I was standing in the middle of the room still holding the glasses of wine and all I could look at was his phone. I couldn't escape the fear that he was cheating on me but I needed evidence before I could go any further. His phone would give me that evidence.

As much as I hated to admit that I was about to snoop into his private, personal things, I had no choice. Angela had been so convinced and I needed to know the truth. Not a truth that he may or may not give me, but the real truth that couldn't be denied.

I took a deep breath and quickly made an action plan. It was poorly thought through but I was desperate.

'You look more stressed than I feel,' I said in a breezy way as I handed him the wine. 'Sorry if I've seemed a bit off. Work's been crazy and it's been getting me down. You know what I need right now: I need some quality time with my gorgeous boyfriend. Why don't you go and grab a shower after all that travelling, and then we can get a take-away and relax? What do you say?'

He hesitated. 'Are you sure it's just work?'

'Of course. Boring work stuff. It's best for me to forget

about it and enjoy my time with you.'

'You know you can talk to me.'

'I know. Later. I've been fretting far too much for days now, it's time I relaxed. Go on, get in the shower. You know where the towels are.'

'I don't like to hear that you've been worrying about anything for days.'

'It's just stupid stuff. Usual work crap. Please, just go. By the time you're out I'll be back to my old self.'

'Are you sure?'

'Will you just go!'

'Okay.' He placed his wine down on the coffee table before kissing me and smacking me playfully on the bum. I found a way to giggle as he headed off to the bathroom.

My smile dropped the second he was out of sight. He was such a good kisser. Why did I have to adore him so much? It made everything I was about to do all the more difficult and all the more important.

I heard the shower turn on and I followed him into the bathroom. As always, he'd dumped his clothes on the floor and I knew that his phone was in his pocket.

'I'm just going to take your clothes into the bedroom,' I said. 'I always worry you'll get them soaked.'

'Decide what take-away you want,' he replied as he grabbed the shower gel. He never minded using my girly stuff. He was very easy going. 'Let's get it ordered ASAP.'

'Okay, I'll have a think.'

I raced into the bedroom, my heart thumping. I grabbed his phone from his pocket and awkwardly dumped his clothes on the bed.

I heard him start to sing. He was always singing to himself. It wasn't just a thing he did in disabled toilets. The vast majority of time it was something by The Beatles, but occasionally he'd burst out with these really weird songs that I'd never heard of, like he'd made them up himself. He was so funny. He was so lovable.

He was so confusing.

I stared down at his phone in my hand. I had to know the truth.

The phone flashed up asking me for the PIN. I'd seen him type it in dozens of times. Surely I must have absorbed the code somewhere along the line.

I couldn't recall anything, though. My mind had gone blank and I was getting jittery with how little time I had. My trembling fingers were poised over the keypad but I didn't even know where to begin.

Something hit my foot. I looked down to see his watch resting against my toes. His trousers were half hanging off the bed from where I'd plonked them and it must have fallen out of his pocket.

I tossed his phone on to the bed and picked up the black device. It told the time digitally, right in the middle of the screen, but it was surrounded by a mountain of other information: facts, figures and symbols that I'd never seen before.

Straight away I surmised that it must have been one of those fancy watches that were like iPads around your wrist.

I pressed a few buttons hoping to find his email or some messages, but all I got were graphs and symbols that meant nothing to me.

Knowing time was running out, I pressed everything I could. Surely there had to be some sort of evidence that he really was cheating on me.

I heard the shower turn off and my breathing quickened. My thumbs were bouncing off the buttons now, I had just seconds left to get the truth. But all I was getting were more meaningless symbols.

'So what are we eating?' Scott called, breaking off from *A Hard Day's Night* for just a second.

'Just thinking,' I called back as my heartbeat doubled in intensity.

I fiddled some more, leaving no icon untouched. Something had to work. There had to be something. There had to be something that could tell me what was going on!

Everything went black. It was like someone had switched the lights of the world off. Scott's singing had also stopped and I was left in pitch black, eerily silent nothingness.

Had I fallen off the earth into space?

I didn't dare move. What had happened?

'Are you there?' a muffled voice said. It definitely wasn't Scott's voice.

I stood still, holding my breath, utterly petrified. What was going on?

Light appeared and I could see that a door before me had opened. A man stood in front of me sporting a crisp white shirt. He looked shocked.

'Who the hell are you?' he asked.

FOUR

I stood stock still, grasping Scott's watch so tightly in my hand that I almost crushed it.

'Who are you and what are you doing in there?' the man asked again, very sternly. He was tall and toned like an athlete.

I glanced behind him and could see quite clearly that I wasn't at home anymore. It was a strangely purple room with just two chairs that sat behind what appeared to be two TV screens. The screens were sort of balancing somehow on what I could only describe as rather sturdy slinkies. I'd never seen anything like it.

'You need to tell me what you're doing in there.'

'What's going on?' a male voice asked. A young, slim man appeared as if from nowhere.

'Call the Superintendent,' the first man ordered.

'Who is she?' the young man asked, shocked.

'Archie, just call the Superintendent.'

Archie turned away from me for just a second as he pressed his ear. I could tell he was muttering something but I couldn't make out what it was.

I was too scared to even tremble. My body had completely frozen and I was struggling to breathe.

All I could think of was that Scott's fancy watch must be fitted with some sort of hallucinogenic button that sent people off on a weird trip. I had pressed just about everything on it. It seemed the only logical explanation.

'What's going on?' a female voice demanded to know from somewhere in the room. Both men just continued to stare at me, their eyes not moving from my immobile frame.

The lady appeared before me. She was also strikingly tall. She was wearing an immaculate dark blue suit that had official looking emblems on each shoulder.

'Who is this?' she asked.

'I have no idea,' the older of the men replied. 'I expected it to be Inspector Lacey but when I opened the door she was there.'

My immobility was broken with a gasp. Lacey was Scott's surname. They had to be talking about Scott. But inspector? Like a hotel inspector? Sales people certainly weren't called inspectors. I would have felt a glimmer of hope except for the terrifying randomness of everything else that was happening.

'How did you get here?' the lady asked me.

I wanted to respond but I didn't even know where to start. Instead I found myself just staring at her, not so much as blinking for fear of what might happen next.

'She hasn't said a word,' the man said.

The lady looked me up and down as if she was somehow processing me.

'Where is Inspector Lacey?' she asked me. She was very commanding and I suddenly felt more scared not to answer.

'In the shower,' I muttered.

The most awkward silence I've ever experienced followed my statement.

I brought Scott's watch around from behind my back to show them. I found myself praying that if I gave them the watch then they might just magic me back home again and I could forget any of this had ever happened.

'You stole it?' the lady snapped.

I shook my head quickly and a dread crackled through me. 'It fell out of his pocket.'

'You stupid girl,' she scowled at me. I swear her piercing eyes could have drilled a hole right through me. I instinctively mumbled an apology.

She swiped Scott's watch out of my hand. 'Get her to room six. We need to sort this out. Now. I'm going to have to tell Seb.'

She marched off and the older man stepped before me. He regarded me with curiosity and his demeanour seemed to soften. 'Can I ask you to take two steps out of the module, please,' he said.

I scanned the pitch black box around me that was apparently called a module. I wasn't sure whether I wanted to leave or not. But I knew I was in no position to argue.

I needed a second to find the strength to move. Slowly I sort of wobbled forward and the full extent of the purple room was revealed. Not that there was much else to see. Apart from four more black boxes identical to the one I'd been in and the weird floaty TV screens, the room was empty.

'Are you going to follow me or do I need to constrain you?' the man asked.

I shook my head and my legs nearly buckled below me. The trembling was now in full force. 'I'll follow you,' I stuttered in reply, trying to work out whether I was actually a prisoner now because they thought I'd stolen Scott's watch. I wanted to declare my innocence but words were too hard to form. I'd never felt further out of my depth.

He led the way and we stepped into a sombre green corridor. 'This way,' he said. I followed him for about a minute, through a couple of doors and past lots of rooms that were either painted in a pastel green or a baby blue colour.

'Here we are,' he said, opening a door. Inside there were just three chairs, two directly opposite the other one. The room was a steely grey colour and not at all welcoming.

'Please take a seat,' he said, pointing directly to the chair that sat alone.

I did as I was told. I was immediately surprised to find that the chair felt like wood although it looked exactly like plastic.

The man shut the door and I was left alone. I sat patiently, expecting something to happen. But nothing did. Nothing happened at all for what seemed like an age.

Finally the door opened and another man entered. He was wearing a similar blue suit to the lady I'd met earlier - sporting the official emblems on each shoulder - and he was also incredibly tall. Where was I?

He took a seat and sat for a moment just staring at me. It was very uncomfortable. I looked to the floor, but I could feel his eyes burning into me.

'What's your name?' he asked in a firm voice.

'Chloe Noble,' I meekly replied, looking up at him.

'Can you tell me how it is you came to possess the CPG?'

I glared at him blankly, completely lost.

He bent his head down slightly as if he was listening to someone before he addressed me again very directly.

'Do you know what a CPG is?' he asked.

I shook my head.

'It's an item like a watch. Do you follow me now?'

I nodded my head.

'We know it's Inspector Lacey's CPG, but what we don't know is why it's in your possession and not his.'

'I'm sorry,' I said. My voice was shaking. 'It fell out of his pocket. I just picked it up for a second and then everything went black.'

The man shook his head and tutted.

'Is he a hotel inspector?' I asked. The second the question came out of my mouth I felt like a complete idiot. I don't even know what made me ask it. I just wanted something to make sense.

'A hotel inspector?' the man said, as if he couldn't quite believe what he'd heard. 'What on earth is a hotel inspector?'

'Like the TV programme,' I muttered.

The man studied me hard. 'Do you know where you are?'

I shook my head.

He sighed. 'I've never known anything like this happen before. This is going to cause us a lot of issues. You're going to have to stay here until we can sort this out.'

He stood up promptly. 'Can we get you something to eat? Perhaps a drink?'

My head was spinning again. Was I a prisoner? What was going on? These people clearly worked with Scott but this was a far cry from anything I'd expected. I was too confused to even figure out whether he'd lied to me or not.

I wanted to ask but I was just too terrified. I fixed my eyes on his but no words would form.

'We'll get you a sandwich and a drink. Okay?'

I pushed a small smile on to my lips. 'Thank you.'

He nodded before disappearing through the door.

I sat in silence again, waiting and waiting, until finally another suited man appeared with a sandwich and a glass of water. He was well-built with floppy brown hair and a pleasant face. He handed me the plate and my eyes widened at the thinly sliced bread that barely covered the mounds of vegetables. I'd never seen a sandwich quite like it.

He watched me carefully for a moment and I could tell he wanted to say something, but then he just smiled in a sorrowful manner and left.

I nibbled at my sandwich full of peppers, courgettes and aubergines, and I sipped at my water. It must have killed a good fifteen minutes, although I had no way of actually knowing. I never wore a watch and my phone was back in my flat.

All I could do was stare at the chairs and the walls and wait.

And I waited and I waited and I waited.

I think time might have eventually halted. I'd even

stopped caring about where I was or what I was doing there. I just wanted the torture to end. I'd walked around to stretch my legs about fourteen times and I'd counted backwards from one thousand twice. That had been a highlight.

A small break from the boredom came when I felt the urge to use the toilet. I sat back and pondered how much of a prisoner I really was. Would I be allowed to use the toilet?

After much internal debate, I eventually decided that not allowing me to use the facilities would be going against my basic human rights. No matter who they were they had to accept nature.

I stood up bravely and I stepped towards the door. I tapped lightly a few times, my courage dwindling with every tap. 'Excuse me,' I said nervously, 'would it be possible for me to use the toilet?'

Nothing happened. I waited in silence deciding how long I should give it before I knocked again, when finally the door opened. It was the same man that had brought me the sandwich.

'Come on.' I followed him just a few paces down the corridor to another door. 'There you go,' he said, pointing to it.

I opened the door and stepped in to a navy blue room. It was light enough to see what I was doing, but it was strangely dark compared to everywhere else. Even my little prison was brighter.

I stepped into a cubicle and locked the door when suddenly a squeaking sound made me jump. It was coming from behind me. I turned and saw that the toilet seat had started to move. It was circling itself around. The only logic I could come up with was that it was cleaning itself for me. It was very bizarre. Polite, but bizarre.

When it finally finished its carousel, I stepped forward with trepidation. Could I use it now?

I swiftly unzipped my trousers and finished my business as quickly as humanly possible. I stood up again ready to exit when I realised that there was no flush.

I scanned every inch of the toilet and the wall behind it but there was nothing for me to press.

I didn't know what to do and I found myself waving around the cubicle, hoping that a sensor might be hidden somewhere. Finally the toilet flushed and the squeaky self-cleaning carousel started all over again. I don't know which part of my wave had worked but I was relieved. I didn't want to have to ask the sandwich man.

I scurried out of the cubicle expecting to find a sink but all I could see were two silver boxes.

Following my earlier success, I waved my hands around with hope again, when a splodge of something wet landed in my palm.

I sniffed the white goo and it smelt gorgeous; like lavender. It must have been soap, although I had no clue how it managed to land perfectly in the centre of my palm.

I rubbed my hands together and then dreaded what was coming next. I needed water but there wasn't a tap in sight.

I hesitantly waved my hands under one of the silver boxes. It seemed the most likely source. And sure enough just as my hands were in the right place, water neatly poured over them, the excess of which was caught in what looked like a smart drainage system below. I hadn't even spotted it before. It was almost camouflaged against the floor.

As if the silver box could read my thoughts, the second all the soap was gone and I was thinking about a hand dryer, a single blast of hot air shot across my hands. They were instantly dry. Not blown dry, but instantly dry, as if the hot air had somehow eradicated the water instead of evaporating it.

I slowly moved my hands away and I stood still. Was that it? That was all I needed to do, but the whole experience had been so strange I wasn't sure if any further surprises might be awaiting me.

After a few seconds, I carefully backed away and exited.

The sandwich man was waiting for me outside and he promptly led me back to my prison. I wanted to discuss my experience with him. Were the male toilets the same? Did he even know that the toilet seats in the ladies cleaned themselves?

I didn't say a word, though. Instead I obediently sat back down in my prison and I let the toilet experience run through my head. I went over it a few times, making sure that I would be ready should I need to go again. It was also a welcome distraction, giving me something else to think about; keeping the boredom at bay.

'Where is she? You can't keep her locked up like that!'

I woke up with a start. My neck was sore from where my head had flopped to the side. I hadn't even known I'd fallen asleep.

'Where is she?' That was Scott's voice! He was here. Finally an end to the hell was in sight.

The door flew open and Scott paced in. 'There you are! Are you okay?' I wanted to run and hug him but something told me this wasn't the time nor place.

'I'm fine,' I nodded. 'What's going on? Please tell me what's going on.' For the first time since I'd appeared in that place, I felt the urge to cry. I'd been terrified before but not upset. Seeing Scott had somehow broken me down, though.

Tears started trickling down my cheeks and I realised that they could be related to a number of emotions, not just fear or relief. Betrayal was definitely high on the list.

'What are you doing?' the man who'd interviewed me asked as he appeared next to Scott. I'd always thought of Scott as tall, but he was just about average in this weird tall person universe. It was so peculiar.

'How long has she been locked up in here for?' Scott demanded to know.

'What else were we supposed to do? She turned up in the module with your CPG. For all we knew she was a threat.'

'She's not a threat.'

'Civilians don't tend to know how to use a CPG.'

Scott looked at me. I'd never seen that expression on his face before. It was grave and full of sorrow.

'She's Donna's friend. She was at the party and I was driving her back home; keeping in the good books.'

Nausea slapped itself on top of my ever-increasing emotional pile as the name Donna echoed across the room.

I had my evidence. He did know Donna. It also appeared that everyone else did too. And no one knew who I was. I was just his bit on the side that he had to lie about.

'I don't even know how to start dealing with this,' the man stated.

'There's no harm done,' Scott countered.

'No harm done? Look at her. Besides, I want to know why you were more than two hundred miles away from your target.'

'I told you-'

'You're lucky I'm not suspending you.' The man cut off Scott with controlled anger. 'It's only because we're already stretched that you're being allowed to carry on.'

'This is wildly unnecessary,' Scott bit back. I'd never seen him so serious. 'There will be no collateral damage.'

'There already is. It's a disaster, Scott.'

'We can just get her back home and I'll straighten it all out.'

'You know that's impossible. We had to pull funding from the Bradbury project to get you back and that's all the spare resource I had. We're too busy and we can't get any extra funding until next year. You know that.'

'I'll take her back. On my CPG.'

'You're not due back for three weeks.'

'But-'

'Inspector Lacey, I'm warning you. None of this is your call anymore.'

Scott exhaled sharply. Both men glared at each other fiercely, their steaming tempers clashing against the icy chill that emanated from the tension.

'You'll need to give her a room,' Scott stated, trying not

to look like he was backing down. 'It's not her fault.'

'Fine. Sergeant Jasper can arrange that. You and I are going straight to my office. I need answers, Scott. We need to get this sorted before Earl finds out.'

'You want to do it now?' Scott asked with disbelief.

'You've left me with no choice.'

'But it's three hundred.'

'And unless we do some damage control, by eight hundred Earl will be hearing all about this. We need to sort this and we need to do it now.'

Scott looked beaten, but I became fixated on the numbers. Had Scott meant three hundred hours, as in three o'clock in the morning?

I sighed as if the realisation had made me even more exhausted. I really had been trapped in that room for hours.

Suddenly I sneezed. It was my usual horse-like sneeze and probably my body's way of jolting me awake.

Scott turned to me but there was no sign of humour. I think it was the first time ever that he'd let my comical sneeze go by without at least smiling.

'All right,' Scott said, turning back to the man. 'Can I just have a minute first, though? At least she knows me.'

Nobody moved as the man contemplated Scott's question. 'Need to know, Scott,' was his reply in a severe tone.

'I understand protocol.'

'Do you?'

More fierce glares were exchanged before the man marched off, letting the door slam shut behind him.

Just Scott and I were left and I became strangely nervous. I knew the body before me but it was obvious I had no clue about the man inside.

'What's going on?' I asked, perhaps more desperately than I intended. 'What are they talking about? Are you really a hotel inspector?' I knew he couldn't be a hotel inspector. I knew he'd lied. I just didn't know what else to say.

He took the seat opposite me. He hung his head,

thinking through his answer, but I didn't want to give him time to lie even more.

'Who's Donna?' I quickly added. 'Are you cheating on me?'

This made him sit up. 'You can't say a word to anyone about how we know each other,' he whispered. 'Things are not as they seem. I know you must be really confused right now-'

'That doesn't even come close to how I feel.'

Scott sighed. 'I know you must be questioning how much you can trust me right now, but I swear I have always had your best interests at heart. Always. You have to trust me. Keep your head down, speak to no one other than me, and I'll do everything I can to get you home as soon as humanly possible. But please, don't say a word to anyone about anything. You could cost us both so much.'

The door opened again before I could even think about what to say in return. 'We've got a room ready,' the sandwich man said. I took a guess that he was Sergeant Jasper.

'Dom here is going to take you somewhere more comfortable. Just get some rest and we'll get this sorted in no time,' Scott told me.

'You want me to go with him?' I asked Scott.

'Yes. Dom will look after you. Won't you, Dom?'

'Yes sir.'

Sir? I tried to catch Scott's eyes. I wanted to see his reaction to this formality, but instead I was taken aback by how crushed he looked. I had never seen Scott so distressed.

As confused and as betrayed as I felt, I knew I had to put my trust in him. I had to listen to him. I didn't understand one thing that was going on but I knew I had to stay quiet. As much as I was finding it very hard to believe a single word that was coming out of Scott's mouth, I still loved him.

I decided that until I had the faintest idea what was happening, I would keep my mouth shut. Scott might be cheating on me but I could also see that things were far from straightforward. I grasped on to the small silver lining that at least I knew more now than I had that morning. Maybe there might be a positive ending somewhere along the line. It was the smallest speck of hope, but I needed something to keep me going.

'I'll source you some clothes for the morning,' Dom said as he opened the door for me. 'Don't worry. Everything's going to be fine.'

I took one last glance at Scott. His head was now buried in his hands and he was hunched over in clear anguish.

I felt a prickle across my skin as my hope vanished. I knew in that instant that everything was going to be far from fine.

FIVE

Dom led me down multiple green corridors until we reached a rather grand set of double doors. He pulled one of the heavy doors open and behind it appeared a different world.

The walls were maroon and homely, and my feet nestled into a soft, velvety carpet. We walked up some warm, shallow steps and I was faced with yet another long corridor, but it was like I'd been transported into a five star luxury hotel. The corridor had rooms either side and the lighting was dim and comforting.

We stopped at the third door on the left. It had "Seventeen" written on it in beautiful italic lettering.

'Look at me,' Dom said. I did as requested and he quickly flashed something into my eyes. He fiddled with a tiny black box and then asked me for my full name.

'Chloe Noble,' I replied and he fiddled around some more.

'You're all set.'

'Thank you,' I muttered, not really sure what I was all set for. He looked at me expectantly but I had no clue what he wanted me to do.

'Oh,' he sighed with a smile, as if the penny had just

dropped. 'Right. Look into that light there.' He pointed to the left of the door where there was a small red light at just about my head height. I stared directly at it and the door clicked open.

'Is that some sort of iris scanner?' I asked.

'Yes, well done,' Dom replied in what I first thought was a rather patronising tone, but when the smile didn't leave his lips I began to think he was being genuine. I'd obviously been unexpectedly perceptive and I allowed myself a moment of smugness.

He gestured for me to step in and I stuck my head around the door expecting the luxury to continue, but I was instantly disappointed.

It was a magnolia room with nothing in it but a bed, a bedside table and a wardrobe. To the right there was a little door that I assumed led off to the bathroom but the excitement ended there.

'Make yourself comfortable. I'll leave some clothes outside so you have something to wear when you get up. I'll be back at ten hundred to collect you for breakfast. Does that sound okay?'

'Am I a prisoner?' I asked him. I had a right to know that at least. Scott hadn't exactly been forthcoming with details.

He smiled sweetly. 'No. But it's really important you follow all of our rules. For your own sake.'

'When can I go home?'

'I'm not sure.'

I wanted to ask more. I wanted to ask why I couldn't go home and why I was being kept there even though I wasn't a prisoner. I had a string of questions, but Scott's words tugged at me. I had to keep quiet.

'When will I see Scott again?' I asked, realising that he was my only hope of getting any answers.

'Again, I'm not sure. Tomorrow probably.'

'Okay. Thank you.'

'Get some rest, Miss Noble. Goodnight.'

'Goodnight.'

Dom closed the door behind him and I sat down on the firm bed.

I took a deep breath and tried to make sense of everything.

With the uniforms and the Sergeant, Inspector and Superintendent, it was definitely like some sort of police station. But not one I'd ever seen before. Actually, not that I'd ever seen a police station in real life before, but I'd seen dozens of them on television. And they were never like this.

I shuddered as it dawned on me that maybe Dom had lied. Maybe this was a high end prison cell. It wasn't exactly like *Prison Break* but maybe female prisons were different. How was I supposed to know?

I swiftly stood up and tried to open the door. It opened with ease. I could come and go as I pleased. At least that confirmed I definitely wasn't a prisoner.

For a second I considered just leaving, but then I quickly decided against it. Firstly, the place was like a maze. And even though my door wasn't locked, if I was in sort some of weird police station, I wasn't going to be able to get outside without difficulty.

Then I admitted the truth. For the past five days I had toiled with wanting to know what was really going on with Scott and now I was closer than ever to getting answers. If I just played this out for a little while longer then I might find out everything I needed to know, and I wanted that more than anything.

But at least I knew I had the option to leave, should all of this get too much. That gave me some peace of mind.

I closed the door and headed to bed.

I tossed and turned through most of the night. It hadn't been a restful sleep. On top of everything else that was plaguing my thoughts, I was worried sick about my job. It was now Thursday morning and I had effectively just disappeared. I really needed to get to work. What was my boss going to say? How could I possibly explain my absence?

There was a little, rather fancy digital clock on the bedside table that I'd been glancing at through most of the night. When it got to nine am I decided it was futile trying to sleep any more and I got up. I still felt dreadfully tired, but I wanted to get the day over with.

I'd slept in my clothes and I was hoping that Dom had done as he'd said. I poked my head outside to find a neatly wrapped brown paper parcel waiting for me.

I brought it into my room and tore the paper away. It revealed white underwear, two white shirts, two white pairs of trousers and some white cotton pyjamas.

I had a quick shower using the complimentary toiletries and then put the ever so slightly baggy clothes on. I stood in front of the mirrored wardrobe to view myself. I looked like some sort of clinical janitor. I couldn't believe that Scott was going to have to see me like this. I looked really stupid.

It was only half past nine and so I sat on the bed and tried to ponder more on where I was, how I'd managed to appear there and why I was being kept there. All I could think about, though, was Donna. Scott had another girlfriend. Scott had a proper girlfriend.

Did I actually mean anything to him?

I loved him so much. We had incredible chemistry and I know we brought the best out in each other. How could he do this?

Before I knew it, there was a knock at the door. I looked at the clock and saw it was bang on ten am.

I opened the door to find Dom there, all smartly suited up.

'Good morning Miss Noble. Are you hungry?' he asked.

'I could eat,' I replied with a shrug. In truth I felt quite sick but I knew I should eat something.

'Good. Follow me.'

'Where are we going?'

'To our food hall. Canteen you might call it.'

'Okay.'

I closed the door to my room and followed Dom back the way we'd come the night before.

'I'm sorry, but is there any way that I could contact my work?' I asked. 'I was supposed to be at my desk in Canary Wharf an hour ago. I really need to speak to someone.'

Dom glanced at me. 'I believe Inspector Lacey is taking care of logistics.'

'Logistics?' I virtually snapped. 'What does that mean? I should at least be able to contact my work to let them know I'm okay.'

Dom stopped walking and I instantly shut my mouth. The tiredness and stress must have been getting to me as I rarely spoke to anyone in that tone.

'I'm just following orders, Miss Noble,' he explained quite calmly. 'Inspector Lacey will catch up with you today, I'm sure. It's probably best to speak to him about such matters. I don't know what else to say.'

I nodded. What else could I do? The only real option I had was to wait for Scott and then demand some answers.

Dom carried on walking and I followed him back through the large double doors and down multiple green corridors again. Finally we stepped in to a very white room that was filled with dozens of tables and a large buffet bar at the back. It was exactly like any canteen I'd seen before.

'Please, help yourself to anything you want. I've credited your account with an unlimited amount.'

'Account?' I asked.

'Of course,' Dom smiled, as if again the penny had dropped. 'Go and choose whatever food you want and meet me at the end.'

'I can have any food?'

'Anything you like. And as much as you like.'

I hesitantly walked to the start of the line and collected my immaculately clean tray. As with the chairs, it looked like plastic but felt like wood.

I picked up a tub that had cornflakes in it and I poured a few into a bowl. Next to it was a jug of milk and I splashed a bit on top of my cereal. Moving on there was a display of fresh fruit and I grabbed an orange, apple and banana, followed by a Danish pastry from the less healthy adjacent section. Despite the fact that I hadn't been feeling very hungry, I couldn't stop putting food on my tray.

At the next station I stopped. There was a machine emblazoned with a picture of a steaming cup of coffee but there were no buttons for me to operate it.

I started waving my hands around, seeing if it was powered like the strange toilets, when Dom came over to help.

'What is it you require?' he asked. I swear he was stifling a smirk.

'A strong black coffee,' I replied, feeling quite embarrassed.

The machine gurgled and out popped a proper ceramic cup with strong black coffee in it.

'Smart,' I remarked, coyly.

'Are you all done?' he asked.

'Yes,' I nodded, looking down at the mountain of food I'd piled up. I didn't know how I was going to eat it all.

'Come over here,' he said. He led me to the wall at the end of the buffet bar where a red light could be found, just like the one next to the door of my room. 'Look into the light.'

I did as requested and it flickered twice.

'Right, you're all done.'

'That's it? What was that for?' I asked.

Dom hesitated. 'Just checking off that you've had breakfast.'

I nodded, but I wasn't quite sure what I'd just achieved.

'Please, sit anywhere you like and I'll return in one hour to take you back to your room.'

'Can I see Scott then?' I asked.

Dom stood still. 'I don't know.'

'Maybe?' I said with hope.

'See you in an hour.' Dom walked off and I felt deflated.

I chose a chair near the back of the room. There were loads of tables free and it was serenely quiet. I sat virtually alone and slowly ate my food, forcing it down more through boredom than anything else. I was starting to really miss my phone.

I helped myself to another coffee and orange juice, making sure to look at the light at the end, just in case I needed to, and I waited for Dom to return.

Exactly one hour after the moment he'd left, Dom escorted me back to my room. He informed me that Scott was in a meeting and he'd get a message to him that I wanted to see him as soon as possible. It didn't make me feel any better, but I could tell Dom was doing all that he could.

I reluctantly entered my room again where I sat with absolutely nothing to do.

I thought that maybe sleeping would pass the time, but all I could manage was a light doze in between the bouts of panic about what I was doing there and what was going to happen.

The knock on my door at precisely one o'clock was a welcome break from the torment and I once again followed Dom, this time for lunch. I piled my plate up with sandwiches, pasta and salad and I nibbled my way slowly through it all before I was promptly escorted back to the boredom one hour later.

I lay in bed, staring at the ceiling, going through my cycle of dozing and panicking all over again, before I was taken for dinner at bang on seven o'clock.

There was still no news about Scott. He was apparently still in his meeting. On top of the boredom and panic, the feelings of rejection and neglect were now burdening me as well. The only bit of salvation I could grasp on to was that at least being an emotional wreck gave me something to do.

I lay back on my bed at just after eight o'clock feeling very full. I'd eaten enough over the day to feed a small village and I'd slept so much that I was becoming twitchy and uncomfortable.

I stared at the ceiling, continuing my search for bumps and marks across the seemingly flawless paintwork, when once again my mind decided to torture me. This time it conjured up images of Scott and Donna.

I recalled pictures of the wedding and wondered if Donna had been in any of them. What was she like? Why was she better than me?

I instinctively reached out my hands to grab my phone. I wanted to text Freya to ask for her opinion, but the emptiness of the room quickly reminded me that I hadn't got it with me.

I was utterly lost without my phone. I bet I had dozens of messages off Freya and my mum. I wondered how long they'd give it before raising the alarm that I was missing.

Just as I was starting to imagine how I'd explain what had happened, I heard a soft tap at my door.

Was it supper time? I couldn't face the thought of eating ever again.

I rolled off the bed and waddled towards the door. I opened it slowly, deciding what to say to Dom, when relief instantly washed over me.

At last.

'I'm sorry,' Scott said, standing before me.

<h1 style="text-align:center">SIX</h1>

He stepped in swiftly as if he didn't want to be seen. He was still wearing the same jeans and shirt that he'd been wearing at three o'clock that morning and he looked absolutely shattered.

'I'm so sorry, Pepps,' he said touching my cheek. 'Are you okay? Has Sergeant Jasper been looking after you?'

'What's going on? When can I go home?'

Scott hugged me and I had every intention of pushing him away. Deep inside I was so angry with him.

But the superficial outer layer of me quickly surrendered to his enchanting scent. I didn't know how he could look so haggard and still smell so fresh.

He kissed me softly on the lips before staring deeply into my eyes. His gaze was so heartfelt and real it immediately snapped me back to reality. I knew for a fact there was insincerity in him and I wasn't going to fall for his convincing façade anymore.

'What's going on, Scott?' I asked firmly, taking a deliberate step away from him.

He took a deep breath. He was obviously trying to think up more lies and I didn't want to give him the chance.

'What was that watch?' I asked. 'How could I just appear

in some box? Where am I? Is this a police station? Are you a policeman? No one around here will give me any answers. You have to tell me what's going on.'

'All right, all right,' Scott sighed. 'Come and sit down.'

'I want to know.'

'I'll tell you. Just come and sit down.'

Scott sat on the bed and gestured for me to join him. I stood still, determined to stand my ground. But then I realised that he wasn't going to talk until I sat next to him, and all that mattered was getting answers.

I joined him on the bed, making a point of leaving a gap between us.

'You're right,' he said. 'This is some form of a police station. It's a bit different to what you may be familiar with, but we definitely deal with law and order.'

'Why did you tell me you worked in hotels?'

Scott shook his head. 'Because I had to.' He paused and I let him find his words, although the more he hesitated the less I was inclined to believe him. 'I'll tell you what I can. That's all I can do. Basically...' Again he paused and I could see him searching his brain for what to say. 'I work undercover. It needs to be secret. I couldn't tell you. Do you see?'

'You're an undercover policeman?' I asked, incredulously.

Scott hesitated. 'Yes.'

'Come on,' I argued, shaking my head.

'Think about it, Pepps.'

I rolled my eyes before realising that it actually made perfect sense. I was so ready not to believe him, but it did fit together all the confusing parts of him very neatly.

'Does Donna know?' The question just blurted out of my mouth. 'Am I your bit on the side?' It was the conversation I'd been dreading but suddenly the words were very easy to form.

'What?' He looked genuinely shocked but I told myself not to believe it. 'No,' he said softly. 'Not at all. I love you,

Chloe. You have to know that. Forget what I said to Seb. You don't need to worry about that.'

'Angela said you'd been dating Donna since Kimberley's wedding. Why would she think that if it wasn't true?'

'Who's Angela?'

'Donna's cousin.'

It was like a shadow of frustration darkened Scott's face. He shook his head and exhaled sharply. 'Shit. Shit!'

'What?'

He lowered his voice. 'Donna is not my girlfriend. She's the girl I've been investigating. Okay? I'm posing as her boyfriend. But for my job. Undercover. It's not real.'

That was the last thing I'd expected him to say.

'I should have known there'd be a connection. Shit!'

'Is Donna a criminal?' I asked, eagerly. I couldn't deny that a part of me really wanted her to be.

'I can't say. I shouldn't have even told you that much. But you need to know that you're the only one I love. Can't you see how hard this is? I should have been with Donna and I've been sneaking off to see you. I could lose my job if they found out. Or worse.'

'You're allowed a personal life, surely.'

Scott shook his head. 'It's a lot more complicated than that. But I can't tell you. I really wish I could, but I can't.'

I scanned his face. It was impossible not to believe him. As ludicrous as it was that my boyfriend was an undercover policeman working for a secret law and order organisation, it actually made everything slot into place.

A startling fear stabbed me in the heart.

'Have you slept with Donna? What does "posing as her boyfriend" actually mean?'

'Of course I haven't! How immoral would that be?'

I felt a wave of relief.

'Posing as her boyfriend is one thing, but we have a strict code of ethics.'

'You've kissed her?' I asked as my jealousy raged at the idea of him being someone else's boyfriend. Even if it was just pretend.

Scott regarded me with sad eyes. 'I had to, Pepps. I'm so sorry. It meant nothing. It was like acting. Think of me as an actor just playing a part. Every minute that I'm with her, I'm thinking of you.'

'How is that okay in your code of ethics?'

'It's only a kiss. I have to do something to convince her I like her. And when you look at the big picture, it's definitely worth it.'

'What does that mean?'

He touched my cheek again, stroking it gently with his thumb. 'I was assigned to meet Donna at the hotel and work my way into her life,' he said softly. 'I'd gone to the disabled toilet to keep out the way while I scanned the area and got some intel. You were never meant to be standing outside. But when I saw you there and you humoured my singing and love of The Beatles, I felt... You made me feel alive. You made me feel things I never knew I could.

'I saw you go outside to get some fresh air and I couldn't resist getting to know you better. I only meant to say hi and enjoy a fleeting moment of me being me, but I... I fell in love with you then and there. You're an incredible woman and I've treasured every single second we've spent together.'

I was speechless. As much as my head was screaming at me to think carefully and not just immediately trust him, my heart believed every single word.

'I shouldn't have done it, though,' Scott added. 'You were a distraction and I hadn't covered my bases. As you lived in London and didn't know Donna, I assumed I could get away with it. It's not like me to be so sloppy.' Scott turned away from me and I was jolted with sudden panic. Was he saying it was a mistake meeting me?

'I love you. We love each other. That's important.'

Scott moved in closer and I could feel his breath. 'I don't know what's going to happen. I hadn't planned any of this and I don't know what to do now. But whatever happens, know that I love you. Deeply. There isn't one inch of me that doesn't want you.'

He kissed me passionately. Within seconds he'd pushed me down on the bed and our hands were all over each other.

He drew out my lustful side like no one I'd ever met. I'd had two boyfriends before him and neither of them had had an effect on me even close to how Scott intoxicated me. I thought I'd been in love twice before but Scott gave the word "love" a whole new meaning.

He backed away from me abruptly. 'I'm sorry. I can't.'

'What? Why?'

'If we get caught...'

He buttoned his shirt and stood up.

I edged off the bed and stood up next to him.

'What about if you take me back home?' I asked. 'We'd be properly alone in my flat.'

He looked at me blankly and I couldn't tell what he was thinking. 'I have a meeting with Seb tomorrow morning. I'll let you know then. I promise, I'll get you home as soon as I can. There's just a lot of red tape to go through when strange girls turn up at a secure facility unannounced.'

'You still haven't told me, how exactly did I manage to just turn up unannounced?' Scott smiled as if the answer was obvious. 'It was like some sort of teleport,' I rationalised. 'Do you teleport?' My eyes widened as I began to think through the possibility. 'Is this a secret government teleportation place that allows you to drop in undercover?'

Scott chuckled. 'You watch far too much sci-fi. I'm sure if you get a good night's sleep it will all become clear. You've been through a lot. Get some rest and I'll speak to Seb in the morning. This will all be sorted in no time.'

His response threw me. Had I been imagining things? Maybe I'd passed out? I had been stressed. But then-

'Seb's the man you met yesterday,' Scott explained, cutting through my thoughts. 'I think he interviewed you. He's our Chief-Superintendent. Giving you answers and deciding when you can go home, it's his call.'

'Then who's Earl?'

Scott hesitated. 'He's the man above Seb, the one ultimately in charge.'

'Are you in trouble?'

'No. It's all fine. Don't worry.'

'I was just looking at your watch. It fell on the floor.'

'It's fine. It's more my fault than yours.'

'Then I just sort of appeared in that box. Was I drugged? I might have knocked a couple of buttons. Is it an anti-theft thing?'

I could see Scott trying not to smirk. 'Nobody has drugged you. I can promise you that. I know it can seem confusing, but get a good night's sleep and I'm sure you'll see things more clearly in the morning.'

'Can I go home tomorrow?'

'As soon as I speak to Seb then we can get this all straightened out.'

'Haven't you been speaking with him all day?'

'As I said, there's a lot of red tape to go through. This is a very secure facility.'

'Is that why I've been left trapped in this room?'

I could see Scott didn't know what to say, but the regret and sympathy was evident in his eyes.

'It's so boring!' I told him. 'Could I at least get a TV? Or a radio? I'm going out of my mind.'

Scott shifted awkwardly. 'I'll see what I can do. I'll ask Dom to source some appropriate entertainment.'

I screwed up my face. What was "appropriate entertainment" meant to mean? It sounded like he was going to get me some sort of educational toy. Just as I was about to ask, a more important question jumped in my head.

'Can I call my work? They'll be wondering what I am doing. I didn't turn up today. I've just disappeared. And then I need to let Freya and my parents know I'm all right too.'

Scott kissed my forehead. 'Everything is taken care of.'

'What does that mean? What have you done?'

'We work with the government. You have nothing to

worry about.'

'Did you speak to my boss? What did you tell him?'

A cheeky grin spread across Scott's face. 'That you're the most beautiful girl in the world and you're spending a few days in bed with me.'

I couldn't help but smile. 'I would love to have been a fly on the wall during that conversation!'

'Stop worrying. Everything is going to be fine. I'm taking care of it. Just get some rest. Think of it as official time-out.'

'This isn't exactly like a holiday.'

He kissed me one more time. 'I have to go. I'll come and find you tomorrow. Sit tight, this will all be over with soon.'

Before I could say anything else he was blowing a kiss to me at the door and he was gone.

SEVEN

I didn't sleep well again that night. The bed was comfortable enough but I was a jumbled mess. I spent the night flitting between delight at how much Scott loved me, concern about my job and my family - and what Scott had really said to my boss - and fear as I still didn't know why I was being held in a weird police station.

By the time Dom knocked on the door at precisely nine am I was pacing around anxiously in a desperate need to get away from the world's most boring four walls and my agonising carousel of thoughts.

'Morning,' I said as I whipped open the door.

'Good morning, Miss Noble,' Dom replied, all suited up in his blue uniform.

He led me down the corridors towards the canteen.

'Did Scott speak to you last night?' I enquired. 'He said he was going to ask you to get me a television. Or anything really to ease the boredom.'

Dom stopped walking. 'He told you I'd source you a television?' From his expression you'd think I'd asked for the deeds of Buckingham Palace.

I hesitated. 'Well I asked for a telly and he said you'd source me some "appropriate entertainment".'

'Oh yes.' There it was: that nod again like he'd just understood what was going on, although I was starting to feel increasingly out of the loop. 'I'm sure I can find something suitable. Leave it with me this morning.'

Suitable? Appropriate? Everything in this world felt a tad patronising.

I carried on following Dom and he dropped me off at the canteen telling me he'd be back in one hour. And I knew it would be exactly sixty minutes, not a second more. He took punctuality to a whole new level.

The canteen was far busier than it had been the day before. I had to queue up, but it didn't take long before I was grabbing my cornflakes, fruit and the biggest pastry I could find. The boredom was definitely making me hungry and the food was actually really tasty.

After I'd looked in the light for reasons that I still couldn't fathom, I scanned the room to locate a good place to sit. I could see a few spare seats at a table near the door.

I placed my tray down and took a seat at the quiet end of the table. At the other end there were a couple of women who must have been about my age. They were chatting about how the coffee had changed and the new supplier was nowhere near as good. I thought it was a great cup of coffee, especially from a machine. The coffee before must have been fantastic.

'Morning,' another girl said, sitting down opposite them. She too was about the same age with long light brown hair and a pointy face.

'What is that smile about?' one of the women asked her.

'We've just had the night,' the pointy faced girl said with bags of enthusiasm. I almost expected her to say she'd won the lottery she was so excited. 'It's finally really happening.'

'You're joking?'

'All that back and forth and not really knowing, but last night was totally different. We spent the whole night together.'

'We're definitely talking about Scott, right?'

I almost choked on my cornflakes. I placed my spoon down, eager to hear more. I glared ahead of me, pretending not to be listening, pretending that I was interested in the antics of the canteen.

'You slept together?' the excitable girl was asked.

'All night long. I can feel it finally happening. This is the start of something really special. It's been a difficult ride, but so worth the wait.'

I wanted to cry. My insides were like a crazy flurry of fluster and panic, but all I could do was sit still and endure it.

I took a deep breath and forced myself to get a grip. Scott was a really common name and there must have been hundreds of people working in the building. I had to stop being so dramatic.

'I'm so pleased for you, Leanne.' So her name was Leanne. The pointy girl who was starting something special with a man called Scott was called Leanne. 'To be honest, we were starting to think he wasn't interested.'

'Tell me about it,' Leanne stated. 'But this job he's on has really changed him. I don't know what it is with this Donna, but ever since he started that assignment he's been totally different. It's like he's realised what matters in life.'

I felt sick. I pushed my cornflakes away as the truth began to sink in. Could it really be my Scott they were talking about? How many people could be called Scott and working with someone called Donna?

I looked around. Just in the canteen alone there must have been a hundred people, and I'd passed dozens more. There was every chance that another man called Scott was working with a woman called Donna. There just had to be.

'So it's proper true love?' Leanne was asked.

She paused. I studied my hands. I couldn't look at her face, although something told me she wasn't shaking her head.

'You know we've always loved each other,' she said earnestly. 'It's only because we work together that he's been cautious. But last night he kept talking about how things were going to change. He seemed so different. He seemed more intense.'

'Scott? Intense?'

'Ooh, what if he proposes?' the other woman asked with a small shriek. 'We'd have our first work wedding. Can I be a bridesmaid?'

'Don't get me excited!' Leanne giggled. 'Mrs Inspector Lacey, how about that?'

It was like someone had punched me in the stomach. The world around me went very quiet as everything dropped into place. I fought hard to control my tears. I wanted to get away but I couldn't. I was stuck in that canteen with no friends and no escape.

I closed my eyes and everything became crystal clear. All the bothersome questions and niggles disappeared as the startling truth detonated before me.

It wasn't that he was sneaking off to see me when he should have been with Donna that Scott was worried about. It was that he was sneaking off to see me when he should have been with Leanne.

I was nothing more than a distraction. When we were at my flat, that was pretend. It was an escape for him. A bit of fun from what must be a stressful life.

Here and now - the surroundings I found myself in - that was his reality. Leanne was his real girlfriend. These people knew him far better than I ever could as they knew the real him.

The only Scott I knew was whatever he'd told me. Most of which was clearly a load of crap.

I glanced over at Leanne's beaming face. She looked thrilled.

A small tear ran down my cheek and I quickly wiped it away. I had to keep control. I would have hours to sob my heart out in about fifty minutes' time, but for now I had to keep it together.

I took a few deep breaths and I clenched every muscle,

desperately trying to keep the tears at bay.

What had I been thinking? As if in reality a love like ours could exist. It was all a fantasy.

I got to meet a man who seemed perfect because he was pretending to be perfect. He'd probably been trained to be the perfect man. He could have his way with me and no one else would ever know. It must have been great fun for him. Until I happened upon his watch.

His watch! So much for sleeping on it. I still didn't have any answers as to how I'd just magically appeared in that stupid box.

'Long time no see,' I heard Leanne purr and it yanked me from my thoughts. I looked up to see Scott standing next to our table. I nearly fell off my chair.

He was dressed in the standard blue uniform. He looked gorgeous. He re-defined the word sexy.

Tears threatened to fall again and my heart started to pound through a horrible concoction of emotions.

I took a very long, deep breath. I had to get through this. I just had to find a way.

'Leanne,' he nodded awkwardly. His eyes glanced desperately between me and Leanne and it gave me all the answers I needed. You could have choked on the tension.

I couldn't take my eyes off him as Leanne's words echoed round my head. He'd left my room last night to go and visit another woman. A woman he'd then spent the night with. The woman that he was actually going to be with as she was his real girlfriend. In his real life.

He took a seat opposite me as I felt on the verge of collapsing. This was all far too much emotion for breakfast.

'I'd better dash,' Leanne said, standing up. She flashed a huge smile in Scott's direction. 'Catch you later?'

'Yeah,' Scott nodded in reply but he was keeping his eyes firmly on me.

'Can I go home now?' I asked, before gripping my lips together so he couldn't see them quivering.

'There's a complication,' he replied without a flinch to

his face.

'What do you mean complication?'

'Seb's agreed to let me tell you more. Tell you the truth. Whenever you've finished your breakfast.'

'I've finished. Tell me,' I replied without taking a breath.

'You've barely even started,' Scott said, scanning his eyes across my untouched food.

'I don't want it. I just want to go home.'

'Are you okay? Did you not sleep well? You look tired.' How did he do it? His face seemed so full of love and concern. It made me sick.

'What's the truth?' I asked, more spikily than I intended. 'The truth?'

'You said Seb had agreed to tell me the truth.'

'We need to go to his office. Are you ready?'

'Just tell me.'

'You need to follow me.'

I reluctantly stood up and followed Scott. He led me down the green corridors for a few minutes until we reached a glass door that had "Chief-Superintendent Wiley" etched on it. At least I guessed it was etched. It actually looked more like the words had formed part of the glass.

Scott opened the door and inside there were four chairs surrounding a virtually floating monitor. It was again delicately balanced on what looked exactly like a slinky.

'Miss Noble, how are you?' Seb asked, standing to greet me.

'I'm okay. Can I go home now?' The urge to cry was subsiding as the desperation to get away took control.

'I take it Inspector Lacey hasn't informed you yet of the situation?'

'I told you I'd wait,' Scott stated.

'What situation?' I asked. I sensed I wasn't in that office to hear good news.

'I'm afraid, Miss Noble, that we aren't going to be able to send you home for another three weeks,' Seb said.

'Three weeks?' I gasped. 'You can't keep me here for

three weeks. What have I done? I have rights!' I could feel my body starting to shake through panic. This nightmare just kept getting worse and worse.

'That's why I told Seb we needed to tell you the truth,' Scott explained. 'We couldn't keep you here that long without it having an impact and without you understanding.'

'For the record, I'm not happy with you receiving this information, Miss Noble,' Seb said. 'But I can see how you not being told will make life very difficult for all of us. Even though we shouldn't be in this difficult situation in the first place.' Seb flashed Scott a stern look, but Scott let it wash over him.

'I think you'd better sit down,' Scott said.

I hesitated. I didn't know if I could move. I felt such a wreck. But maybe sitting down would be better. I didn't know how much longer my shaking legs could support me.

I took a few steady steps forward, hoping that Scott and Seb wouldn't see me wobbling, and I slowly sat on the seat closest to me.

Scott took the seat next to me and Seb returned to his seat opposite. Both of their eyes were fixated on me like they'd set a timer on me and they were waiting for the explosion.

'I wasn't lying last night when I told you my work relates to law and order,' Scott finally began. 'We're very much an extension of the police force you'd be familiar with.'

I watched Scott. Even though I could tell he was deeply uncomfortable, he was still sitting up straight and speaking confidently; all with such an air of authority. He was a remarkable man.

For a two-timing shit-bag, that is.

'We do very important work,' he continued. 'Work that is essentially saving lives. Millions of lives.'

I glanced behind Scott's head as a picture caught my attention. It said "Changing the Past to Shape the Future" and there were photos of lots of happy people. It was like some sort of propaganda.

Scott took a breath. He turned to Seb, but Seb remained very still, clearly not in any mood to support his Inspector.

'I don't know how to say this and make you believe me,' Scott said. I watched him struggling for words until finally I almost witnessed the metaphorical light bulb spark above his head. He reached into his pocket and pulled out a gadget. It was some sort of black box, similar to what Dom had had. He fiddled with it for a moment and a screen lit up.

'Tell me what it says,' he instructed.

I took the little box from his fingers. The screen looked very much like a driving licence. It had Scott's picture, address, date of birth. I glanced angrily as I realised that he did live in Bedford. How could he not tell me that when I'm from Bedford? I moved on to check his age. I was eager to see what else he'd lied about. But it wasn't reading right.

'Your date of birth is all messed up,' I said, handing the box back to him. 'It's got confused with your expiry date or something. Why are you showing me fake stuff? Why can't you just be honest with me?'

Scott shook his head slowly. 'I am being honest. My date of birth is correct.'

I screwed up my face as I studied the image once more. 'It says you were born in 2053. The 14th May, 2053. That's got to be your expiry date.'

'No,' Scott stated. 'I *was* born in 2053. And I'm thirty-three years old.'

'What?' I asked. I turned to Seb for support, but his face was deadly serious. 'That would mean you're living in 2086.' I shook my head. 'What are you playing at?'

'This is 2086,' Scott said.

That did it. I had no words left. What was I supposed to say to that?

'We're a form of law and order that travels back in time, preventing people from making costly mistakes,' Scott explained. 'We effectively rehabilitate people before they commit a crime, thereby saving lives and creating a better world.'

I glanced again at the framed picture on the wall. I didn't know what to think. It had to be a joke.

'Miss Noble,' Seb added, 'you've managed to transport yourself forward to the future. It is 2086. Everything Scott's saying is true. Now do you see why we can't just take you home?'

EIGHT

My jaw dropped open. There was nothing I could do about it. Not one single word came to mind. I was just sitting there agape. Scott and Seb continued to stare at me, eagerly waiting to see what my reaction would be. It was like I was still that ticking time bomb but now no one knew what the fallout would be. I didn't even know myself.

The first sensible thing that came to mind was to double check how serious they were. It didn't feel like a wind-up but could it really be true?

As much as I wanted us all to laugh and for them to move on to tell me the real truth, it actually made perfect sense. I hated to admit it, but it made everything about Scott and these last couple of days add up. In fact it was eerily comforting.

'You weren't travelling the world, you were travelling to the future?' I said directly to Scott. It hardly seemed like the most important question but it was the first thing that popped out of my mouth.

He sat back awkwardly, obviously not expecting me to say that. He glanced at Seb and I knew I'd said too much. He was having an affair with a girl from the past. God I'd be ninety-seven.

Complicated was an understatement.

'Am I still alive in this time?' I asked, again not really thinking through the words that were rolling out of my mouth.

'We don't know that,' Scott said.

'I could be, though. This is so weird. Is this all for real? Oh my God. This is the future? You're not joking?'

'This is far from a laughing matter,' Seb said.

I experienced a fleeting moment of excitement before grave panic set in. 'I'm so far from home. Am I really that far from home? You have to be joking! Oh my God! You've got to get me back home!'

'Calm down, Chloe,' Scott said. This was the time when he'd normally stroke my cheek and soothe me, but he was keeping a firm distance. It made me want to go home even more.

'Why are you making me wait? I don't want to wait three weeks to go home. I got here easily enough. Can't I just use that watch again to get home? Why can't I go back home? Will I ever get home? I'm not trapped here forever am I? I want to go home!'

'Please, calm down,' Scott said. 'It's going to be all right. You're not trapped here, but there are complications as to why we can't send you back right away.'

'It wasn't complicated getting here. Wherever here is. Where are we? Are we still in London? We're not on the moon are we? Are people living on Mars?' My lips were now working all on their own. I'd lost complete control of my thoughts.

I noticed a small smile curl up on the side of Scott's mouth, but before he could say anything Seb warned, 'The less you know the better, Miss Noble. It's one thing you knowing this facility exists, but we need to keep you away from the world around you. If you know too much about what happens in the future it could have catastrophic consequences.'

'How?' I asked, surprising myself. 'If I find out we're

currently sitting in a Martian police station, what difference does that make?'

'You could change the course of history,' Seb stated. 'Believe me, you'd only have to mention to one person that time travel is possible and we're all destined to live on Mars, and it could cause a string of events that stops us ever getting to Mars in the first place.'

'So we are on Mars?' I asked with a gasp.

'We're in Bedfordshire,' Scott said. Seb flashed him another one of his stern looks. 'Oh, she can know that much. We can't have her thinking she's on Mars.'

'Why didn't you tell me you were from Bedford?' I snapped.

'Because you know too much already,' Seb answered firmly and it shut me up. I needed to remember that Scott was in his work place.

Everything went uncomfortably quiet. It was horrible.

After a few moments of nobody knowing what to say, I realised I had to know more. 'Are there flying cars?' I asked.

Scott could barely hide his smile this time. I wasn't meaning to be of such entertainment.

'Again, Miss Noble, we can't tell you anything,' Seb said and I could see his patience diminishing. 'We can't hide what you can see around you, but we can limit your knowledge to a need to know basis.'

'You're not going to zap my brain with a memory wiping flash thing, are you?' I asked.

'What?' Seb replied. He glanced at Scott as if he was hoping Scott might be able to translate my nonsense.

'Nothing like that is going to happen,' Scott said as he continued his efforts to stifle his laugh. 'We can't stop you knowing what you know, but we can prevent you from knowing too much. Time travel's difficult. We go through months of training. We have to be very careful.' The humour in his face disappeared. 'Mistakes come at a high price.' Was he talking about me?

'Mistakes that can affect generations,' Seb added but I

didn't want to listen. Scott had told me that meeting me was a mistake. It was humiliating.

'Why haven't you stopped Hitler?' I asked, trying to gain some sort of control over a situation that dwarfed me in so many ways.

'If only things could be that easy,' Seb said but I wasn't really listening. I was trying to make sense of everything.

I was a huge mistake.

'We have a dedicated ethics committee driving what we do,' Scott explained. 'We have to make careful choices. Stopping Hitler would have an indeterminable effect on all time that followed it. The world wars are incredibly significant periods of history. We have to be careful about what we change.'

'So you just pick stupid piddly things to change, like some kid nicking an apple from the supermarket?' The bitterness of reality was now burning me. 'What's the point in having a police force that can go back in time to change the world if you don't stop massive, bloody events like wars? What about terrorism?'

'Chloe, calm down,' Scott said. His humour had now completely vanished and his concern for me was evident, but I was riddled with nerves. I felt all over the place.

'What's poor Donna done? She's a nice girl, I'm sure. Even if she's not perfect, why her? How is she worse than Hitler or Stalin or all of those horrible terrorists that kill innocent people year after year?'

'Chloe, are you okay? Do you want some water?'

The tears were now filling up my eyes. I was so angry, but I knew it had nothing to do with the fact that they weren't tackling terrorism. I knew it was all to do with the fact that I was utterly heartbroken by the truth that I wasn't allowed to talk about. Scott clearly shouldn't have been messing around with me. He had work to do.

I wondered how many girls he'd slept with back in time.

Scott hopped to his feet and came back a minute later with a glass of water and some toilet roll. I took a few pieces of tissue. It was lovely and soft and it made me feel even sadder, although I had no clue why.

After I'd tidied myself up a bit, he handed me the water. I was shaking so much I could barely hold it. He quickly took it off me and placed it on the floor. There was nowhere else to put it.

Why were there no tables in this stupid future building!

I bounced between anger and heartache for the next few minutes and Seb and Scott just watched me. Scott placed a caring hand on my shoulder but that was about as affectionate as it got.

I sobbed as I realised my relationship was over. I'd met the man of my dreams but he lived seventy years ahead of me and had a real life girlfriend.

Then I became angry as I reflected on how badly he'd treated me. He'd got me to fall in love with him and then he was going to disappear from my life forever. Probably with no word. And it's not like I'd ever have a chance of seeing him again. He lived seventy years away from me.

That thought then brought on the tears again.

Finally I realised that I had to stop this madness. I was getting nowhere and it was becoming embarrassing. Seb couldn't have looked more awkward if he'd tried.

I picked up the glass of water and somehow managed to take a few sips without spilling it.

'I'm sorry,' I said at last.

'Please don't apologise,' Scott said, soothingly. 'Time travel takes its toll. It has done on all of us.'

I blew my nose and dabbed my eyes and tried to gain some composure.

'Why have I got to wait three weeks to go home?' I asked, calmly.

'Time travel is hugely expensive,' Seb replied. 'To refer back to your earlier question, there are millions of things we could change. Believe me, all of us have grappled with how much power we actually have. That's why we have an ethics committee. They work through mounds of data and choose the events that will have the least impact on the world's timelines and the most impact on building a better future for our society. It's the best we can do. Once they've identified a suitable assignment, at that point we have to raise funding. I've known it take months from the time that we find a problem to any of our team going out to tackle it.'

'I'm not a problem or an assignment, though. I just made a mistake.' I turned to Scott. 'A big mistake.'

'It costs around half a million pounds for every journey we make through time. Unless you have that sort of money lying around, you're going to have to wait until Scott next goes back in time.'

'My CPG can carry both of us back,' Scott explained.

I quickly calculated exactly what I was being told.

'If I go back with you on your next scheduled time travel visit, then you're not going to take me back to the point I left, are you? How long will I have disappeared for? I'll have lost my job. What am I going to say to people? They'll start doing experiments on me. I'll be like that boy from *Flight of the Navigator*!'

'What boy?' Seb asked.

'It's a film from the 1980s,' Scott explained as once again he battled to stifle his laugh. It was nice to know I'd returned to being amusing. 'And he disappeared for eight years.'

'He still just vanished with no explanation.'

'Nothing like that is going to happen to you,' Scott said through his smile. 'That's another thing I've been discussing with Seb. I'm owed some annual leave, so I've agreed to go back with you to the night you left and then wait out the three weeks in 2018 until I need to see Donna again. Archie is putting me together a plan. I'll need to keep a low profile so I don't interrupt the time lines too much, but it will be nice to have some time out. Even if I'm just reading a few books.'

I didn't know what to say.

Did time out mean time out from me? Does he not want to see me again?

No, what if he wanted to spend three weeks with me back in 2018? Would I want that too? Knowing that ultimately he'd be coming back to his real life with his real life girlfriend, could I honestly spend three weeks with him?

'Do you feel better now?' Scott asked but I couldn't reply. I didn't know if I'd ever feel better again.

'Pep... Chloe?' Scott nudged.

I shrugged. 'I guess I've got no choice. I'm guess I'm stuck here for three weeks. You're not going to lock me up in that room, are you? I'll go mad.'

'You can't leave this building,' Seb said.

'But that room is so boring! There's definitely no chance of a telly? Do you still have TVs? Do people still watch television?'

'You don't need to know that,' Seb replied. 'We have to minimise your exposure to as much of this time as possible.'

'But you can't lock me up for three weeks! It's inhumane!'

'I concede that,' Seb nodded. 'I suppose considering the fact that most of our work around here is based on history, this is probably the safest place for you to be. Therefore I don't see any harm in you spending time around this facility. Inspector Lacey, she's your responsibility, so you can take care of her until you return her home.'

Scott looked shocked and my heart sank further.

'She can shadow you. And I'm sure you can manage to keep her knowledge to a need to know basis.'

'But I've got work,' Scott argued, making me feel worse by the second.

'And I have no doubt that Miss Noble will be an asset. Maybe you could utilise some of her knowledge of the twentieth century while you can. You and all the team.'

'The team?' Scott all but spat.

'Yes. It's our team meal tonight. What a great place to start the introductions.'

'But that's a team event,' Scott argued. I had never felt less wanted. Being stuck in that room for three weeks was beginning to seem like the more desirable option.

'Exactly. We'll introduce her as a visiting consultant. An expert in the late twentieth century and early twenty-first. It makes sense to bed her in with a social event.' Seb turned to me. 'We have to work long, hard hours together, so every fourth Friday we have a meal together to break some of the stresses and bond as a team.'

'But I thought you said she couldn't leave the building,' Scott argued, stabbing me in the heart over and over.

Seb considered his response. 'Quite right. We'll have the meal here. We've done it a couple of times before.'

'Why is it a problem?' I asked Scott, challenging his obvious aggravation.

'It's not,' he said, forcing a smile. 'It's not a problem at all. I just want to protect you. I don't want anything to happen to you. Liaising with the team causes added complications. I'm just worried about that.'

'So kind of you,' I replied, controlling my sarcasm. 'I'll make sure I don't leave your side. I'll follow your lead every step of the way. Is that okay?'

Scott nodded with another forced smile. 'Sounds perfect. Will that be all, Seb?'

'Yes, that's all. Unless you can think of anything else?'

'No. That's all good. Right.' It was quite bizarre to see Scott so uneasy. He was the most confident, self-assured person I'd ever met. As much as it broke my heart to know how much he wanted to avoid spending time with me, it totally served him right that he was now stuck in an awkward situation. That should teach him for being a two-timing shit-bag. I didn't know what was going to happen over the next three weeks, but I knew I wasn't going to make life easy for him. He deserved nothing less.

'Do I go with you now?' I asked.

'There's a briefing in ten minutes with Superintendent Ackerman,' Seb said. 'Miss Noble, please follow Inspector Lacey. I'll inform the team of your presence. Let's say you've been sent from HQ as a historical consultant, but be as vague as possible. The fewer people that know about this the better. We need to avoid any unnecessary questioning.'

'Can I ask who does know the truth?' I asked.

'Only the people you've met so far,' Seb replied. 'Anyone you met on the first night you arrived is privy to the information, but we've kept it to that. We've been very lucky in that the whole affair has seemingly gone unnoticed. Isn't that so, Inspector Lacey?'

'Very lucky,' Scott stated. 'Come on then,' he said to me. 'You'd better get ready for your first official Shape the Future meeting.'

NINE

'Why don't you want to spend time with me?' I asked as I walked with Scott down the corridor.

'What? What makes you say that?' I didn't need to respond. I just glared at him until he gave in. 'It's not that I don't want to spend time with you. Believe me, that's really not the case. I'm just worried about you. This is a very different world to what you're used to. Anyway, I want to know where your wild imagination comes from.'

'Imagination?'

'Flying cars and living on Mars?'

'It's the future. They were valid questions.'

'It's only seventy years in the future. Like you said, you could still be alive.'

'I forgot about that. Do you think there really could be two of me here? How freaky is that?'

'I was tempted, you know.'

'Tempted?'

'To look you up.'

'Really? But you didn't?'

'I couldn't.'

'Why not?'

'Because then I'd know. I didn't want to...' Scott's face

became uncharacteristically serious.

'Know what?'

For a second he looked quite upset, but then a smile sprung on to his face again. 'Why flying cars? In which year exactly did you think we'd altered gravity?'

'Aeroplanes fly.'

'They're a bit more expensive than cars.'

'But it's the future.'

'No, that's *Back to the Future II*, isn't it?'

'It's still the future.'

'Yes, but didn't he go forward to 2015? You've lived through that time and there were no flying cars.'

'Doesn't mean it's not going to happen.'

'So in which film do they do the memory wiping flash thing? I forgot how obsessed you are with science fiction. Fiction being the operative word.'

'I still think they were all valid questions.'

Scott chuckled. 'I think you'd find it all a bit disappointing if you were to venture outside.'

'Well then, why can't I?'

'Are you kidding? I'm in enough trouble as it is.' Scott stopped. 'Here we are. This is my office.'

He opened the door to reveal a very light blue room that contained four floating slinky monitors in front of four chairs. That was it.

'This is your office?' I said stepping in. 'Why are there no desks anywhere?'

Two people standing to the left of the room suddenly caught my attention. One was the woman I'd seen as soon as I'd arrived in that box and the other was a man I'd not met before. He was handsome but seemed young, although his deep blue eyes indicated more maturity than his youthful face suggested.

'Why would we need a desk?' the woman asked quite sharply.

I just smiled and shrugged.

'No, come on, I want to know what's so important about

a desk,' she insisted.

'To lean on. Rest stuff on,' I meekly replied. 'How do you ever write anything down?'

'You need to pull her into line,' the woman warned Scott, which left me quite indignant. She'd asked.

'Write things down?' the man queried with confusion. 'Do you mean like with a pen and paper?'

'Pen and paper?' A female voice appeared behind me and it immediately gave me chills. It was Leanne from breakfast. I looked across at Scott and he stiffened.

'This is Chloe, everyone,' he said. 'She's here's from HQ. An expert in the late twentieth century and early twenty-first. Part of her remit is to challenge us, so don't be thrown if she appears to ask strange questions. It's all about how we answer.'

Leanne looked me up and down. I felt so uncomfortable in my white janitor-like uniform. 'Do you still use pens?' she asked like it was the most absurd prospect on the planet. I couldn't believe that something as simple and as useful as a pen had been made obsolete.

'Of course not,' I mumbled.

'Enough of this,' the strict woman said. 'Chloe, you are welcome to join us but please sit at the back and stay very quiet.'

I closed my mouth. I could see she wasn't a woman to be messed with.

'Sorry I'm late,' another man said coming in. 'HQ is being unusually slow.' I recognised him. He was the man that had opened the door to the black box. The first person I'd met in this time.

Scott walked to a cupboard at the front of the room and pulled out a chair. He put it down at the back of the room away from everyone and gestured for me to sit on it. I did as requested. He then sat down in front of a monitor, as did Leanne and the two other men. The stern woman stood at the front, like she was about to lecture them.

'Updates first, please' she said. 'Leanne, Bradley?' I

noted that Bradley was the man who had been there before we walked in. 'How are things in 2023?'

'We still can't get him to bite,' Leanne said.

'There's something we're missing. He's just not interested,' Bradley detailed.

'Theo?' the stern woman said, turning her fierce gaze in his direction. Theo was the man who'd been late for the meeting.

'I gave them everything I had but it was limited. There were three years missing that I couldn't account for.'

'Did you try an alias?' Scott asked.

'All the usual tricks.'

'People always leave a footprint. Do you want me to escalate it?' the stern woman said.

'No, not yet,' Theo replied, quite assertively. 'There are a few scenarios I want to run through. Perhaps look at it differently.'

'When are you due back?' the stern woman asked Leanne.

'Eleven days,' she replied.

'I'll give you seven to find the missing link, Theo. Then I'm escalating it.'

Theo just nodded before typing something into the monitor.

'Scott? How is it going in 2018?'

A chill ran through me. That was my year. That was where I belonged. Not sitting here in some strange room with people who hadn't even been born yet. Bloody hell, I was probably sitting with people whose parents hadn't been born yet.

'Donna's easy,' he said. 'It's just babysitting really.'

'Any sign of the target?'

'No, not yet. It was her birthday at the last visit and we were expecting something then, but it went like clockwork.'

'Not quite clockwork,' she said, glaring at me.

'Why? What happened?' Leanne asked Scott.

Scott stiffened again. I could only see the back of him

but I could sense the tension.

'Donna asked me to do her a favour that sent me off course. It wasn't a disaster, but off track, that's all.'

'Is that what you meant last night? About you making a mistake?'

The jabs of sadness and hurt struck my heart.

Scott turned his head to acknowledge her, but he said nothing.

'We have two new assignments just in,' the stern woman said, thankfully changing the subject.

Scott, Leanne, Bradley and Theo all started to type on their monitors.

'These are two twentieth century tasks, so Scott I want you to take the lead.'

'Of course,' he replied.

'Firstly, we have a hostage situation in 1971 that we need to eliminate. We believe it to be the catalyst to larger activity. Two hostages die and one is sent on a destructive path.'

'On scene or build up?' Scott asked.

'We believe disabling the car may be enough. Theo?'

'Profiling the two targets reveals that they aren't confident. Having this job go wrong may be enough to dissuade them from future activity.'

They all spent a few minutes looking at their monitors. I was desperate to see what they were reading, but I couldn't make it out. It was fascinating.

'When are we ready for logistics?' Scott asked.

'Not for two weeks. Scott, I'm leaving it all in your hands, okay?'

'Sure. I'll have it mapped out this afternoon.'

'No you won't. I need you to be ready for the second assignment by nine hundred tomorrow.'

'What's the urgency?' Leanne asked.

'There's another flicker in the timeline,' Theo replied. 'I can't get a consistent reading.'

'Again?' Scott asked.

'It's getting worse,' Theo said.

'With such uncertainty, we need to get the job finalised without delay. Just in case,' the stern woman instructed.

'Are they still blaming the upgrade?' Scott asked.

'Apparently so,' Theo replied.

'It's been a year,' Scott stated.

'And it seems to be the only difference the upgrade has made,' Theo added.

'Let's focus on our jobs, team,' the stern woman said. 'HQ is on the case with these problems. They'll get it sorted as soon as they can.'

'We go in on target date?' Leanne noted with surprise, reading her monitor.

'We haven't got any time here,' the woman explained.

'This profile is sketchy. It's not enough to work with,' Leanne remarked.

'You're the best team here,' the woman said. 'There's going to be a lot of thinking on your feet, but what's the point in you being trained if you're fed everything all the time?'

'So Leanne and I are going to be a married couple again?' Scott asked as my stomach knotted. 'I can see how that could work. But what about children?'

'Over to you,' the woman said. 'It's 1993. How would you play it?'

Scott thought for a moment. 'It would be much simpler in the early twenty-first century.'

'One boy, one girl?' Leanne suggested, turning to Scott. I noticed a little grin flash across her lips.

'I think that would work,' Scott agreed.

'What about the rest of the back story?' Leanne asked, once again referring to her monitor.

'I've only had two days,' Theo replied, defensively. 'You'll get it by thirteen hundred. Will that do?'

'You're going to fill all these gaps by thirteen hundred?' Leanne asked Theo, sceptically.

'It'll be your fourth time in the 1990s, Leanne,' Scott said. 'We can do this. It's not a new era for us.'

'Is that why we've got this consultant?' she added, turning to me. All the heads in the room pointed in my direction.

'She's here for ongoing training,' the woman stated. 'And we don't have time to consult our guest right now.'

Leanne sighed. 'Right. If you're the lead, Scott, I know we'll be fine.'

'Good work,' the woman said. 'Logistics said they'll be ready at sixteen hundred. Any other questions?'

Everyone shook their heads and the stern woman promptly left. Theo followed shortly after, just as Leanne stepped over to Scott.

'It's been a while since we've been married,' she grinned, placing her hand on his shoulder. Scott just nodded. 'Married with kids again. And a night in a good old-fashioned pub.'

She stroked his hair and he didn't even budge. He just sat there letting her play with him while he worked on his computer.

Finally he moved her hand away, very gently. 'Shall we meet at thirteen hundred?' he asked her.

'Sounds good. Do you need help running scenarios?'

'Looking at this, I can't see the point. It's a complete mess. But I might drop by and see Theo. It can't hurt, I suppose.'

'Do you want me to come with you?' she asked.

'No,' he replied, quite sharply. 'I've got to look after Chloe, anyway.'

'Why is she your responsibility?' Leanne asked, turning to face me.

'You think Gloria's going to do it?' he smirked.

With each passing minute, I was feeling less and less important.

Scott stood up. 'Are you ready to move on?' he asked me. He had no idea how ready I really was, but I just nodded politely. I stood up and followed him out of the room.

We walked down a corridor in silence. I couldn't think

of anything to say. That whole session had been quite confusing, in many different ways.

I finally recognised where he was taking me. We were going back to my room. That small, boring room. So much for him looking after me. How on earth was I going to get through the next three weeks like this?

TEN

'You're ditching me here now?' I asked with a bitter tongue.

He looked at me with surprise. 'Of course not. I just thought you might appreciate a few minutes of time alone. Believe me, Pepps, we're not going to get a lot of it.'

I was absolutely gobsmacked. I'd just seen him all over his girlfriend not minutes before and now he wanted some alone time with me. The nerve of him!

We waited outside the door and I stared at the light to open it. It popped open and he walked straight in.

'Do you think I could get some other clothes?' I asked, snappily, heading straight to the back of the room to keep my distance from him. 'If I walk around looking like a janitor all the time I'm worried people will start asking me to clean stuff.'

'A janitor?' he asked before chuckling. 'Oh, I see. Now you say it.'

'Is there anything else I can wear?'

'Of course. I'll sort it. I suppose you'll need something for tonight's meal as well.' He was edging closer to me and I didn't like it.

'What do women wear in 2086?'

'Too many questions, Pepps. I definitely can't tell you about future fashions.'

'Why not? I'll find out tonight anyway, won't I?'

This made Scott stop. He shook his head. 'Seb was right. You go back with too much information, it could change the future. We've never been in this situation before. We can't take the risk.'

'None of this is my fault,' I replied, perhaps far too defensively.

'I know. I know it's not.' He stood in front of me, virtually pinning me up against the wall. He touched my hand. 'You do see why I can't tell anyone about us?'

I looked him square in the eyes. 'Yes. It's pretty obvious.'

'I could get into serious trouble if anyone finds out that I was seeing you when I should have been with Donna.'

'Why risk it, then?'

He hesitated. 'Because I love you. Because you make me happy.' He paused for another second. 'Because I couldn't stop.'

'They think I'm one of Donna's random friends that you dropped off home that night?'

'As soon as I saw that you were gone with my CPG, I knew it could be bad. I had to think of something. I had to keep it on target.'

'What does that mean?'

'I had to relate it to my assignment. If it kept Donna happy then who could argue?'

I didn't know what to say to that. He had it all so nicely planned out. I stepped aside to get away from him and walked over to my bed. 'Would you rather I didn't go to the team meal?' I asked, sourly. 'I can see how it could be complicated for you.'

'No, it would be great to have you there. We just need to be careful. You need to keep our secret. Will you do that for me?'

As much as I hated being a secret, I had to concede the truth. That's all I was: a secret. I knew I had the power to make life difficult for him, but it wasn't in me to be so spiteful. I would be gone in three weeks; gone forever. What would I gain from stirring up trouble other than a fleeting moment of satisfaction? Satisfaction that I'd probably regret in a few weeks' time anyway, knowing me.

'Fancy dress!' he blurted out with far too much excitement.

'Fancy dress?'

'Logistics can come up with something.'

'What is Logistics?'

'That's the department that gives us our period dress, money, tips on culture, popular slang. All the bits we need to properly fit in to the time we're visiting. The whole team had to work on an assignment in 1987 just a few months ago. They've got loads of eighties clothes. We could have a 1980s party.'

I was horrified but he seemed full of joy.

'You want me to walk around looking like I'm from *Pretty in Pink*?' I asked. I'd never been a fan of fancy dress. Most days I felt awkward in my own clothes, let alone dressing up like somebody else.

Scott sat down on the bed next to me. 'What's *Pretty in Pink*?'

I rolled my eyes. 'Do you ever watch films?'

'Honestly, Pepps, I love films.' He sighed. 'It feels so good to be able to tell you that.'

'Well, why haven't you before? We've sat through dozens of movies but you always say you've never heard of them.'

'That's because to me the ones we've watched together are really, really old.'

'Oh.'

'*Back to the Future* is like a hundred years old to me.'

My jaw literally dropped open at this. That sounded so weird.

'I'm guessing *Pretty in Pink* is from the 1980s too?' he asked.

'Yeah. So that's like a whole century old too. Does no one watch classic movies anymore? What about classics from my time? Like *The Wizard of Oz* or *Mary Poppins*? Do they still come on the telly at Christmas or are they now just lost in the archives?'

'I can't tell you, Pepps. You know I'd love to, but I can't say anything.'

'How is me knowing if *The Wizard of Oz* is still on the telly going to threaten history?'

'I can't take the risk. I've messed up enough as it is.'

'Right,' I nodded, taking the hint yet again that I was a mistake.

'You were born in the 1980s, weren't you?' he asked with a nostalgic grin.

'1989.'

'You're so lucky.'

I could tell that I'd lost him. This was so typical of him. He was a ball of energy most of the time, then every now and then he'd just switch off into his own world and go really quiet.

'What are you going to make me wear?' I asked, snapping him back to reality.

'What? Oh. Something from your time,' he said, standing up. He could never sit still for long. 'You'll love it.'

'I didn't even live a whole year in the eighties, it's not really my time. Can't we wear clothes from 2018?'

'Not when I know there's a whole wardrobe from the eighties. It'll be fun. It's only for tonight.'

'What about the rest of the time?'

'I'll get you a uniform. I can't see why a historical consultant can't be from the force.'

'So it's a proper police uniform you wear?'

I looked him up and down in the blue suit he was wearing. He looked amazing in it. It made it all the more difficult to be angry at him when he looked so incredibly sexy.

'You like me in my uniform?' he asked with a cheeky

grin.

'It's just different,' I said, determined not to let on how flustered it made me. 'What did Donna do?' I asked, eager to change the subject. 'Why is she of interest to the future time police?'

'Future time police?' Scott smirked.

I shrugged. 'That's what you are, isn't it?'

'We're officially called the Shape the Future branch. Virtually everyone here has come through the ranks of the police force, but it's run as a separate entity. We get specially chosen to move over if we meet the right criteria. Do you remember us talking about Earl?'

'Yes,' I nodded.

'He's one of the few people here that's not from the force. It was his team that developed the CPG in the first place. When the government found out about it they wanted to use it to aid their fight with law and order but Earl would only licence it to them if he could run the branch. It's an unusual set up, I'll grant you, but Earl is a brilliant man and I think everyone agreed having him in charge would only benefit the programme. A lot of people owe their lives to him.'

'Changing the past to shape the future,' I said, recalling what I'd seen in Seb's office.

'You've seen the posters?' Scott queried. 'They're designed to keep us motivated. Don't get me wrong, it's a real honour being chosen to go back in time and make such a difference to the world, but it's also a really tough job. You sacrifice a lot to be a part of the team. We all have to live here and we rarely see our families and friends. I've seen and done things that have been incredibly challenging. But it's your job, so you just have to get on with it.'

'How often do you see your family?' I asked. 'I take it you're not the orphan you implied you were?'

Scott sat on my bed again. 'I didn't lie as much as you might believe. I only deceived you when I absolutely had to. And I'm very sorry for that.'

'So you are an orphan?'

'No, not technically. My parents are both alive, but I have no relationship with them. I see them perhaps once a year, just to check in, but they pretty much despise me.'

'What? Why?'

'Having a son in the police force is highly embarrassing for them.'

'Are they criminals?'

'I have no evidence of that. But there are many things I question about the way they live their lives.'

'Do they know you time travel?'

'Absolutely not. This is a highly secure facility and very few people know of its existence. Another reason why you being here is a nightmare. But we had to tell you the truth. I couldn't see another way.'

I felt a huge weight lift off me as I finally started to get some answers. It made me realise how much I'd placed question marks over things before. I knew things hadn't always added up, but I'd been too loved up to pay attention.

It was on the tip of my tongue to ask about Leanne and get everything out in the open, when he said, 'Donna met a man in 2018. A man that became very dangerous. It's a story knee deep in death and destruction.'

'What?'

'We believe their meeting was the catalyst to the dark path they both went down.'

'Oh my God.'

'She wasn't really to blame. It seems she was so devoted to him, she couldn't really see what was happening.'

An eerie sense of familiarity crept through me. I was definitely starting to understand the meaning of "love is blind". 'What happened to her?' I asked with trepidation.

'Amongst other things, he ended up using her hairdressing business as a front for a lot of other stuff. Fraud, money-laundering, tax evasion, you name it. That's before it developed to GBH and, sadly, murder. He was a truly evil man but he never got arrested. He let her take the fall for everything and she got twenty years in prison.'

'What?' I was shocked.

'It far from happens overnight, but that's how the story goes. It was only when she was released from prison that much of the truth came out. It was a bit late for her then, though. That's why she was identified by us.'

'So you try to stop innocent people from going to prison? Is that what this place is all about?'

'Our goal is to prevent crimes before they happen, thereby freeing up prisons and taxpayers' money over time. It's a complex process but I think we're making a difference.'

'How are you helping Donna, then?'

'All we could trace back was that she meets him in 2018. He travels a lot and we identified that he was in London up to early March 2018 but after that we don't know. We know they're together in January 2019, so at some point between those two times he visits Harrogate, meets Donna and they fall in love.'

'It doesn't sound like love.'

Scott touched my hand. 'I guess some people aren't as lucky.'

I pulled my hand away. There were far too many mixed messages and my head couldn't take much more.

'I was sent back to date her,' he explained. 'To be a distraction. If she's dating me then I can prevent her from dating him.'

'That's awfully big headed of you, isn't it?' I snarled.

'Excuse me?'

'What makes you so brilliant that any woman would prefer to be with you rather than any other man? I mean she did fall in love with this man. Is it not possible that she might choose him over you? Over God-like Scott Lacey?'

Scott was clearly taken aback by my outburst. Although, to be honest, so was I. He regarded me very gravely. It wasn't a look I was used to and it pinned me to the spot.

'I'm a trained undercover operative. We spend weeks,

sometimes months researching people before we travel back. I've deliberately been sent back in time to get her to fall in love with me and I am using the best information on the planet to make that possible.'

I felt a small stab in my stomach. 'Is that how I fell in love with you?'

Scott grabbed my hands. 'No. Haven't you realised yet? You're the one person that has seen the real me. I've travelled across hundreds of years pretending to fit in with people and changing who I am to get them to act in a certain way. But when I met you, I was being totally me. It felt so good to be me. When I'm with you I know I'm the best version of myself and I don't want that to go away.'

He stopped abruptly and the air became tense. I didn't know how to react. His expression seemed almost regretful.

He stood up, cutting the moment off. 'We'd better get going. I've got to run through scenarios with Theo.'

'I can come with you?' I asked, my head still spinning.

'Of course. You're going to spend the whole day with me. I'll have to leave you with Theo when we go out on assignment tomorrow, but you'll see me leave in the module and you'll see me arrive back there.'

'Is that the black box?'

'Yeah, what you arrived in. It must have been weird for you, everything just suddenly going black.'

I stood up and sighed. 'And it just keeps getting weirder and weirder.'

'You'll get used to things,' he said before kissing me softly on the lips. 'Come on, Pepps, you're going to love this. Prepping for assignments gives me such a buzz.'

ELEVEN

He couldn't have been more wrong. Prepping for assignments was mind-numbingly boring.

I followed him to a light blue room with about twenty-five floating monitors in it. This was the busiest room I'd seen yet, alive with the buzz of blue suited people zooming their hands around their monitors, talking in great depth and scurrying in and out.

We stood and talked to Theo for a while, and I was able to follow about ten percent of what they were discussing, and then Scott led me back to his office where I watched him work in silence for about half an hour.

At one o'clock, as agreed, Leanne came to meet him. She giggled at everything he said and stroked his head and arms quite unnecessarily, all while discussing the pretend marriage they were going to have with their two adorable kids. I wanted to throw up.

When Scott finally managed to get away, we went for a very quick lunch, before we returned to his office for more silent work. Then at four o'clock on the dot we went to the Logistics department.

I actually thought that might have been fun, but it was just a lot more serious discussion. While we were there we picked up our outfits for the 1980s party that everyone had to suffer through that night, before returning to Scott's office for more silent work.

By the time six o'clock arrived and he announced that we'd better get ready for the evening, I was struggling to stay awake, but Scott was pumping with adrenaline. He clearly loved his work.

He dropped me back at my room and told me he'd collect me at seven o'clock. And I knew he meant bang on seven o'clock. Punctuality was majorly important at this place. No one was ever late for anything.

I threw the electric blue puffy dress that I'd been given down on the bed. I had leggings to wear underneath it and a bright red beaded necklace.

It was horrible.

I had a shower to refresh myself before slipping in to the awful blue outfit. It wasn't exactly comfortable and I looked ridiculous. Did people seriously wear stuff like this to impress?

I was ready for five to seven and I sat quietly for exactly five minutes before there was the very expected knock at the door.

I opened it to find Scott sporting a huge grin. 'We should definitely do this more often,' he said.

He was wearing a light grey suit with a black T-Shirt underneath. He looked nice but I'd seen him look a lot better.

'You look great,' he said, twirling me around. 'Eighties fashion suits you.' Normally his twirls made me giggle but on this occasion I was struggling to find any amusement. 'Are you ready?' he asked.

'I suppose.'

'Come on, Pepps. This will be fun!'

I nodded to his face and then rolled my eyes the second his back was turned. We left my room and I followed him down the endless corridors again.

'Why is everything so colourful?' I asked, pointing to the

green walls.

Scott hesitated. 'I suppose I can tell you what I can't hide from you. It's all to do with a vision a man had in 2072.'

'He painted them?'

Scott chuckled. 'No. I'd better not say too much, but basically he found a way to reduce certain anxieties through the use of colour.'

'So green walls help you feel better?'

'Different colours have different impacts.'

'Green is good for the police force?'

'We have very stressful jobs so this is meant to help relax us.'

'It hasn't relaxed me,' I said.

'How can you know for sure?'

'Trust me, I've been anything but relaxed since I came to this place.'

Scott nudged me. 'But you don't know how you would have felt without the green walls. Maybe you're far more relaxed than you might have been.'

I thought about this for a second and was about to continue the debate when Scott opened a door to our left.

Inside the unusually white room there was a table with eleven chairs around it: five either side and one at the top. It was all set for dinner. The room was already full of people, all dressed brightly in eighties fashion.

'I hear this was your idea?' Theo said to Scott. He was dressed in a green shell suit and I had to stop myself from giggling. He didn't look good at all.

'It's great, isn't it!' Scott beamed. 'We always do the same thing every month. I thought, why not have a theme!'

I glanced around the room and my eyes halted on Leanne. She was chatting to another girl and she looked stunning in a white strapless dress. Why was she the only one not looking stupid?

'Sit here,' Scott said, pulling out a chair for me at the end of the table. 'I'll be back in a second.' I did as he asked before I watched him make a beeline directly for Leanne.

They immediately started laughing together and the jealousy raged inside of me. She sat down and she pulled him to sit next to her. He started telling her something and she was hanging on his every word.

Suddenly everyone started to take their seats. Before I knew it, Bradley was sitting next to me and Theo was opposite. Scott was stuck right down the other end of the table.

'Can we have some quiet please?' Seb said, standing up from the head of the table.

Scott flicked his head up from his deep conversation. I saw him glance right down the table at me before he turned straight back to Leanne.

'I want to thank Scott for tonight's idea of dressing up,' Seb announced. 'It's a bit of fun and Logistics were thrilled that they were getting more wear out of their wardrobe. I say let's have a theme every month. We can all take turns to vote for our favourite era. I would like to nominate the forties for next month.'

Everyone sniggered but I didn't get the joke. I was trying to recall what wartime fashion was like when I realised he must have meant the 2040s. That was a very strange concept: that they were laughing about something that I wouldn't understand for twenty years.

'For those of you who haven't met our guest, I'd like to introduce Chloe Noble.' Seb gestured in my direction like he was presenting me. 'She's here from HQ as a consultant on the late twentieth and early twenty-first centuries, mainly working with myself and Scott. Please make her feel welcome. Although I do need to say that as a consultant her clearance level is minimal.'

'Need to know,' everyone mumbled in response. It made me feel about three centimetres tall.

'Maybe we could all introduce ourselves. Let's go round the room. Theo?'

'Hi Chloe,' Theo said. 'I'm Sergeant Theo Harringdon. As you probably learnt earlier, I do the research, compile back stories and make sure these guys know exactly what they're walking into when they travel back.'

'Hi Theo,' I said, nodding at how his summary matched everything I'd seen him do that day.

'I'm Francesca,' the girl next to him said with a squeaky voice. 'Or Sergeant Edmundson if you want to be precise. I'm hoping to make Inspector in the next year.'

'You will,' Theo muttered supportively. She seemed lovely. She was full of smiles that lit her round face.

'We've met,' Dom said from next to her. 'I hope you're settling in well?'

'I'm Superintendent Ackerman, second in command,' the stern woman from the meeting earlier butted in before I could respond to Dom. 'I think that's all you need to know.'

'She's also known as Gloria,' Bradley whispered next to me.

'I'm Constable Archie Travis,' the man at the end said. He was the man I'd seen with Theo when I'd first arrived in 2086. He was clearly the youngest of the group. 'I'm a trainee.'

'We've all got to start somewhere,' I said with a smile.

'You know me,' Seb said, still standing up, before he turned to Leanne next to him.

'I'm Inspector Donnington,' she announced, glaring down the table at me with the fakest grin I've ever had the misfortune of witnessing. 'But you can call me Leanne.'

'Hi Chloe,' Scott said from next to her, not allowing me any chance to reply. (Not that I had intended to). He had that awkward, stiff look about him again. 'I'm Inspector Lacey, as you know. I'm one of the more experienced Inspectors. It's us Inspectors who go back to tackle the assignments.'

'He's the best this branch has ever seen,' Leanne gushed with an adoring smile. I couldn't see her hand but I just knew it was stroking his leg all seductively. She had that look on her face and I wanted to slap it so badly.

'That's a bit patronising,' the woman on the other side of Scott said. 'She might be a consultant, but if she's from HQ then she'll know what an Inspector is.' This woman was larger than life. Her voice boomed across the table and I could feel her energy from two seats down. 'Sorry about that, chicken,' she said, smiling in my direction. 'I'm Barbara Hoggard. That's Inspector Hoggard. And now you know all about Inspectors, don't you; thanks to Scott.' She winked at me.

'I disagree,' Scott said. 'There was a chance she might not have known. To assume, after all, makes you an ass.'

'I think that's you and me,' she said.

'No, in this instance I think it's just you.'

There was a second when I was worried a fight might kick off until they both burst out laughing. 'You've got to love him!' Barbara said and then she kissed him square on his cheek, leaving a bright red lipstick mark.

'Do I get my go?' Bradley asked with a grin and for the first time I started to see the dynamic of this group. They were so close and had such respect for one another. Leanne wasn't just Scott's girlfriend, I was realising. She was his family.

'Patience is a virtue, darling,' Barbara said. There was a short pause. 'Now you can go.' Everyone laughed again and Bradley rolled his eyes.

'I'm Inspector Bradley Stainthorpe,' he told me. 'Nice to meet you properly, Chloe. We didn't really get a chance to talk earlier.'

'Nice to meet you too,' I said. I scanned the faces across the table. 'Nice to meet all of you.' *Except you, Leanne*, I thought to myself.

I sat back in my seat. Multiple conversations developed, in-jokes were thrown around and laughter could be heard in bucket loads. I couldn't fight the pinch of jealousy. Scott might have had a high pressured job and a lot of responsibility, but he also had solid support from a close-knit team. None of their smiles were fake. All of the relationships in the room were sincere and caring. It was obvious.

I found myself longing for a working team like that myself. It was the complete opposite of the cold, harsh environment I spent all day in. If I had a conversation that wasn't work related, it was probably someone trying to get gossip out of me. No one gave a crap about what I'd done at the weekend. No one cared about me at all.

The starters arrived and we were each given a glass of sparkly stuff that tasted like elderflower. It wasn't alcoholic but I knew that Scott and Leanne were heading back in time at nine o'clock on the dot tomorrow morning, so being sober was probably the wisest choice. Although I was dying for a bottle of wine or two to help me get through the evening.

It was simple food, well presented. We had fishcakes for starters followed by beef with fondant potato and carrots for mains. The meal was finished with a creamy white dessert that tasted a bit like vanilla but with a bitter aftertaste that I didn't like.

While we ate I attempted some small talk with Bradley and Theo, but generally I just listened to their joking around and reminiscing. And I kept my eyes firmly on Leanne at the end. Her hands were far too free and easy when it came to Scott and no one seemed surprised.

As I watched her through my envious eyes, one question circled round and round my head. Would Scott have ended things with me in 2018 when his assignment with Donna had finished or would he have just disappeared from my life leaving me to never know the truth? That would have been awful. Well awful for me, but incredibly easy for him.

I knew I couldn't ask him. It's not that I was afraid of the answer, it's that I was convinced he'd only ever tell me what he thought I wanted to hear. I'd never know the actual truth - that life didn't exist anymore - so why would he hurt me unnecessarily?

As awkward as it was being in the future with him,

maybe it had all turned out for the best. At least I could make peace with it now and I'd never be left wondering.

I was taking the last sip of my after-dinner coffee when Scott finally came down to see me.

'Did you enjoy that?' he asked. I shrugged. I didn't know what to say. As much as I wanted to be brave and logical, this whole experience was proving to be nothing but heartbreaking.

'I'd better get you up to bed,' he said.

Leanne appeared at his side. Her face was full of expectation.

'I definitely need to get a good night's sleep tonight,' he said very firmly, not taking his eyes off me. I, however, got to witness just how disheartened she seemed by his determination to sleep. I took some pleasure from that.

'I'll see you at eight hundred then?' she asked. I could sense she was wanting more of an answer than yes or no.

'See you then,' was all that Scott said and again it gave me a dash of gratification. 'Are you ready?' he asked, looking down at me still in my chair. I nodded and he led me out of the room without turning back.

We walked in silence back to my room. I stared at the light to pop the door open and Scott stepped inside first.

'They're a good team, aren't they?' he said.

'You and Leanne seem close,' I said, shutting the door behind me.

'We've worked together for a long time,' he replied, although he couldn't face me. Instead he sighed and opened my wardrobe. 'Has Dom not brought you a uniform yet?' he asked, studying the contents of my virtually empty wardrobe with far too much intensity.

'No,' I replied feeling a weight pull down inside of me.

'I'll get it sorted before I go to bed.'

Scott closed my wardrobe again and we both hovered for a moment. It was rarely awkward between us and this was horrible.

'Do you really love me?' I asked, cutting the silence.

He stepped over to me and stroked my face. I loved it when he did that. I stared up at his enchanting brown eyes. 'I have never loved anyone like you,' he said.

'Just bad timing, then?' I muttered, trying to make sense of everything.

He shook his head. 'I'd better go. I've got a really big day tomorrow.'

'Okay.'

He kissed me and I could feel the love right through his lips. My heart tore a little as I justified how this was probably nothing more than a sad and unfortunate situation. A love out of time that never should have been.

'I love you too, you know,' I said.

He stroked my face one more time. 'I know.'

He stepped away before adding. 'We'll have to go for breakfast at seven tomorrow. Is that okay?'

'That's fine.'

'Goodnight, Pepper Pot.'

'Oh, hang on. You don't have an alarm clock, do you? I usually use my phone, but...'

'Yeah, you've got...' He stopped and studied me. 'You know what, I'll set it for you. It uses new technology. Well, new for you.'

Scott fiddled with the clock on my bedside table. 'Six, six-thirty? What time do you want?'

'Six-thirty will be fine, thanks.'

'There you go. All set. All you need to do is hit the button on the top to disable it. I'll set it for you again tomorrow if you like.'

'Thanks.'

'My pleasure. Night Pepps.' He kissed me one more time before slowly opening my door. It was the least rushed I'd seen him all day. As soon as the door closed I slumped on the bed.

I grabbed the alarm clock, determined to see if it really was that complicated, but when I couldn't actually find any buttons at all except for the one on the top, I decided that maybe Scott had been right.

I started to question what sort of new technology it could be, but I quickly realised that I didn't care. I was trying to think of anything really other than the awful mess I'd got myself into.

I placed the clock down and flopped backwards on the bed.

I had three more weeks of this torment and I could only see it getting worse.

TWELVE

I was wide awake well before the alarm went off. I was actually watching the last couple of minutes go by, poised over the clock, ready to strike the button to disable it.

It gave me something to do.

I got straight up and poked my head outside my door. Sure enough, Scott had done exactly as promised and he'd arranged for me to have a uniform.

I picked up the very neatly folded and sealed package and I brought it into my room.

Half an hour later and I was showered and ready for action. I studied myself in the mirror. The blue trouser suit looked far nicer on Scott, but at least I didn't look like a janitor anymore. At least I'd blend in.

At seven on the dot, Scott knocked on my door and we headed down to the canteen for breakfast. The canteen was really busy and we didn't say much to each other as we munched our way through our cereal.

At eight o'clock we arrived in the Logistics department and Scott got ready – along with Leanne – for his visit back in time.

'Am I allowed to ask what this assignment is about?' I said as I sat in the corner of the salmon coloured room. It was a simple room with just a couple of mirrors, a floating monitor, a bench, and now my seat, which Scott had kindly sourced for me. Scott was dressed in a pale pair of jeans and a blue stripy shirt and we were waiting for Leanne to appear in her denim wonder.

'I suppose there's no harm in you knowing,' Scott said after a moment's pause. He checked himself in the mirror one more time before turning to face me. 'We're going to try to stop a man from killing his family.'

I was shocked and instantly nauseous. 'God, that's awful. Why would he do that?'

'It wasn't deliberate. He was an alcoholic and one night when he got home from the pub he passed out with a lit cigarette.'

'Oh. Oh right.'

'What is it?' Scott asked, reading my confused expression.

'I don't mean to be unsympathetic. I mean that is horrible and such a shame for his family. But why him? Why are you saving his family? Surely there are worse criminals out there you could be focusing on?'

'All heart, you, aren't you,' Scott gibed.

'Don't be like that. It's just that it seems you have a lot of power to change history for the better. I was expecting you to be dealing with mass murderers or rapists. Not a drunk.'

'Believe me, he ended up far worse than just a drunk. That event was the catalyst to a viciously destructive path. Being the only one to survive, the guilt devastated him and he quickly spiralled down to a very dark level. He ended up hurting quite a few people.'

'He killed other people?'

'No, but you don't need to kill someone to ruin their life. Trust me, it got quite brutal towards the end.'

'Do I want to know?'

'Definitely not.'

'So what's the plan? How are you going to save him?'

'We've run a few scenarios-'

'What does that mean?' I asked.

'Part of Theo's remit is to run theoretical outcomes in the system to see what the best course of action should be. We call them scenarios. There are often multiple ways we can handle a situation so this helps us identify the one most likely to succeed.'

'Do you always succeed?'

'We always get there in the end, but sometimes it can take a few attempts. As they say, hindsight is a wonderful thing.'

'What did it say was the best course of action on this job?'

'That we need to get his wife to come to the pub with him. There are problems in his marriage, so we've calculated that if we can get her to spend a night with him then it will likely have a positive knock-on effect. If nothing else, it means he's not on his own when he gets home and therefore he won't set light to the place. But there were strong indications that it will put him on a better course to resolving his issues. Not overnight, obviously, but if she goes with him once, it's likely she'll go more often and that will build a stronger bond between them.'

'Wow, okay. That doesn't sound too bad.'

'Not if we could properly profile it.'

'What does that mean?'

'Do you remember Gloria saying that this was urgent?'

I thought back to the meeting when they'd first been discussing it but I hadn't followed most of what they were talking about. 'Not really.'

'This is a very odd assignment. Well, assignments like this used to be odd, but there's been an increasing number of cases where we're going back without actually fully knowing what happened in history.'

'How can you not know what happened in history? It's like history. It's already happened. Except, I suppose, when you've gone back and changed things.'

'Yes, if we've changed things, that's fine. But events that we've not altered should be static. However, over the past year there have been multiple cases where the timelines have been fluid; actually changing in front of us. The end result is usually the same, but things happen on different nights and in different places, and so on.'

'It must be the knock-on effect of what you've been changing, surely? Like the butterfly effect.' It seemed pretty obvious to me.

'Not at all. We have sophisticated systems that track the fallout of every single event we alter. We wouldn't set foot back in time if we couldn't manage the knock-on effect. Remember the ethics committee? That's their whole job, to ensure a minimised impact.'

'So what's changing history?' I was now sitting forward, utterly captivated.

'We have no idea. HQ has told us it's related to the system upgrade they've implemented. They're saying there's nothing actually wrong in history, there's just a glitch in how our data is reading it. But I'm not convinced. Nor is Theo. But whatever the reason, the timelines appear to change every few days, so in these instances we have to act immediately or we'll never be able to pinpoint the exact time, location and circumstance in which to travel back to.'

'Why bother at all? There must be a gazillion things you can change in time. Why choose these difficult cases? You must have far less chance of success.'

'Did you just say gazillion?' Scott smiled.

'It's a word!'

'Call yourself a mathematician.'

'I'm not, I'm a data analyst. That's completely different.' I stuck my tongue out at him and he chuckled.

'To answer your question,' he continued, 'I don't know. It's not up to us. HQ sends the cases through to Seb. They're like orders. We don't get to pick and choose, we just know that HQ is sending us back because they've identified an event important enough to change.'

I had a hundred more questions all ready to roll off my tongue, but I was halted by Leanne's entrance. She appeared through the door in the back. A door I wasn't allowed to go through.

'I don't think I'm keen on the fashion of 1993,' she said with a grimace. She was wearing stonewash jeans and a black crop top. She had a stunning figure and a gorgeous tan. I instantly hated her more.

'You look great,' Scott said with a smile.

'Aww, thank you hubby,' she said, kissing him on the cheek.

A middle aged skinny man appeared from the back door and he put down a box on the bench. It was the same man that had given us our eighties outfits the night before.

'Here's your currency, your plastic bits, your accessories,' he said, grabbing bits from the box. Scott and Leanne started rummaging through what they needed.

'Why do you need children?' I asked, breaking through their concentration. I recalled Leanne's many ramblings about their happy pretend family and I was desperate to know.

'Why are you asking that?' Leanne said.

'People trust a family unit more than an older couple with no children,' Scott replied.

'Although I am only thirty-one, I'd like to add,' Leanne said.

'But we're talking 1993,' Scott countered. 'It's a little bit different to today.' Scott glared at me and I knew he didn't want me to say anything else.

'Are you taking children with you?' I asked, ignoring Scott's clear signals that I should shut up.

'Are you serious?' Leanne asked with disbelief.

'It's her job to challenge us,' Scott told Leanne. 'No, Chloe, we're just pretending to have children. Pubs weren't generally child friendly in 1993, as you well know. Our little ones will be at home with their babysitter.'

'So you have a complete back story? You really do this

properly!'

'And I hope you'll be reporting that back to HQ,' Scott nodded, before quickly adding, 'It's time to go.'

I knew I should be playing more of my consultant role, but it was all too fascinating. This was such a bizarre job. I had to ask my questions while I could.

I followed Scott and Leanne down the many green corridors again. She was wittering on about what she'd wear on her actual wedding day, but I was more interested in the fact that Scott kept turning around to check on me. Other than to make sure he didn't walk into things, his eyes were fixated on me.

We finally arrived at the room where I'd first appeared, with the purple walls and the five black boxes. Scott and Leanne immediately stepped over to Theo and they all analysed something on his monitor. Next to them was Archie. He handed them both the time travelling watch things and they discussed technical stuff that went completely over my head.

Gloria appeared in the doorway. 'Are we all ready?' she asked. She glared at me standing awkwardly by the wall. 'You are to wait in here until you are either escorted out or Inspector Lacey arrives back. Do you understand?'

I nodded. I had no intention of messing with her. She was far too scary.

'Have you got everything?' she asked, approaching Scott and Leanne.

'Here you go,' Dom said, appearing next to me, carrying a chair. 'Perhaps we could sit you at the back.'

I followed Dom to the back of the room where he placed down the chair right in the corner. I felt like such a naughty school girl, but I wasn't going to argue.

Gloria and Dom scurried off and Scott stepped over to one of the black boxes, which I remembered were called "modules". He opened the door and then hesitated. He quickly turned his head and scanned the room before resting his eyes directly on me.

'I'll see you soon,' he said with a confident smile.

'Good luck,' I replied.

He stepped in the box and Leanne took her place in the box just next to him. Theo checked both of the doors – I assumed to make sure they were closed properly – before he made his way back to his monitor.

'Ready whenever you are,' Theo said, and I found myself holding my breath.

I was jittery with excitement and nerves. I was about to witness time travel. I know I'd travelled to the future myself, but it was now different. I now knew what was going on.

I didn't move my eyes from the modules. I was ready for the action.

When was it going to happen?

Theo and Archie watched their monitors and I was literally sitting on the edge of my seat, poised to witness the marvel of time travel.

But absolutely nothing happened. We all just sat in silence.

After about ten minutes, Archie stood up. 'Anyone want a coffee?' he asked.

'Yes please,' Theo said.

'Chloe?' he asked.

'I'm sorry, have they now gone back in time?' I asked, ever so politely.

'Yes. Of course,' he replied, looking at me like I was stupid.

'It's very simple then?'

'What were you expecting?'

'I don't know,' I shrugged. Doctor Who's TARDIS popped into my head, but I was far too embarrassed to admit it.

'Why haven't they instantly come back?' I asked.

'They've got work to do,' Theo replied, now also looking at me like I was stupid.

'But they're time travellers. Surely it wouldn't matter if they were doing stuff for a decade, they must be able to transport back to the time they left?'

'Oh I see,' Theo said, now sporting that same "the penny has dropped" expression that Dom had had many times in my presence. 'No, we have to preserve their individual timelines. You know that time isn't linear?' He studied my confused face for a second before shaking his head. 'It's very complicated. Anyway, all that aside, if they went for a week somewhere, or even an hour, and then came back at the time they left, they'd be a week or an hour older and forced to repeat the time that they'd already lived through. So, essentially, however long they're gone for, that's how long it is until we see them again.'

'You mean so they won't grow old prematurely?' I asked, trying to keep up.

'Basically, yeah.'

My brain began processing Theo's explanation. It seemed a total contradiction. By his definition, time *was* linear. No matter where they were in time, minutes and hours of their lives passed by the same. So that made it a straight line by my calculation.

There was so much to consider when it came to time travel.

'Coffee?' Archie nudged, interrupting my thought trail. He was now standing next to me and I hadn't even noticed.

'That would be lovely, thank you. White no sugar, please.'

'On its way.'

I watched Archie leave and I went straight back to my contemplation. At least it would give me something to do. I had no idea how long Scott would be gone for. I'd figured it would be pretty instant, but now I was worried he'd be gone for an hour or two.

THIRTEEN

Scott was in fact gone virtually all day.

I'd been brought drinks, escorted to lunch and dinner, and, very annoyingly, I'd had to ask to be taken to the toilet.

Theo and Archie had been lucky enough to get regular breaks. After the first hour had passed, they took it in turns to work for a couple of hours while the other one disappeared off somewhere else. I was the only one who had to endure the torture of just waiting, endlessly.

My contemplation of time travel had got boring very quickly. Mainly because I wanted to ask lots of questions but I didn't want to be bothersome to Theo or Archie. Having lots of questions and no answers was very dull, so deciding exactly what shade of purple the walls were soon became my pastime of choice.

Thankfully, after what felt like hours of naming shades of purple in my head, but may have only been ten minutes, Dom came in to check on progress. As soon as he saw me tucked away in the corner, practically dribbling with boredom, he remembered that Scott had requested some "appropriate entertainment" for me.

At least now I understood that meant "nothing from the future".

It took him a while to source something suitable, but eventually he appeared with a pack of cards. It was the safest option he could find, apparently. They looked pretty much like cards from my time, but they felt terribly coarse. They weren't exactly easy to shuffle.

Shuffling became the least of my worries, though. I might have been gifted a pack of cards, but I spent the next half an hour wondering how I could play solitaire without anything to lean on. Why were tables so overlooked in the future?

I finally gave in and crouched on the floor. However this caused all sorts of commotion. Theo got straight on the phone and before I knew it he had half the building trying to locate me a table.

I was highly embarrassed when Dom placed the tiny desk in front of me. It was very dusty. I don't know where they'd dug it up from. But I was also very grateful. Now I could pass the time with solitaire. I'd always loved a bit of solitaire.

Two hours of solitaire was far too much. It was also making my back ache as the chair was too high for the table and I was having to lean over. All in all, this day was proving to be really crap. Far from the thrilling vision of time travel I imagined it would be.

By eight o'clock in the evening I was going out of my mind.

I missed my phone badly. I could be texting my mum or Freya, or catching up on Instagram. Hours would flit away when I had my phone in my hand. I'd never known time to feel so stagnant. Which was truly ironic considering my company.

'Oh, here we go, here we go,' Theo said, breaking the tedious silence. My heart fluttered with hope.

The door to one of the modules opened and a very tired looking Scott stepped out. Leanne opened the module next to him and I jumped to my feet. It was over!

'Can you check the timelines?' Scott said, immediately

pacing over to look at Theo's monitor.

Theo put his finger to his ear. 'They're back,' he said.

I wanted to run over and hug Scott. It was an incredible feat. It was one thing to know he was a time traveller, but to witness him re-emerge like that was amazing.

I remained still in my corner, though. He was clearly exhausted and Leanne was hovering around him like a needy dog.

'Yep, yep,' Theo nodded, swiping his hands across his monitor. 'It looks good. It looks better than good.'

'I'd call that a win!' Scott said and Leanne threw her arms around him. They embraced for a moment and she kissed him right on the lips.

Scott exhaled, gently pushing her away. I could almost see the relief pouring through him. It must have been a hard trip.

But then maybe they always were.

'Give me the news,' Seb said, entering the room, shortly followed by Gloria and Dom.

'It's straight,' Theo replied. 'The timeline has stabilised. And it's good news.' Seb glanced at the monitor and I was dying to know what the outcome had been. They must have stopped that man from killing his family.

Wow. They'd just saved the lives of a man's family. Those people were now living because of the heroes standing in front of me. It was remarkable.

'Great work, team. Excellent work,' Seb said. 'But we have more to celebrate than that.' Seb addressed Scott and shook his hand. 'Congratulations Inspector Lacey. That's your one hundredth assignment complete.'

I was gobsmacked. One hundred assignments? Scott had saved one hundred people? No, it would be more than that. Hundreds, maybe even thousands of lives had literally been changed because of him. I was becoming more and more in awe of their work by the second.

Cheers and laughter started to fill up the room. The rest of the team slowly began to join us, and before I knew it I could barely see Scott so many people were surrounding him.

Still stuck in my corner, I didn't know what to do. Eventually Dom came over to me. 'I'm really sorry, you're not going to be able to join in the celebrations,' he said, and I could hear his genuine regret.

'Really?'

'They're heading out into town and you're under strict instructions not to leave the building. Come on, I'll take you back to your room.'

I hesitated. Scott hadn't even so much as acknowledged my existence. I looked over one more time. I could just about make out his beaming face, thanking his peers for their congratulatory comments.

I was rippled with emotions as I turned back to Dom. I felt sad that I wasn't going to see Scott, angry that he was now ignoring me, especially after I'd sat patiently waiting for him all day, and most of all jealous that I wouldn't get to go out with him and his friends.

'Let's go then,' I said, trying to pretend that I didn't care.

I followed Dom out of the room, desperately making a last attempt to catch Scott's attention, but he was in deep conversation with Barbara. He wasn't interested in me.

I was led down the endless green corridors to my room and Dom left me at the door to scan my eyes. I sensed he was eager to get back to the party.

I went straight in and sat on my bed. It wasn't even nine o'clock and I was about as bored as a person could be.

I'd also left my pack of cards in the module room, so I had absolutely nothing to do.

I took my new uniform off and got into my pyjamas. I lay in bed but I was even too bored to sleep.

I lay awake for ages, wondering what Scott was doing at that moment and wishing I could be with him.

No doubt he was in a bar somewhere with Leanne, and they were all over each other like lovesick teenagers.

I tried not to think about her. Instead I closed my eyes

and thought of home. Would my life be the same, now that I'd seen the future? I couldn't imagine going back to my mundane data analyst job after seeing how Scott was literally changing the world for the better. It made me feel quite insignificant.

Finally, as I thought of my friends and family and my life as it was, I drifted off to sleep.

My eyes snapped open as I thought I heard something. I glanced at the clock next to me and it said two twenty-six. Maybe it was just pipes or something.

I listened out and within seconds I heard it again. Someone was knocking at my door.

I stepped out of bed feeling momentarily cautious, until I remembered that I was in a police station. Well, sort of. But at least I could be sure there wasn't a criminal at my door.

I opened it slowly to find Scott standing there. He pushed me back into the room, almost swiping me off my feet, and kissed me.

He pulled away just so he could kick the door shut with his foot, and then he swiftly turned back and kissed me again.

In my dazed state in the middle of the night, I wasn't sure if it was a dream. It was a warm and loving kiss, as so often the kisses from him were. When we were apart, I'd spend hours fantasising about his lips against mine, and for a second I believed this was all my imagination and I was still fast asleep, enjoying the sort of dream that you never want to wake up from.

I threw my arms around him and melted into his embrace, letting the sparks of delight dance through me.

Very slowly, though, as the taste of stale beer became apparent, the spell broke and I snapped back to reality.

I stepped away from him, once again muddled with emotions. He was so good at making my head spin.

We stood staring at each other and I could see he was

on the verge of kissing me again. He was hungry for it and I really wanted his lips on mine.

No. He wasn't treating me right.

Not knowing what else to do, I quickly retreated back into bed. I pulled the duvet over me but kept sitting up, just in case he thought it was an invitation for him to join me.

He came over and sat next to me, his eyes droopy from the alcohol and the exhaustion of his day. He looked incredibly smart, dressed in a black suit with a dark tie.

'Have you been somewhere nice?' I asked.

'Just a few bars,' he said, holding my hand. He was slurring his words.

'They must have been fancy ones. You're very dressed up.' He looked down at his clothes.

'Oh no. This is what people wear in my time. Casual clothes are very old fashioned.' He leaned in to kiss me again and I tried to pull away, but I was conscious that if I went too far I'd fall out of bed.

'Did you have fun?' I asked, pushing him back against the head rest.

'It was a celebration. I've been on a hundred... one hund... hundred assignments.'

'I know, I was there. Not that you noticed.'

He looked down. 'I'm sorry. It was a bad day. It was a very tough assignment. By the time we got back I was all over the place. I'm sorry.'

Without even knowing it was coming, I loudly sneezed. A clear sign that I'd been interrupted in the early hours of the morning.

'You have the best sneezes,' Scott smiled. 'I love your sneezes. Neigh!' It was only when he was drunk that he actually mocked me with horse impressions. It had always made me laugh before but at that moment it just made me sad.

He pulled back the covers and slipped in next to me. I wanted to argue, but I couldn't resist the feel of him. He wrapped his arm around me and kissed me again. This time it was a softer kiss and I was instantly enjoying it far too much to object.

'I missed you tonight,' he whispered. Then he sighed. 'What a fucking mess.'

He pulled me in closer and lay on his back. He stared up at the ceiling in thought and I rested my head on his chest. I didn't know what to say. All I could think about was how good he smelled and how much it hurt that this would have to end soon.

Within a few seconds I heard him snore. He was out cold, and it didn't take long before I was fast asleep next to him.

He woke with a jolt a few hours later and it shocked me awake too. He looked at me still wrapped up in his arms. 'Shit, what's the time, what's the time?'

I glanced over at the clock. 'Half five.'

'I'd better go,' he said, leaping out of bed.

'Is there a problem?'

'If anyone catches me here, coming out of your room in last night's clothes. Oh Chloe... I've got to go.'

'Right.'

He quickly kissed me goodbye and darted off.

I lay on my back and sighed. I realised that I'd probably just spent the last night I'd ever have with him. I couldn't continue this when I got home. It was one thing playing along when I was literally out of time, but it was another thing putting myself through pain for no gain at all.

I wanted to sleep, but I had no idea what time Scott would be back for breakfast, and I didn't want to make him late. Especially knowing how important punctuality was to these time travelling cops.

I got up and decided to have a leisurely shower. At least I'd be ready for whatever o'clock Scott was going to reappear.

I hoped it would be soon.

FOURTEEN

It wasn't soon. Continuing the day of boredom I'd just had to suffer through, I had to wait until ten o'clock before Scott tapped on my door for breakfast.

I'd been lying on top of my sheets, trying not to crease my uniform, falling in and out of sleep. Ever since I'd arrived in this place, time had done nothing but drag.

'Hello,' I said as I opened the door. It was the first time I'd ever seen Scott look that tired. I'd seen him hungover before but this was more. He looked like the weight of the world was bearing down on him.

'Let's go and eat,' he said.

We walked side by side to the canteen in silence. I didn't know what to say and Scott seemed a million miles away.

As soon as we got there, I chose my fruit and cereal while Scott opted for a huge fry up. He clearly needed it.

I couldn't help feeling a few sparks of joy as I watched him devour his scrambled eggs. Having a man sneak into your room in the middle of the night, when his girlfriend was probably waiting for him just down the corridor, was quite thrilling. It was heartbreaking too, but I chose not to dwell on that.

I sat trying not to smile too much, munching on my

cornflakes, when I heard the soft sound of Scott humming to himself.

'Is that *Yesterday*?' I asked.

He looked across at me. 'What about yesterday?'

'No, you were humming to yourself again.'

'Was I? Oh right, yeah.'

'So, was I right?'

'About what?'

'Was it *Yesterday*?'

'Erm, yeah, I think so. Yeah. It's been going round and round my head all morning.'

I'd known very little about The Beatles before Scott had come into my life, but in the last few weeks I'd been successfully able to guess every single song that he'd been singing to himself. He'd opened my eyes to a wonderful new range of music. And also a wonderful new game. I'd been loving "guess that song" and I was winning on a regular basis.

I was yet to share my game with him. I'd been secretly keeping score to date. It was on the tip of my tongue to tell him that I was in the lead, when I stopped myself. Now really wasn't the time. He was eerily distant and far from his usual cheery self.

'Scott, you're needed,' Dom said, appearing next to our table.

'For what?' Scott replied.

'Emergency meeting.'

'But Seb said we could have the day off.'

'Believe me, this is urgent.'

Scott reluctantly nodded. There was no denying the stress across Dom's face.

I scoffed the last of my cornflakes and followed Scott to his office. The whole team was already there, including an older man that I'd not seen before.

Leanne, Bradley and Barbara were sitting at the monitors and everyone else stood at the back. Scott took the last remaining seat, which I'd calculated must be his 'desk', and

I stood next to Archie in the corner.

'I know you were expecting a few hours off today after last night's celebrations, but we've got a problem,' Seb said, addressing the room. 'I'll leave it to Earl to explain.'

The man I hadn't recognised stepped forward and I made a note that this was Earl. I'd heard a lot about him, as the ultimate man in charge from Headquarters, but his physical presence didn't mirror his reputation. He wasn't very tall, like virtually everyone else, and he had a bit of a beer belly. In fact he was the polar opposite of the fit, agile, physically dominating superbeings that surrounded me. I hadn't realised just how superior they all were until now.

'We find ourselves in highly unexpected circumstances,' he began. His voice was grave and firm, but his shuffling on the spot made him appear anything but confident. 'We need to work as a team now more than ever.'

Glances were shared across the room and I could tell a situation like this wasn't normal.

'A highly sensitive document has been placed in the office of a legal firm in central London,' Earl continued. 'For reasons that we cannot explain, the timelines keep moving, but what remains constant is that a person with great power and questionable connections has been given the opportunity to use this information to the detriment of... To great detriment.'

'Why can't I pull up any information?' Scott asked, flicking through his monitor.

'We're working on it,' Theo said from the back.

'We need to ensure that this document never gets seen,' Earl said. 'After a great deal of investigation, we've found that the timelines are going around on a loop. We've run the scenarios and we've narrowed down that the best chance of success is in a very tight window that we're currently in. We have to act now or face potentially losing completely.'

'What's going on?' Scott asked. 'Does this relate to your so-called computer glitch?'

'We're working on that. That's for my team to worry

about. What you need to do is ensure that this document is destroyed.'

'Get it and bring it back here?' Barbara asked.

'No!' Earl snapped. 'It won't work.' He was getting sweatier by the second. 'Extraction scenarios always fall down as the person is expecting to find this document. We have to destroy it and make it look like an accident.'

'Are these timeline issues ever going to get sorted?' Scott asked.

'I've said, that's for my team to worry about,' Earl replied, assertively. 'You need to put into action the only thing that will save us.'

There was a moment of stiff silence before Scott asked, 'What's the play?'

'It's March 2014 and you need to set fire to the building. Logistics are working on how to make it look accidental. They'll have the answer within the hour.'

'We don't set fire to things,' Scott remarked, clearly surprised by Earl's instruction. 'That's not how we work.'

Earl shifted again.

'You need to tell my team everything,' Seb warned. It was getting uncomfortably tense.

'We have no choice but to start a fire,' Earl explained, trying his best to stay calm. 'Every other scenario leads to disaster.'

'Disaster?' Barbara asked. 'What sort of disaster?'

'You can't let them go back without knowing,' Seb said.

Earl took a deep breath. 'My team identified that a fire was the only way we could be confident to secure the future. We need to secure the future. There is a very small window of opportunity for success at twenty-two seventeen when the Security Guard leaves his post. We can transport you in at that point to start the fire and you'll have three minutes and twelve seconds to get out.'

'Security Guard?' Scott said with agitation. 'There's somebody in the building? Will he get hurt?'

Earl hesitated. He couldn't look at Scott. 'No.'

Scott glared at Earl. 'Somebody else gets hurt?'

'There is one other person in the building that is working late. There's no way around it. He will die.'

'No way!' Scott said, standing up. 'We don't do this. I'm not going to be responsible for someone's death.'

'It's one life to save hundreds,' Earl argued. 'No, actually, thousands.'

'We can't make judgements like that,' Scott bit back.

'Sit down,' Earl demanded fiercely.

Scott did as he was told but he was clearly seething.

'You're being instructed to go back in time and start a fire. You're the best team I have here. You will have three minutes and twelve seconds to start that fire and you will be going back within the next three hours. If you fail to do any of this the implications will be very serious.'

'You need to tell them why,' Seb urged again.

'Fine,' Earl replied with frustration. 'We don't know how this has happened. I have all my resources on it. The document that appears on this desk is... it's a list...' He sighed, trying to find his words. 'It's a list of all the families of everyone in this branch. If it's not destroyed then all of our grandparents and great grandparents are going to face implications that we can't get a hold of. We have no idea how bad this can get, but it will undoubtedly strip this facility of everyone.'

There was a horrific silence as everyone absorbed the news. 'How has someone in the past put all of our names together?' Bradley asked. 'Do we have a leak? Is that even possible?'

'You don't need to worry about any of that,' Earl insisted, wiping his brow with a tissue. 'My team is working on it. All you need to do is make sure that this list is eradicated. Is that clear?'

'At the cost of an innocent life?' Scott said, poking further at Earl's slowly erupting state.

'We have no choice,' Earl replied.

'We always have a choice.'

'Not this time.'

'There are always other options. Can't we run some more scenarios?'

'There's no time!'

'I've been at it since eight hundred, Scott,' Theo said. 'If we're successful in destroying the document then either you get out of there and the man dies or you try to save him and you both die.'

'Can't we go back sooner?' Scott asked, getting desperate. 'Can't we stop him going into the building?'

'No!' Earl bellowed. 'The only reason we have this window of opportunity in the first place is because he falls over and gets trapped beneath a bookcase and the Security Guard is alerted to it. We believe he calls the Guard from his mobile phone. When the Guard leaves to find out what's happened, we have a rare chance to get about unseen.'

'But-'

'If the Guard sees you he will arrest you. You need to move about freely.'

'But-'

'We have no more time to plan anything else!' Earl roared. 'We have four hours left before this window is closed. We've been trying to find every other way around this, but we haven't even come close to another alternative. There is simply no more time.'

'We're fucking time travellers!' Scott yelled, once again rising to his feet. 'How is it that we have no time?'

'I don't know!' Earl snapped back. 'We will find out, but for now we need to secure all our futures.'

'And burn a man alive?' Scott shouted.

The tension had reached a suffocating peak as everyone watched Earl. Scott was shooting daggers in his direction.

'I'll need all the Inspectors on this,' Earl said, refusing to acknowledge Scott's persistent questioning anymore. 'Please go and wait in Logistics. They'll get you ready and will give you details of how and where to start the fire. Light the fire and return immediately. This is a very dangerous assignment. Do not cross me.'

Scott was still glaring at Earl with venomous eyes. I'd never seen him so angry. I really was getting to know him better in his own time. He was so much more than the cheeky, lively man I'd grown to love. He was passionate and fiery with a deep moral code. I had a whole new level of respect for him and it made me love him all the more.

'This could cost us everything,' Earl stated, scowling back at Scott. 'Do not let that happen.'

FIFTEEN

'Scott, you'll be lead in the field, but I'll be closely overseeing everything beforehand,' Seb said, trying to calm things down. 'We need to get on with this now. Are you going to do your job?'

Scott didn't move. He was still glaring fiercely at Earl, while every other pair of eyes in the room was staring at him; waiting to see what he was going to do.

Finally he nodded. 'I'll do what needs to be done.'

'Good,' Seb said, but I could tell he wasn't convinced that Scott was actually going to comply. And, to be honest, neither was I.

But what could he do? Orders were orders and this was life and death for all of them. As awful as it was, there was much more at stake than one man's life.

'Right,' Seb announced to the room, 'you all know what needs to be done. Let's get on with it.'

The room quickly emptied as the team set off in their different directions, ready to manage whatever role they had in this grave assignment. Scott slowly turned around and placed his eyes on me. He didn't say a word but I knew it was time to follow him.

I walked with all the Inspectors and Seb to the Logistics

department. Not one person spoke.

'We've figured it out,' the skinny man said as we arrived and it was nice to hear a voice. 'Where's Theo? He needs to know.'

Seb pressed his finger to his ear and summoned Theo. As we waited, my mind started to question what was inside everyone's ear. It was clearly some sort of futuristic telephone system.

I made a quiet note to ask Scott next time we were alone. If that would ever happen again.

Theo came hurtling into the room a minute or two later and everyone's attention once again turned to the skinny man.

He held up a small, metal, rectangular box. 'Place this on any plug socket in the room. It will start the fire and make it look like an electrical fault.'

'Will it be traceable?' Seb asked.

'This technology didn't exist until the sixties. There's no way anyone will detect it in 2014. And the fine exterior will burn very easily, removing any evidence of its existence. It's the best option we have in such a short space of time.'

'Theo?' Seb asked. Theo started to fiddle with the little black box in his hand. They all seemed to have these black boxes. I guessed they were like new age iPads.

'Yeah, I concur. By far the best chance. In fact, if we do it right then this could be hugely successful.'

'I've just got you simple black clothing,' the skinny man said. He disappeared for a moment and reappeared with four black shirts and four pairs of black trousers. 'And a torch each,' he said, placing four torches down next to the clothing. 'The building will be dark.'

'Right, get yourselves ready and we'll work through the play,' Seb said. He turned to walk off when suddenly he placed his eyes on me. 'Chloe, please come with me. Scott has work to do.'

I glanced at Scott who nodded gently and I followed Seb and Theo. We walked back through the corridors towards the module room. For the first time I was starting to get a feel for where everything was. It wasn't so much of a maze when you thought about it.

I wasn't given a chair this time. Everyone was far too busy to notice. I just stood in the corner and watched their anxious bodies work at about a million miles an hour.

Around half an hour later, Scott, Leanne, Bradley and Barbara all appeared, dressed in their black outfits.

'Are we ready?' Scott asked. I'd never seen his face so dark and angry.

Theo was still working away on his monitor and Seb stood forward to address the Inspectors.

'We've found that the document is somewhere in a Douglas Atkinson's office-'

'I'm sorry, say that name again,' Leanne interrupted.

'Douglas Atkinson,' Seb said.

'Douglas Atkinson?' she repeated. 'A lawyer in 2014?'

'Yes.'

'Not the office of Hobson Pierce? Near Bank?' Leanne had turned pale.

'How did you know?' Seb asked.

'That's my Great Grandfather. What has this got to do with my Great Grandfather?'

'There's something going on here,' Scott said. 'I don't like any of it. As much as I don't buy any of that computer glitch crap.'

'I agree,' Barbara added. 'We're not being told the full story.'

'Maybe not,' Seb said. 'But it's not for us to worry about.'

'Why not mention it at least? HQ must have known that this man was related to Leanne. Why not tell us?'

'I'm sure they had their reasons.'

'Come on.'

'Maybe it's because it's not our job!' Seb asserted, putting Scott firmly in his place. 'Earl has made it very clear - on several occasions - that his team is working on these issues. The best thing we can do to support them is make problems in the field disappear. Do we all agree on that?'

No one said a word.

'Good,' Seb stated, taking their lack of arguing with him as agreement. 'Now, let's get on with this assignment.'

'We know his office is on floor two but you'll need to find out the exact location,' Theo explained. 'Earl wants the blaze to begin as close to the document as possible to ensure that it's properly destroyed, so you must find his office. I'll land you by the staircase at the start of the corridor. That's the best I can do.'

'The man gets trapped under a bookcase?' Scott asked, as if he hadn't heard a word Theo had been saying.

Theo regarded him with hesitation. He turned his head to Seb who nodded for Theo to reply. 'Yes.'

'What happens?' Scott asked. He was so deadly serious.

'It's not important,' Seb said.

'What happens?' Scott demanded to know.

Theo sighed. 'The Security Guard tries his best but he won't have time to release the man. We suspect that he'll run out to get help when he's aware of the fire, but it'll be too late. At least it will only be one casualty.'

'It's not what any of us want,' Seb muttered.

I couldn't take my eyes off Scott. He seemed deeply pre-occupied, no doubt tearing himself to shreds over what he was about to do. What he had no choice but to do.

The greater good must seem of little comfort when you have to knowingly take a man's life. I couldn't even begin to imagine how he was feeling.

'How do we track down the right office?' Leanne asked, breaking some of the tension.

'The certificates on the wall,' Theo replied. 'He definitely had certificates on his office wall with his name on.'

'Open the door and check, open the next door and check,' Seb said. 'Keep it speedy but thorough. I need three of you checking the rooms and you, Scott, following with the device. When you get a positive location, place the device on a socket in the room and come straight back here.

Not one of you is to delay. Do you understand?'

'It seems simple enough,' Bradley said.

'And be quiet,' Seb said.

'The man who is trapped is one floor below you,' Theo added. 'If you stomp around too much you'll catch the attention of the Security Guard. We can't afford to invite questions. It has to look like an electrical fault.'

'Be invisible,' Seb warned.

'Your CPGs are ready,' Theo said, handing them out. 'End of the stairs, go straight to your left.'

'Rooms either side of the corridor?' Scott asked.

'Yes,' Theo replied. 'It's a significant building.'

'That we're about to torch,' Scott followed with very quickly.

'For all of us and every person we have ever saved,' Seb bit back.

Scott turned away from Seb, his face full of fury. He addressed his fellow Inspectors. 'Bradley on the left, Barbara on the right.'

'What about me?' Leanne said.

'I want you to use your wits. Let's see how long this floor is. We'll do whatever we can to speed it up. Any questions?'

Everyone shook their heads and Scott took a deep breath.

'Three minutes, twelve seconds is the maximum amount of time you can have,' Seb ordered. 'Failure is not an option.'

There was a very small moment where no one moved. The tension was so palpable it was almost suffocating.

'You'd better go,' Theo said.

Finally Scott took a step towards his module, and soon after the other Inspectors followed his lead. They all entered their respective black boxes and Theo checked the doors of each one, before sitting back down at his monitor.

'Time,' he said after a few seconds and I could see on his screen a clock ticking back from three minutes twelve.

I'd never been more scared. Although I didn't know

exactly what of.

I suddenly noticed that I wasn't breathing and I took a few short breaths. I needed to calm myself down.

What if they weren't successful? Would everything instantly change around us?

Theo had said time wasn't linear. I hadn't got a clue what that meant, but I was becoming very fearful that it would somehow impact our imminent future.

My legs felt weak beneath me as I realised I had far too many questions and very few answers.

A minute had gone by and I was still breathless.

I imagined the four of them running down a pitch black empty corridor, searching for a certificate hanging on a wall with the name Douglas Atkinson on it. Barbara would wave to indicate she'd located it and Scott would race in, skidding on his knees, before slapping that metal device on a socket right at the back of the room. They'd all share a mutual satisfactory nod before hitting their watches and appearing back in 2086.

Or maybe it wouldn't be that easy.

One minute left.

What if they hadn't even found the office yet?

They were highly skilled operatives. They must be able to remain calm under pressure. I bet it's just like any other job for them.

Except for the fact that every other member of the team was now in the room with me and they all looked just as terrified as I was. I knew this wasn't business as usual.

There were just twenty seconds left.

I felt the urge to cry. I didn't even know why.

My heart was pounding and it was all I could hear against the silent tension. I wanted to close my eyes but I couldn't stop staring at Theo's countdown.

We were approaching the last few seconds.

Where were they?

Seven, six, five...

Leanne's door suddenly flew open. They were back!

She raced over to Theo. 'Did it work? What's the outcome?'

Next Barbara appeared and then a millisecond later Bradley opened his module door.

All of the team scurried over and huddled around Theo's computer, waiting for him to determine if the mission had been a success. All except for Bradley who was standing just outside of his module in very deep thought.

I stared at the module that Scott had stepped in but the door didn't open.

'It worked,' Theo said with very obvious relief. 'As far as I can tell, a huge success.'

It wasn't so much a celebration as more supportive hugs that were shared around the room. Still no one had noticed that Scott hadn't reappeared.

The team started to talk, but I wasn't listening. My eyes were fixed on Scott's module. Why hadn't he reappeared?

Francesca, Barbara and Archie disappeared off with purpose and everyone else carried on speaking to Theo, as if there was still more to learn.

Where was Scott?

I could feel the panic set in. My breathing was erratic. Why was no one paying any attention to the most important person in their team?

I looked across at Bradley who was still standing apart from everyone else. Had he noticed? He glanced at the team with a worried face and then darted out of the room as quickly as he could.

Did he know something? Was it bad?

I focused my attention fully on Scott's module again. My heart was racing uncontrollably. This wasn't right. Was he in there? Had guilt made him do something unthinkable?

The remaining people were still huddled around Theo's monitor, discussing facts and figures. No one acknowledged me stuck in the corner, and no one seemed to care at all about Scott.

Fear and dread started to consume me. This couldn't be

right.

Could it?

Maybe they knew he wasn't coming back. Maybe he'd been transported somewhere else. Maybe he'd...

Oh God, what had he done?

'Where's Scott?' I bellowed out, far too loudly. I couldn't contain it. I had to know.

All eyes turned to me.

'Scott hasn't come back,' I said, meekly.

'No!' The fear across Leanne's face nearly cut me in two. She raced to his module and flung the door open.

'No!' she shrieked and I lost all of my senses.

SIXTEEN

The module was completely empty. I couldn't get my head to work out why, though. What did that mean?

'Where is he?' Seb demanded to know.

Leanne looked distraught. 'He was just doing his job.'

'What did he do?'

'Oh God!' She started to wail dramatically and it was highly alarming.

'Leanne, you need to tell us.'

'I... It's... A few seconds after we got there, he said he saw someone at the end of the corridor,' she whined. 'He told me to take the device and work with the others while he went to check it out.'

'There was no one else in the building,' Theo stated.

'I didn't have time to question it. Why would he lie?' She started to cry uncontrollably and I turned giddy with desperation. Why was she so upset? What could have happened? I needed answers.

My mouth went dry as I watched Seb consult Theo again. Theo was flicking through information on his monitor quicker than I'd ever seen him move before. Everyone watched him for a few minutes, and then he slowly started to ease the pace. Eventually he stopped and stared at Seb. There was the slightest shake to his head.

'What is it?' I asked. My heart was thumping so hard it could have cracked my ribs.

'He's dead!' Leanne shrieked.

At first her words seemed to bounce off me. I couldn't process them. He couldn't be dead. She must have got it wrong.

I cast my eyes around the room, unable to escape the mortified faces of all the team.

'You can't know that for sure,' I said, glaring at Theo; desperate for him to agree with me.

'There were two bodies found in the wreckage,' he told me.

'That could be anybody!'

'There was no one else in the building.'

'What about the Security Guard?'

'He made it outside.'

'That doesn't mean anything.'

'The second body was never identified-'

'So there you go. It could be anyone.'

'It isn't,' Seb said, firmly but softly. 'It's Scott. There is no other explanation.'

'But...' I gasped for breath as the horror crept over me very slowly, paralysing me to the spot.

Scott was dead?

No; he couldn't be. He couldn't be.

The desperate excuses dissolved away from my head as I was forced to admit the horrendous truth.

Scott was dead.

Tears suddenly threatened to appear but I didn't want to cry in front of these people. These people that I didn't know.

I couldn't move. I didn't know what to do with myself. I was completely overwhelmed. It was only my frozen fear that was preventing me from collapsing.

Oh God. I was so far from home. I was all alone, so far from home. I didn't know how to deal with it.

It couldn't be true.

I looked around at his peers again as I felt my body begin to tremble.

'My boyfriend's dead!' Leanne howled.

The tears started freeing themselves and I looked to the floor. They couldn't see me like this. Other than Leanne, everyone else was just quietly mournful, keeping a firm grip on their emotions. I couldn't get into a mess. Not in front of these people. Not when they all knew Scott so much better than I did.

Leanne threw herself against Scott's module door and sobbed heartily into her arm. Dom walked over and placed his hand on her shoulder and I knew I couldn't bear this anymore. I wanted to be alone. I needed to be alone.

I started gasping for breath as the panic and sorrow became more and more intense. I could barely contain myself.

'Is he really dead?' I asked, still clinging on to some sort of hope that they could have got it wrong. They must have got it wrong. How could he be dead if I still loved him?

'We ran the scenarios,' Seb muttered. 'We ran them for hours. No one could have survived that fire.'

'It's not definite it's Scott, though,' I meekly suggested, not even convincing myself anymore.

'Stop being so stupid!' Leanne screeched in my direction. It made me feel so small and insignificant.

I could barely breathe. I looked down to the floor again, trying to block out Leanne's bawling. I had to keep my composure but everything around me was getting darker and darker and harder to process.

I took a deep breath in an attempt to halt the tears, but they were falling thick and fast. I couldn't let them, though. I knew as soon as I gave into them, the Nile would seem tame in comparison.

I needed a tissue. I looked up to see virtually all eyes in the room now firmly fixed on me. No one was watching Leanne's dramatics at the front, everyone was watching me.

Watching me with pity in their eyes.

I felt my lip quiver under the pressure of being such a spectacle, and more and more tears trickled down my cheeks.

I had to leave. I couldn't stay there. All I wanted was to curl up in bed and cry for years. But I wanted my own bed, not the horrible bed I was forced to sleep in, trapped seventy years ahead of my own life.

I closed my eyes and felt the pain.

I was never going to see Scott again. I'd lost him. I loved him more than I could ever imagine loving anyone, and in the shortest time he'd just gone.

He was gone forever.

My whole body was shaking with sorrow now. I wanted to sit on the floor; to let the grief take over. Nothing else mattered. Nothing else would ever matter again.

He was gone.

It was so unfair.

'Was there a funeral?' Seb mumbled to Theo. It was like being kicked really hard, right in the centre of my gut.

I gasped for breath again as flashes of Scott's seared body haunted my imagination. He was such a good man. He didn't deserve that.

He was the best man alive. In any time.

I glanced across to see Theo's fingers darting around his monitor once more. But I didn't want to know. There might have been pictures. I didn't want to see. I looked down again, taking deep breaths. I had to find a way to calm myself. At least for now.

'What is it?' Gloria asked, urgently.

My head flicked up. She was glaring at Theo who was shaking his head, but more through confusion.

'Theo?' Seb nudged.

'Hang on,' he said, concentrating hard on the screen before him. 'It's changing. This doesn't make any sense. I've never seen anything like it.' His speed of swiping through his monitor had risen to new levels.

My tears halted as I watched him work. I was shivering with anxiety and my fists were clenched firmly with hope.

'Oh God,' he whispered, looking up at Seb. Seb peered over to read the monitor.

'What is it?' Leanne demanded to know, wiping her face with her sleeve. 'What is it!'

'He's alive,' Seb said after a short pause.

'What?!' Leanne screeched.

I don't know how I didn't collapse this time. It was more than overwhelming.

'Where is he then?' Leanne asked. 'Why didn't he come back? What's he playing at?'

Theo and Seb shared a look of concern.

'What is it?' Gloria pushed.

'He was arrested for arson.'

SEVENTEEN

'Arrested?' Leanne screamed before I'd had any chance to process what Seb had just stated. 'He's been arrested?' She fell back against the module door, presenting more unnecessary dramatics. I couldn't look at her anymore. I turned my attention fully on to Seb hoping that he would elaborate.

But no one said anything.

'You have to go back and get him,' I said. It seemed pretty obvious what needed to be done.

Seb regarded me, full of regret. 'I'm afraid it's not that simple.'

'Why not?'

'Is this like your first day of time travel or something?' Leanne asked, scornfully.

I didn't know how to respond so I just ignored her and continued to focus on Seb.

'Scott is now a part of that history,' Seb said, softly. 'With an arrest comes records. We can't lift him out of that time without inviting a lot of undue attention. He's going to have to see it through.'

'See it through?' I asked with disbelief. 'See it through? See what through?' The second I'd said it, I was horrified by what the answer could be. 'He hasn't done anything.'

Everyone in the room glared at me and I realised that he was, in fact, guilty. They'd lit the fire. It had been a deliberate arson attack. Whatever the justification, they were guilty.

But, no, Scott wasn't!

'He didn't do it,' I argued, as if my words were about to change everything. 'You said it yourself, Leanne: he went off. He didn't actually start the fire. And I bet we can all figure out where he went.'

'He said he saw someone,' she replied and it instantly made my blood boil.

'Do you even know Scott?' I asked with more contempt than I knew I could muster up.

'Excuse me?'

'He was told that one person alone couldn't save the man under the bookcase. It's obvious where he went.'

Leanne flashed me the dirtiest of looks. 'I was trying to protect him,' she hissed.

I couldn't look at her. Everything about her made me angry. I turned to Seb again.

'There won't be any evidence against him,' I stated. 'He didn't do anything. He was saving that man. Surely that will work in his favour?'

Theo scanned his monitor. 'I suppose it won't look good that he was there at the time, but you're right there's no way they'll be able to prove he started it.'

'So when he's free, can we go and get him?'

Seb turned to Theo. 'How did it play out?'

'That's what I'm trying to find out,' Theo replied. 'But I can't get a grasp on the timelines. It's not making any sense.'

'You've got to give me something, Theo,' Seb said. 'Earl is going to find out very soon. We need to be one step ahead. We need to limit the damage here.'

'I just... Hang on...' We all stood in silence watching Theo's fingers dart around his monitor like he had some sort of super-speed robotic hand.

Minutes went by and he still couldn't tell us anything. My

heart started to pound as I grew concerned that no news meant bad news.

After what felt like an age, Theo finally said, 'Right, I have a trend. I can't get a grasp on any sort of outcome, but there is one thing that seems to have definitely happened.'

'What's that?' I asked. Words were freeing themselves from my mouth in a way I'd never known before.

Theo shifted himself in his seat before he addressed Seb directly. 'He's charged with arson, but he isn't in a position to post bail so he has to stay in remand until his hearing.'

'But surely they find him innocent!' I exclaimed.

'In remand?' Leanne screamed, like the world had ended. 'My boyfriend's in remand? How could he be so stupid?'

'Stupid?' I spat back at her. 'Is trying to save a man's life stupid?'

'Don't give me that,' she retorted. 'He had a job to do. His orders were clear. But no, instead he had to go running off like Reginald Jackson, trying to save the day.'

'Who's Reginald Jackson?' I asked. What was she wittering on about?

'What's wrong with you?' she sneered.

I turned to Seb who shook his head slightly and I remembered that I was in the future.

'He wasn't being like Reginald Jackson,' I bellowed back, confidently. 'He was being like Scott Lacey. A truly decent man who was more concerned with saving another man's life than risking his own. We should be celebrating him not bad-mouthing him.'

'He had orders!' Leanne shouted back. 'We have orders for a reason. And now he's locked up. He's so stupid!'

'Stop calling him stupid!'

'Cut it out!' Gloria demanded. She was so firm, Leanne and I both immediately backed down. 'We need to focus on the facts, not our own feelings about Inspector Lacey's behaviour. As a starting point I think it would be very helpful to know if Scott was even successful. Theo, did the man survive?'

'Yes, I believe so,' Theo said as he flicked around his monitor again.

Suddenly his face went pale and his hands dropped.

'What is it?' Seb asked.

'This can't be right. When I looked earlier... It...'

'What?' Seb urged.

'It said Scott had been charged with arson. But it's changed. How can it have changed? This is nonsensical.'

'He's been found innocent?' I asked with hope.

Theo just shook his head with dismay.

'What is it?' Seb pushed, almost as desperate to know as I was.

'He's now been charged with arson and murder.'

A tense silence gripped the room. No one knew what to say. Even Leanne wasn't over-dramatising it.

'I can't get a handle on it,' Theo said. 'It now appears that the man didn't survive. He died in the fire. The fire they believe Scott started.'

I couldn't process it. 'He was trying to save that man's life,' I insisted. 'He's not a murderer. He didn't want to kill anyone. You made him do it! Out of all of you, he was the only one that was trying to do the absolute right thing and look what's happened to him. It's not fair. It's not fair! You have to go back and help him. You owe it to him to go back and help him.'

'Why do you care so much?' Leanne hissed at me.

I became distinctly aware that all eyes in the room were very much focused on me again, like my answer was going to be of grave importance.

'We should all care,' I said, thinking as quickly as I could. 'He's a part of this team; this family. He's a good man who was trying to live a moral life and the most unspeakable thing has happened. We should all care.'

I wasn't sure whether this had satisfied Leanne's curiosity or not but she didn't challenge me further. To my relief.

'Are you going back to help him then?' I asked Seb.

Seb shook his head. 'We can't,' he muttered.

'You have to! He's all alone, stuck in time. He was trying to do the right thing. You can't let him suffer for that.'

'He's been charged with a serious crime. If we lift him out of that time, there will be huge implications.'

'But...' I didn't know how to argue with Seb. There had to be a way around it but I didn't know enough about time travel to find a logical answer. All I could manage instead was, 'You have to!'

'Scott knew the risk he was taking when he made his decision,' Seb stated.

'You have to at least go back and see him. Someone has to at least visit him.'

'We can't,' Seb said.

'What planet are you living on?' Leanne asked with a bitter tongue. 'You're as bad as that stupid boyfriend of mine.'

'He has a name!' I screamed at her so loudly, it almost shook the room. I couldn't remember anyone annoying me more in my life.

'You're like some sort of emotional wreck,' she spat. 'Do you see what being all emotional does? It gets you into trouble. It gets you trapped seventy years in the past and it means you're going to be all alone for the rest of your life. Don't you see what's happened? I've lost my boyfriend. We had such a promising future, and he's gone. I'm the one who should be upset, not you.'

Her words resonated hard with me. It was like she'd poisoned me, leaving me with a sharp, unbearable pain in my chest. All I could do was cry.

No one said a word for ages and I looked to the floor again, staring at the same tiny mark on the vinyl. It was my focus point although I was yet to even take it in. I had no clue if it was a scuff, a hole or just a bit of fluff. All I needed was something to look at that meant I could evade the eyes around me. I needed something to focus my attention on to help me calm myself. I was so far out of my comfort zone yet it felt like I was Scott's only hope. No one else seemed to care at all.

'As you know, Chloe,' Seb said, 'every journey costs a substantial amount of money. We literally haven't got the resources. I stretched every contingency I had to get him back last time.'

'What do you mean get him back last time?' Leanne asked. I flicked my head up with urgency. Was the truth about to come out? Well, not the whole truth, but at least that I was not from this time.

'It's not a big deal,' Seb said casually. 'Scott had CPG issues. We had to pull extra resource to sort it.'

'CPG issues?' Leanne queried. 'What sort of issues?'

'It's not the time now,' Seb said in a tone that told her the conversation was over with.

I took a deep, relieved breath. I knew if the truth was going to come out then I'd need Scott next to me. This thinking on my feet malarkey was not easy at all.

'So you're not going to do anything?' I asked, but no one was willing to respond. 'Can we at least find out what happens to him? He can't be found guilty. It's not right!'

Theo flicked around his monitor again. 'The timelines are a complete mess. I'm struggling to even find a court date.'

'Maybe he doesn't go to court?' I said, realising that I was grasping on to the faintest speck of hope again.

'I don't know.' Theo rubbed his forehead with frustration.

'We need to give Theo some space,' Seb said. 'We all need answers, but we're not going to get them like this. Dom, will you please escort Chloe back to her room.'

'I don't want to-'

'You will do as you're told,' Seb said. It was the first time he'd raised his voice to me. 'We will let you know if there is any news. But for now we need to let Theo work in peace and I think you need some time to calm down.'

I looked down at my shaking hands.

'Will you keep me posted?' I asked, not meaning for it to sound quite so pleading.

'When and if we have news,' Seb replied. 'Now please go with Sergeant Jasper.'

Dom waited by the door and I realised I had no choice. I reluctantly followed him. My head was spinning with what-ifs and horrible thoughts about where Scott was right at that moment. Did time even work like that? Would he actually be dead now in 2086?

It was all far too confusing.

'We'd better get you something to eat first,' Dom said.

'I'm not hungry.'

'I wasn't asking.'

Dom led me to the canteen where I picked up a sandwich. It was a choice of beans and kale or pepper and spinach. Both further turned my already somersaulting stomach, but the pepper one seemed like the safer option. How I missed egg and cress or ham salad.

Dom led me back to my room with my food on a tray. I wasn't given the option to eat in the canteen. I guessed he was following Seb's orders to the letter.

We reached my door and I looked at the light to let myself in.

'I'll collect you for dinner at nineteen hundred,' Dom said and then he left.

I slumped down on my bed with no clue in the world about how to feel or what to do.

EIGHTEEN

I nibbled at the corner of my far too heavy sandwich. The filling was so thick it almost made the bread redundant. After digesting a few tiny morsels, I couldn't face it anymore and I put it aside.

My head was heavy with a million thoughts. So much had happened in such a short space of time. I had to find a way to logically process it all.

My immediate concern was for Scott. He was all alone, trapped in some prison somewhere, being treated like a criminal. But in reality he was a heroic policeman who had saved thousands of lives.

I imagined the moment he was arrested and how scared he must have felt. He must have arrested people in the past himself. How awful to be on the other side. Especially when he was innocent.

For the first time it dawned on me what difficulties he must have faced. He didn't belong in that time. Who had he even said he was?

I told myself that he must have known what to do. After one hundred assignments he was clearly no stranger to undercover time travel, but it couldn't have been pleasant for him.

It devastated me to think about how lonely he must be feeling. And how cast aside. What if he was waiting for someone to reach out to him, never knowing that no one was even willing to try?

Since I'd met Scott, we'd had very little time together. A week or two could easily go by between his visits. I'd certainly missed him before, but suddenly I felt a hole in my heart in a way I'd never thought possible. It ached so severely that I didn't know if I could breathe.

I sobbed into my hands. It started off quietly but then I had to let it all out. I curled up on the bed and cried relentlessly into my pillow. I was mournful and angry and so without hope. I'd never felt so desperately low.

I don't know how long I'd been weeping for, but eventually the tears subsided. I'd cried more than I'd ever cried before and it was as if my tears had finally run out.

I took a deep breath and closed my eyes. I remembered how, not twelve hours before, Scott had been lying next to me. We'd fallen asleep in each other's arms. Now he was lying in some cold prison cell. It wasn't fair!

I sat up. There had to be something I could do. I couldn't bear feeling so hopeless. It wasn't like me. I was a problem solver. It pained me that everyone could so easily give up. Well I certainly wasn't going to.

I felt a surge of determination. There had to be something I could do.

I thought through the problem in my head.

Scott was trapped in 2014. It was obvious that he himself wasn't able to return to 2086, so someone had to get back there to help him.

At the very least if one of the team could speak to him then they could find out first hand what had really happened. Surely that was better than looking on some stupid floating monitor. Why had his genius colleagues not figured that out?

An idea hit me. If Scott couldn't get back then could they speak to his older self in 2086? It might be a start.

How old would he be?

I quickly did the maths and realised that he'd be one hundred and five. Even if people did live to over a century more regularly in 2086, he still wasn't going to be in a position to remember something that had happened over seventy years ago. It could all get very complicated. And far too weird.

No, someone needed to get back in time.

Turning my mind to that, I recalled that Seb had said resource was the issue.

From what I'd understood, he'd had to pull funding from another project to get Scott back to 2086 when I'd accidentally travelled through time. So Seb wasn't in a position to get more money, but he could certainly shift budgets around.

I felt like I had something to work with. I crossed my legs, feeling more energised.

What projects did I know about?

The one with Donna. Obviously. I knew that very well.

I knew that very well!

That was it!

How could that work to my advantage?

I sat and pondered on it for a few moments when the most obvious answer in the world came to me.

I had it. I had the perfect idea. All I needed to do was speak to Seb.

I consulted my clock. It was only quarter past two. Dom wasn't picking me up until seven.

I couldn't wait that long. I would go stir crazy sitting with this gem of an idea.

I stood up. I may have been told to wait, but Scott didn't follow the rules and I knew he wouldn't want me to either. I'd walked around those corridors enough now, I felt confident I knew where I was going.

I marched on.

My confidence halved the second I stepped out of my room, and then another quarter fell away as I meekly scuttled around the corridors trying to remember where Seb's office was. I thought that seemed a sensible place to start.

I finally found the door with "Chief-Superintendent Wiley" etched on it and I took a deep breath. I had to do this. I was doing it for Scott.

I opened the door and stood with purpose. Seb was sitting at his monitor and he looked positively gobsmacked by my presence.

'What are you doing?' he asked.

'I need to talk to you about something.'

'Who escorted you here?'

'Nobody. Like I said, I have something very important to talk to you about and it can't wait.' My body was like jelly but I wasn't going to let absolute fear stop me from saving Scott.

Seb studied me silently before I swear I saw the fleck of a smirk appear in the corner of his mouth. Just for a second, then it was gone.

'Take a seat,' he said.

I sat down on one of the two chairs facing him and I immediately missed the presence of a desk. Desks were great for hiding behind.

'What is it?' he asked, moving his chair so he could properly face me. 'Because I have no further news for you and nothing has changed from earlier.'

'I have a proposition,' I said, trying to hide my trembling hands.

'What sort of proposition?'

'I think it's very important that someone goes back to see Scott. We need to check he's okay and he needs to know that we haven't forgotten about him.'

'He's trained for instances like this. It won't be easy, but-'

'I think we also need to get first hand information. We need to know exactly what happened from his perspective. You keep saying that the timelines are messed up. So therefore, having a first hand perspective, out on the front line, will be massively beneficial.'

Seb didn't reply immediately and I could tell that I'd got his attention. He sat for a short while considering my plea.

'There is sound logic there, Miss Noble, but it still doesn't change my funding situation. It could take weeks, if not months for me to find a way to get back to him. If we can do it at all.'

'Maybe not,' I said.

'You've come into money since you've been here, have you?'

'No, but I am in the perfect position to help. Scott is working on a case with a girl called Donna.' It had dawned on me that I was meant to know her. He'd told Seb that I was Donna's friend. 'A good friend of mine,' I lied.

'Apparently so.'

'That case is going to be in disarray now that Scott is... well, absent-'

'Not at all, Chloe. Things go wrong. We will find a way to make it right.'

'Let me make it right.'

'I beg your pardon?'

'How many more times was Scott meant to go back to 2018? You must have budgeted for it already?'

'Of course. He had a maximum of three more journeys planned in. I believe it was October when you interfered with his CPG?'

I couldn't reply. Three more journeys? There were only going to be three more times that I would have seen him?

'He was going back twice in November and then from early December through to the new year. We know that the events happened in 2018, so that should be enough.'

'You said maximum?' I mumbled.

'Yes.'

'Why maximum?'

'If Scott had been successful earlier, there would have been no reason for him to return.'

'But... but what about that man? When Scott disappears out of Donna's life what's to stop her meeting up with that man afterwards?' I could feel my tone becoming desperate.

'All of our intelligence indicates that the target was only ever going to visit Harrogate for a couple of days. It was meeting Donna that made him stay. If they don't connect then he will leave and the issue will be resolved.'

I couldn't move. The threat of tears was stinging my eyes as the truth of how little time I had left with Scott hit me. We were so close to the end. It was only by pure chance that we'd been gifted with as much time together as we'd had.

I needed to see him. Really badly.

'Why didn't he just stay back in time?' I asked, as the question jumped into my head. 'Why keep travelling back here?'

'Because we couldn't lose our best Inspector to just one case for months. The team is often working on four or five cases at a time. Although, to be honest, he did spend more time in 2018 than any of us expected.' Seb's face was expressionless but his words made me feel momentarily better.

I sat upright trying to regain my composure. I needed to be confident and get back to the point. 'What if I finished the assignment for Scott?'

'What?' Seb's surprise told me that he'd far from expected me to say that.

'Send me back as agreed in a couple of weeks on my own and I'll make sure that Donna doesn't end up with that horrid man. Whoever he is. Scott told me the basics and I'm sure you can fill me in on the rest.'

'And how exactly do you propose you're going to achieve such a task?'

'With girl talk,' I replied, firmly. I hadn't really thought it through, but all that mattered was convincing Seb and saving Scott. The rest I'd worry about later. 'Let's face it, she's going to be heartbroken that her boyfriend has died. As that's what I'll be telling her. And you can't be dating someone new when you're in mourning.'

'Or she'll be looking to move on to ease the pain,' Seb countered. 'This man had quite an effect on Donna. I don't think it will be as easy as you believe.'

I shifted myself forward in my seat to address Seb quite directly.

'Scott is all alone, trapped in a prison, serving time for a crime he had no interest in being a part of. That you and your team made him guilty of. If there is any way that I can free up some resource to make it possible for us to go back, to ease just some of the anxiety that he is inevitably going through, then I will do everything in my power to make that happen. Believe me, Chief-Superintendent Wiley, I will not let Scott down. I will make sure that Donna never has anything to do with the awful man that she's supposed to meet, and I will make damn sure that I do Scott proud and finish the assignment just as he'd expect me to.'

Seb didn't move. He seemed quite blown away by my speech. Although, to be honest, so was I.

'Very well, Chloe,' he said, much to my surprise. 'But I agree to this only on the understanding that you go through strict training first. You will not be leaving this facility until I am satisfied that you are well enough equipped to take on this task. Do I make myself clear?'

'Absolutely,' I replied, still not able to believe I'd convinced him. 'If we can get to Scott then I will do anything you say.'

'Right.' Seb put his finger to his ear. 'Get the team together, we have a plan,' he said into his invisible telephone. Then he focused on me again. 'Good work.'

NINETEEN

Feeling the buzz of my achievement, I followed Seb to Scott's office where all of the team swiftly arrived, one by one. I stood at the back, as before, and the Inspectors took their seats at the monitors. There was just one left that no one dared to touch. It was very sad.

'It seems we have some resource that's just become available,' Seb announced. 'This means we can visit Scott in 2014. Theo, do you have an update?'

'It's still a mess,' he said from nearby me at the back. 'I can't get a grasp on anything concrete. There are possible signs of a custodial sentence, but it's like time is changing around him. I have no clue how it's possible, but it's happening.'

'Do you think it's because Scott is fighting it?' I asked, instantly wishing that I hadn't. All I received in return were bewildered looks. 'Or maybe it's because of something we're doing or going to do?' I followed up with, trying to save face.

'It doesn't work like that, Chloe,' Theo said and I shut up. I realised that I was actually way out of my depth and I felt my cheeks burn up.

'Going back to see Scott is the best thing we can do,' Seb

said. 'We need his first hand perspective on what happened and what is happening. It might give us some well needed intelligence.'

My fleeting embarrassment faded and pride took its place. All that had come from my head. Maybe I wasn't so out of my depth after all.

'For it to work, we need Scott to be alone. Theo?'

'On it.' Theo dashed over to Scott's seat and he started to flick through the monitor.

'Leanne, you'll be lead-'

'No!' I yelled. It just came out of my mouth. As was becoming a deeply uncomfortable regular event, all eyes in the room stared at me again. I couldn't let it happen, though. She couldn't go back. It hadn't occurred to me before exactly who would go back. I'd been so pleased that I was getting Scott a connection to his life, I hadn't thought through the logistics. But this had been my idea and Leanne clearly didn't know him anywhere near as well as I did. There was no way I was letting her visit him.

'Is there a problem?' Seb asked.

'Let me go,' I said. The idea filled me with unnerving excitement. What was I saying?

'You?'

I paused. What could I say now? All the eyes burning into me were flushing my cheeks again, but I had to be strong. 'You see, the way I see it,' I started, hoping it would lead me somewhere. I glanced around the room, praying for inspiration. They were all seasoned, trained time travellers. Who was I? Nobody. In their eyes, I was just some crummy consultant.

Oh, consultant! Of course!

'As you know, I am an expert in the early twenty-first century,' I continued with feigned confidence. 'In fact I guarantee that I know that time period better than any other person here.' I smiled, knowing how true that was. 'There are certain things that one needs to be aware of in 2014 and I think this mission will be safer if a real expert goes.'

'I've had multiple trips to the early twenty-first century,' Leanne argued.

'I've spent years there,' I retorted, in a strangely posh accent that I'd somehow adopted for reasons that I couldn't explain.

Leanne shook her head. 'This needs a professional,' she said to Seb. 'A proper Inspector, not a consultant.'

'I've got it,' Theo announced.

'Yes?' Seb asked.

'There's one night when his cellmate is taken to hospital, so Scott's alone. That's our window.'

Just Theo saying it made me want to cry. Could I really see Scott locked up in a prison cell?

'All night?' Seb checked.

'It's clear all night,' Theo responded.

'We could use a proofer,' Seb stated.

'On it,' Theo said. He swiftly put his finger to his ear and started muttering.

'Okay, Chloe,' Seb said, addressing me directly, 'as an expert in all things 2014, it seems wisest that you take on this assignment.'

My mouth dropped open. Half of me wanted to jump for joy and the rest of me wanted to collapse on the floor in a heap.

'Seb!' Leanne screeched.

'I'm thinking about what's best for Scott and the entire team here,' Seb replied to her, very firmly.

'She comes across like she's never even heard of time travel,' Leanne argued. It was the first astute thing I'd heard her say.

'Isn't it funny how the appearance of a situation can be so different to reality?' Seb said, then he looked at me again. 'Come on, Chloe, we need to get you to Logistics.'

I didn't move for a second. I was going back in time. I was going back in time!

Although, actually, I was going back to my own time. Well, four years before.

I would have been twenty-five. I remembered it well.

I quickly knew I had to stop thinking about it. I knew it wouldn't take long before it completely overwhelmed me. I decided the best thing to do was just go with the flow.

Switching off my thoughts, I followed Seb to Logistics. I wanted to thank him and ask him why, but I was too scared that he would change his mind. I was going to see Scott and that was all that mattered.

'Jeremy!' Seb called out as soon as we arrived. The skinny man appeared and I was happy that I finally knew his name. 'Do you have the items?'

'Are these for you?' Jeremy asked him, clearly confused.

'For Miss Noble here.'

I could see the shock blatantly slapped across Jeremy's face. But he did as requested. He appeared several minutes later from his secret door carrying a green jumper and a denim skirt.

'Will these suffice?' he checked, handing me the clothes.

'Yes,' I nodded. I don't know how, but he'd got my exact size.

'And here's your proofer.' He handed me a small silver cube that looked exactly like a dice, except there were only dots on one side. I studied the dots and realised that they were six tiny holes.

'I'll explain it all,' Seb said, reading my expression. 'Get changed and we'll see you at... the room we were in earlier, with the modules. Could you find your way?'

I was delighted I was being so trusted. 'Definitely,' I said, nodding.

'Good.'

'Do you want to come back to the changing area?' Jeremy asked.

'No!' Seb cut in rather abruptly. 'Need to know,' he said, offering me a small smile. 'Perhaps you could stop off at the ladies?'

'Yes, of course.'

Seb took the silver dice from me and I dashed along to

the toilet. I got changed as quickly as I could and then I took my uniform with me to the module room.

There was only Seb and Theo present and I was relieved. I was nervous enough with Leanne's interference.

'Are you okay?' Seb asked as I joined them by Theo's monitor.

'Yes.' In truth, I'd stopped trying to acknowledge how I was feeling. It was far easier that way.

'It's only right you go,' he said as he took my uniform from me. 'But just talk to Scott and come straight back. Don't try anything else. Even if you're not sure what use his story is, report it back and let us determine how it can help. Do you understand? Keeping it simple is the only way to help Scott.'

'I understand, don't worry. All I want to do is be helpful.'

'Here's your CPG,' Theo said, handing me the watch thing.

'How does it work?' I asked, strapping it to my wrist. 'I really don't know what I did last time.'

'If I said flick-switch technology, would you understand?' Seb asked.

I looked at him with concern. Did I need to?

'Don't worry. Just ask Scott to send you back.'

'Okay,' I said, before panic struck. 'But what if there's a problem? What if I accidentally get sent somewhere else? What if Scott can't remember what to do?'

Seb smiled. 'None of that is going to happen. However, should the impossible take place and you are stuck, just hit the button at the bottom five times.'

'It's twice fast, once slow, then twice fast again,' Theo added.

'Is that how I get back?'

'No, that just sends us an alarm to say you're in trouble. We'll be able to track you then and bring you back from this end. At least we'll know you're ready.'

'Can you track everyone's movements with these things?' I asked, holding up the watch.

'If we need to,' Theo replied. 'Don't worry.'

'Is there anything else I need to know?' I asked.

'Scott will have been there for just shy of six weeks-' Theo started.

'Six weeks?' I gasped. 'Six weeks! He's been all on his own for six weeks?'

'It's the first opportunity there is to get to him,' Theo justified.

'He's a highly trained Inspector,' Seb said. 'He'll be fine. He's more than capable of coping in a situation like this. Just get every bit of detail you can and come back. That's what the proofer is for.'

'Is it a voice recorder?' I asked, taking the silver cube from Seb's hand.

'No, it's a soundproofer. The second you get there, place it on the ground near the centre of the door with the holes facing up. It will soundproof the whole room allowing you to speak freely. You're our voice recorder. You need to remember everything that Scott tells you.'

'Can't I take a recorder? Won't that be useful?'

Seb regarded me hesitantly. 'Do you want every word recorded?'

I imagined my pending conversation with Scott and swiftly realised that a recorder was a very bad idea.

'Let's allow Scott some privacy, shall we,' Seb said. 'He may say things that he doesn't want everyone to know.'

'Of course. Soundproofing will more than suffice,' I said, relieved that I hadn't just scuppered my chances of some time alone with Scott. 'So I just place it on the ground? Do I need to press anything to activate it?'

'No, just place it on the ground by the centre of the door and it will instantly work. As long as the holes are facing up.'

'That sounds easy enough,' I replied, breathlessly. The nerves were really kicking in.

'Are you ready?' Seb asked.

'I suppose. It's not hard, is it?'

'Not at all.'

'We'll send you back,' Theo explained. 'Just step in the module and tell us when you're ready. You've done it once. It doesn't hurt.'

'I remember.'

'I'll send you back at twenty-three fifteen. Lights are out at twenty-three, so that should be fine.'

'Okay. That's eleven pm, right?'

'Yes.'

I took a deep breath and headed over to the module, just as the door flew open and Leanne raced in.

'Tell him I love him!' she shouted at me. 'Tell him I'm thinking of him. Tell him I wanted to be the one to see him but I wasn't allowed. You tell him all that.'

I stood, motionless. I didn't know how to respond.

'Not now, Leanne,' Seb said.

'She needs to tell him I won't forget about him. He has to know. He has to know how I feel.'

'Not now!' Seb ordered. 'Please leave.'

'I just need to make sure she's going to tell him. Will you? Please?'

She glared at me sharply and I found myself nodding in agreement. What else could I do?

'Leanne, we need to get on.'

'You won't forget?' she practically begged.

'No. Of course not,' I replied, meekly.

'Thank you.'

Leanne glanced at me one last time before heading off, closing the door behind her.

'Are you okay?' Seb asked. I found myself nodding again although I knew I was far from okay. 'It's time,' he then said, softly.

I shakily stepped in the module and Seb closed the door.

'Say when you're ready,' Theo called through.

It was completely black and the only thing I was aware of was my own heartbeat pumping through my ears. It was thumping hard and fast and I could no longer ignore how terrified I was.

All that mattered was Scott.

This was for Scott. He was all alone and no doubt frightened too. I was on my way to give him some support.

If ever I had to be strong, now was that time.

'Ready,' I called back.

TWENTY

In the blink of an eye, everything became slightly less black and a small chill prickled me.

I was there.

I was immediately taken aback by how different it was to my expectation. Thanks to the moonlight that seeped in through the barred window at the end of the narrow space, I could see how white and bright the walls were and how simple but not unpleasant the area actually was.

I glanced across at the bunk bed set against the right hand side of the room. A man was sleeping with his back to me on the bottom and, thankfully, above him there was no one. Just a tidily made bed.

I really hoped it was Scott.

Before doing anything else, I turned around so I could put the proofer in place by the door. I had to pass a toilet and a sink, offering no privacy whatsoever, and my heart went out to Scott. How could it be that a man as good as him ended up being treated like a criminal? Where was the justice in that?

I set the cube down on the floor, just as Seb had instructed, and then I checked it again about four times. It seemed far too easy. I couldn't believe that it was actually going to work. Well, I was about to find out.

I headed back to the man sleeping. I arched my neck over to check if it really was Scott. I saw the edge of his snoozing face and I immediately started to calm down. At least I was in the right room and we were properly alone. So far so good.

I tapped him gently on the shoulder and he instantly jolted back towards the wall. He looked terrified.

He studied me fearfully for a few seconds before his face softened. Then he leapt out of bed and threw his arms around me.

He held me tightly and I wrapped my arms around him in return.

It wasn't like a hug we'd ever had before. The confident, strong man I'd seen leave in that module just hours before was not the same man in my embrace.

It was hardly a surprise, though. Not only had he been arrested in a time where he technically didn't exist, but he hadn't seen anyone that he knew or was even connected to for six weeks. He hadn't even known if anyone was coming.

I let him hold me for as long as he wanted. We had all night and I just wanted him to feel some happiness.

Finally he edged backwards, but he didn't take his hands off me.

'What are you doing here?' he asked with a whisper. He cupped my face and kissed me.

I knew I was on the verge of falling to pieces. Up close, I could see the darkness around his eyes and the distress across his face. For all of Seb's assurances that Scott was well trained to handle such a situation, the man before me had lost all of the sparkle of the real Scott Lacey.

I took a deep breath and decided to take emotion out of it. I needed to be strong for him.

'We needed to see you,' I said, keeping my words factual and light.

Scott immediately tensed. He put his finger to his lips to shush me.

I shook my head and pointed to the door. 'Seb sent me with a proofer,' I whispered, just to be sure.

Scott turned to the door as I screwed up my face. I didn't feel comfortable using futuristic words.

He paced over to the dice and touched it gently with his finger. I could almost see the weight physically lift off his shoulders.

'My gorgeous Pepper Pot,' he said in a normal voice. I scanned him, for the first time able to see my Scott head to toe. He was dressed in a white T-Shirt and dark pyjama bottoms and I swear his stance was somehow wilted, as if the tall, self-assured man I knew had been etched away at.

He stepped back over and kissed me. 'You've set it perfectly. You never fail to surprise me.'

'It wasn't that hard,' I replied.

'So, what are you doing here?' he asked again. It was the first time he'd looked happy.

'The timelines are in a mess. If there is any way to help you then we need first hand information. So Seb sent me back to speak to you.'

'Seb sent you back?' he asked with astonishment.

'Who else in your team would know 2014 better than me?' I smiled. 'Visiting consultants are very useful.'

Scott hesitated. 'Was it Seb's idea?'

'No, not quite. But I made a very convincing argument.' Scott paused.

'What is it?' I asked.

'Nothing. I'm really glad you're here.'

Scott took my hand and guided me to sit on the bed next to him. I didn't exactly melt into it, but it wasn't rock solid either.

'So what happened?' I asked, getting right down to business. 'We all assumed that you were trying to save that man.'

'I had to, Pepps. How could I knowingly let a man die? All this greater good crap.'

'I know. You're a good man. You don't deserve to be

trapped here.'

'The way I figured it, saving him was the less risky option. If we'd have killed him then the guilt would have been a life sentence anyway. It was a risk worth taking.'

'Of course,' I said before stopping myself. Something about what Scott had said didn't add up.

'The Security Guard was pretty shocked to see me, as you can imagine,' Scott continued. 'It would have been funny in any other circumstance. But when he realised he needed my help to save the man, he just let me carry on.' Scott looked back at me, reading my expression. 'What? What's the matter?'

'You saved the man?' I asked.

'Yeah, that's part of the piss-take really, isn't it. Rather than acknowledging that I saved a man's life, they've put my heroics down to unexpected guilt. If only they knew the truth. Anyway, I'm pleading innocent, of course. And they're struggling to find a motive. Although believe me, they're trying. I keep repeating my story that I was passing by and I saw the flames, but no one's convinced. But what else can I say? I don't exist on any of their systems and it's driving them mad. It's not been fun. I'm having to pretend that I'm a travelling person of no fixed abode with my main comment being that I don't have one. Even my legal aid is getting frustrated. I think that alone will send me down for a while. But what can I do? I tell you, Pepps, from the moment Earl opened his mouth with this assignment, I was doomed. It was riddled with problems and it was inevitable that I was going to suffer whatever the outcome. It's not right. It's not right at all. He shouldn't have put us in that situation.'

Scott finally took a breath and I squeezed his hand. 'Why didn't you just travel back to the future?' I asked.

Scott smiled warmly. 'You know why. You also know that two people can travel on one CPG, but I'm under no illusion that I'll be travelling back with you.'

'Seb said because you now have a record in this time you

can't leave without it inviting too many questions. I get that, but couldn't you have escaped the second it happened? Like before any records were created?'

'Not if I wanted to save that man. I did the right thing but it means I'm well and truly stuck here now.'

'But couldn't you-'

'I've caused a mess anyway. The last thing I want to do is unravel things completely. This is just the way it's got to be. I'm really sorry.'

'Hang on, you keep saying you saved the man.'

'Yes. Why? That's the second time you've asked me. What is it?'

I hesitated.

'What is it?' he pushed.

'It's just... Well... according to Theo... The man died.'

'What?'

'But, like I said, there's a lot of confusion at our end.'

'He died?'

'What have they charged you with?' I asked, cautiously.

'Arson. My court date is next week.'

I shook my head.

'What?' Scott was becoming visibly worried.

'I...'

'Tell me. Just tell me straight.'

'Theo said the man died-'

'No he didn't.'

'I don't know the details. It's just what Theo said. He said the man died and...'

'And what?'

'And you were charged with arson and murder.'

'What? No, I've been charged with just arson. I haven't killed anyone. You know that, Pepps.'

'Well of course I know you haven't killed anybody. Theo's obviously got it wrong. I told you everything's in a mess.'

Scott shook his head. 'Theo doesn't get things wrong.'

'Tell me what happened. Talk me through the events.'

Scott thought for a second. 'I left Leanne with the device telling her that I'd seen somebody and I wanted to check it out. I didn't give her a chance to question it. Then I raced down the stairs to the first floor where I could hear a man yelping in pain. I walked in and, as I said, the Security Guard was a bit surprised to see me.'

Scott jolted to his feet, as if something had alarmed him.

'There was someone else there,' he said with urgency. 'Who was it? There was someone else there!'

'It's okay, take your time.'

'No... it's... It's all a blur.' Scott paced the floor. 'I don't remember what happened. I remember everything up to that point and then... I don't actually remember what happened. I have this strange feeling that I was really shocked to see this other person. But it's like it was a dream. Oh my God, I can't even remember how we left the building. I can barely remember getting arrested. It's like it's all fuzzy in head. How can I not remember?'

Scott was becoming increasingly panicky in a way that was most unlike him.

'I'm sure just being in this place has fogged up your mind,' I assured him. 'It couldn't have been an easy few weeks for you.'

Scott glared at me and there was definite fear in his eyes. 'What if I go to court next week and I'm charged with murder? What am I supposed to say? My gut tells me I saved that man. I know I saved him. I just can't remember. What am I supposed to do with that?'

I stood up next to him and held his hands firmly. 'It's going to be fine. We might not have the answers yet but at least I have information to take back to the team now. The fact that you can't remember has got to be helpful in itself, right?'

Scott addressed me square in the eyes. 'You go back and you tell them I saved that man. Whatever I can or cannot remember, I know my gut is right. I know I saved him. You tell them that.'

'I will.'

'They have to figure out what's going on. I'll serve my time for arson, but I will not be deemed as a murderer. I save people, I do not kill them.'

'I know. We're going to sort this out. Just focus on getting through this and let us worry about the mess. You have to stay strong.'

Scott shook his head. I knew my words were of little comfort. But at least I had information now. Information that would surely help. Hopefully.

There was only one way to find out.

'Right, will you help me get back? I don't know how these watch things work. Seb said you'd be able to send me back.'

'You're going now?' Scott asked.

'I'm going to get you help. Unless there's anything else you need me to know?'

'I don't... I don't think so.'

'Then I'll get back and we can get this thing sorted once and for all.'

'You're just going; just like that?' There was obvious sadness in his voice.

'Don't you want me to get on with things?'

'I haven't seen you in six weeks.'

I didn't know what to say. He hadn't said it as if he'd missed people in general, he'd said it as if he'd missed me. Just me. Where did that leave Leanne? Her declaration of love began echoing through my mind.

'You know I couldn't have let that man die, right?' Scott said. 'You know I had to try.'

'Of course I know. I wouldn't have expected anything else.'

'Then why the rush to leave? No one is going to be disturbing us for hours. And whether you go back now or you go back tomorrow morning... At least we'll have had some time together.'

Leanne's words of "tell him I love him" became louder

and louder in my head.

I had no intention of telling Scott a thing she'd asked me to. As much as anything, I would never have been able to find the words. It hurt far too much.

'What's going on, Pepps?' he asked after I'd not replied.

I looked at the floor. I didn't know what to do. I wanted to stay but it didn't feel right. As much as I wanted to be there for him, this pretence couldn't continue. I'd been sent back to help him. That was all.

I glanced up at his face. It was strained and sad. Deeply, deeply sad. I didn't want to leave him like that, but what would my staying really accomplish? The sooner I got back, the sooner we could free him. That was obviously the most rational thing to do.

I studied his despondent eyes and it tore my heart in two. One half was desperate to stay and comfort him, while the other realised that I could never be more than second best in his life, and staying there would only prolong my agony.

'Will you please stay?' he asked, so meekly.

What was I going to do?

TWENTY-ONE

'Why do you want me to stay?' I asked. I didn't expect to ask it. The words just popped out of my mouth.

Confusion and hurt grasped his face. 'Because I thought we loved each other.'

I couldn't help the small scoff.

'What's that supposed to mean?' he asked, offended.

I sighed. 'Don't you think this is complicated enough?' I was trying to be gentle. I really didn't want to start an argument.

He nodded and this time it was he that looked at the floor, unable to hold my gaze. 'I know. I've made a mess of everything. But please don't let it ruin the little time we do actually have together.'

I shook my head as the frustration built up inside me. 'Why can't you be fair to me?'

'What?'

'You make me feel so used.'

'What?' He seemed completely perplexed but I wasn't falling for it.

'What exactly am I to you?' I asked. I knew it was the worst timing in the world to have a heart to heart, but I also knew it could literally be now or never. It was time to get this out in the open so at least we could both move forward with the air cleared.

Scott seemed stunned. He looked at me for a few moments as if he was trying to work out exactly what I was asking him. 'You're my girlfriend. I thought so anyway.'

'What, your 2018 girlfriend?' Then a horrible thought hit me. 'Do you have a girlfriend in every time period? Like a 1970s girlfriend and a 2040s girlfriend?'

'What are you talking about?'

'And then you've got your present day girlfriend, haven't you.'

'What?' Scott's puzzled expression was very convincing, but I couldn't forget that he was trained to lie to people.

The pretence had to end, and now. It was time I was told the truth. I had to stop avoiding it, no matter how bad it was about to get.

'You're my girlfriend,' he insisted. 'Present day, 2018, whatever the date. I only have one life, no matter what the time period.'

'Oh just cut the bullshit,' I said. 'I know all about Leanne.'

The confusion dropped from his face. Instantly his eyes became darker and his expression grimmer. 'What exactly do you think you know about Leanne?'

'I know it all. I'm not stupid. You wouldn't believe the wailing we've had today. "My boyfriend's in prison! My boyfriend is selfish! My boyfriend can't follow orders!" It's been sickening.'

'She said what?'

'I know all about how you left me on that night when I'd first travelled to the future. You left me and then spent the night with her.'

'She told you that?'

'You slept with her!'

'I slept next to her.'

'What's the difference?'

'There's a huge difference!' Scott exhaled sharply. He

placed his hands on my shoulders so he could get my full attention. 'I am not dating Leanne. She's delusional. She might be a great Inspector, but she's got major issues in her personal life.'

This silenced me.

'Look, let's sit down. Let me explain.'

I hesitated. My head was warning that he was about to tell me everything I wanted to hear and none of it could possibly be true, but in my heart I couldn't help but believe him. I decided the best thing to do was listen to what he had to say and take it from there.

I sat down on his bed and he joined me.

'A few weeks before I met you, Leanne and I were on a very difficult assignment,' he began. 'It wasn't the first time we'd had to pretend to be husband and wife, but it was a really emotionally taxing case and it brought us closer together.'

'So you started dating?' I asked, aware that I was putting words in his mouth.

'We had one kiss, on the assignment, and there was something about it that felt right. At the time. I don't know, like I said it was a really emotional case. Anyway, we decided to see if there was more to our relationship.' Scott shifted so he was looking me straight in the eye. 'You have to understand that I've been very lonely. All I ever wanted was to be in the police force, and when I got the chance to join the Shape the Future branch, I grabbed the opportunity with both hands. But it's isolating. You start to lose your identity. I've spent more time in different time periods than I have in my own present life. And I'm always pretending to be someone I'm not. So when I saw the opportunity to start something with a person who was in exactly the same situation as me, it made perfect sense.'

'I get that.'

'But she's a nightmare,' he declared and I had to stop myself from smirking.

'We went on one date, had one kiss at the end of it, and

suddenly she was talking about marriage and kids. She started telling everyone that we were in a relationship and I was the love of her life. I couldn't believe it.'

'Did you put her straight?'

Scott sighed. 'This is where my working life becomes difficult. I have days off, but mostly my life is my job. We're all so closely knit together, how could I tell her I wasn't interested? It would have caused a lot of tension across the whole team. Believe me, I fully regret ever going out with her. The only thing I could think to say was that, although I liked her, I'd come to realise that it was too difficult to do the job and be in a relationship. She was upset but at least she had comfort in the knowledge that she thought I had feelings for her. It seemed to work.'

'You still let her call you her boyfriend, though?'

'She didn't.'

'She has been, believe me.'

'She might do now, but she wasn't then.'

'Well, what changed?'

Scott hesitated. 'You.'

That was the last thing I expected him to say. 'What did I do?'

'Just as I was desperately trying to keep my distance from Leanne – well as much as I could in our line of work – I stepped back into 2018 and met you.'

'And that made you realise that Leanne was the one for you after all?'

'No, Pepps, I realised that I'd met the love of my life in you. I stepped out of that disabled toilet expecting just to get on with my recce, when you were standing there. You were stunning. I couldn't resist asking you about The Beatles. I always knew my perfect woman would like The Beatles. I expected a yes or no reply, but your answer made my day. It made my year. No, it just about made everything I'd ever known complete. I couldn't stop thinking about you after that. We never should have met. It was dangerous and stupid, but I fell in love.'

I didn't know what to say. His words had blown me away. I squeezed his hand and we sat for a moment in silence.

Finally I asked, 'What's that got to do with Leanne?'

'Meeting your soulmate and falling in love changes you. I couldn't wipe the smile from my face when I returned, but I also couldn't afford for anyone to get suspicious. If anyone found out about what I'd done...' He stopped talking and studied the floor.

'Yes,' I nudged.

'The consequences are worth it, I suppose. Anyway.' He looked back up at me and smiled warmly. 'It occurred to me that I could use Leanne as my defence and turn an awkward situation into a beneficial one. I played upon the idea that I was in love with Leanne but kept repeating that we were in an impossible situation where we couldn't be together. I knew it would mean that I could walk about smiling or be caught daydreaming and no one would question it. Do you see what you've done to me?'

I smirked. I never realised how soppy he was. I loved it.

'It was all working perfectly until you stole my CPG.'

'I didn't steal it.'

'All this worry you've had, Pepps. Me dating Donna, me with Leanne. The reality is that you're the only woman I've ever wanted to be with. You're it. If we lived in the same time, I would have married you by now.'

My heart skipped a beat and I couldn't control my grin.

'I was terrified that Leanne would mess things up when you arrived in 2086. I knew she'd tell you that we were in love or some crap like that. She tells everyone. It had never mattered before, but suddenly it did. So I went to her room that night in an attempt to manage the situation. I didn't really know what I was going to say. Something like I wanted it to be more secret, our couldn't-be relationship. I was willing to say anything to shut her up.'

'Like sleep with her?' I nudged with concern.

'No! I will admit it all back-fired but my intention was

good. She was absolutely thrilled to see me knocking on her door at night, but nothing happened. All we did was chat about nothing much for five minutes as I tried to find my words, and then she said she needed to freshen up. The next thing I knew I'd woken up next to her to find her beaming smile dazzling my eyes. I hadn't slept in two days, you must understand. I was sitting on her bed and I must have just drifted off. I couldn't help it. But that was about as exciting as the night got. For me, anyway.'

'Didn't you talk to her in the morning?'

'I had no time. I wanted to catch Seb first thing to talk him into telling you the truth. That was far more important. I really wanted you to know the real me. I wanted the pretence to stop. I didn't know how we could be together, but I at least wanted you to know the truth. It really was a gift, you travelling to the future. Finally I didn't have to lie. I was desperate to get Seb's consent to tell you everything. That had to come first.'

'Why didn't you tell her after?'

'When Seb said he wanted me to look after you, I was at first horrified. I work so closely with Leanne, I was convinced it would all go wrong. But then I figured maybe I could control it. Like at the team dinner. I wanted to sit next to you more than anything. I only went to speak to Leanne so she'd keep her distance from you. Then she started rabbiting on and before I knew it all the seats had been taken. I hated not being next to you. You're all I can ever think about.'

I squeezed his hand again.

'I love you, Pepps. There is no other person in the world that I could love more. Nobody else matters. Meeting you changed me, and so much for the better.'

'I feel exactly the same way.'

Scott kissed me. I felt his love through his lips and I knew every word he'd spoken was the truth. At last, everything slotted into place and every question mark disappeared. The relief was massive. Not only had all my concerns been alleviated, but the answers I'd so desperately wanted to hear were the exact answers I'd got.

We were in love. A proper true love story. It was an impossible relationship but somehow, against all the odds, we'd found a way to make it work.

He cupped my face and kissed me deeper. It didn't take long before I knew where the kiss was going and I had no desire to stop it. In fact I wanted it more than anything.

He nudged me gently and I lay on his bed. Our hands were all over each other, and within a couple of minutes we were stripping each other's clothes off.

It was the most intense sex I'd ever had. It was like our passion for one another had gone into overdrive. I'd never adored the feel of him more and we locked ourselves against each other as if we never wanted to part.

As our bodies calmed down after a rapturous climax, we didn't leave each other's embrace. I curled up next to him on the tiny bed and we kissed some more.

I had never felt more in love and I refused to acknowledge that time was ticking by. I told myself that it was all about the here and now and I nestled my head into his chest.

The reality was just too harsh to comprehend.

TWENTY-TWO

My eyes were drooping but I didn't want to fall asleep. We had just a few hours together and I knew I had to make the most of every minute.

I looked up at Scott and I could tell he was a million worlds away. At times like these he'd normally be humming, but there was a strange silence and it unnerved me. The man lying next to me was not the man I knew. Although it quickly occurred to me that there was a lot about Scott that I didn't know.

I knew what his personality was like, and I knew what made him laugh and what made him shake his head with disgust. But there was a great deal that I had to learn.

I flicked through questions in my mind. I could ask about his childhood, his family, what hobbies he had, what life was like being a policeman. There was a menagerie of questions all ready in my head, waiting to be set free.

But one question niggled at me more than anything.

'What were you going to do?' I asked.

'About what?'

'When your assignment with Donna had finished. What were you going to say to me? Or were you just going to disappear out of my life?'

Scott stared up at the ceiling. He couldn't look at me. After a few moments he exhaled deeply. 'I have no idea. It was too hard for me to process. I should have made a plan, but... Look, it doesn't matter now anyway.'

'Is there no way we can be together?'

'I don't want that life anymore, Pepps,' Scott insisted. 'I used to love it. I used to think it was all that mattered. But you've given me so much more to love. I feel like I'm living life for the first time with you and I want to actually be me. I would happily give it all up to be with you.'

'Would you have just disappeared out of Donna's life too? What were you going to say to her?'

'Things with Donna were getting complicated. She was falling in love with me. We didn't think I'd be there for that long. But I couldn't sleep with her. I'd told her that I didn't believe in sex before marriage and we knew her profile would accept that after her string of abusive relationships. But it was still difficult.'

I frowned. 'It seems so cruel.'

Scott shook his head. 'If you could read about what happened in the original history, you wouldn't say it was cruel. I might temporarily break her heart but he destroyed her completely.'

'The lesser of two evils?'

'Saving people isn't black and white.'

'Like setting fire to a building.'

Scott didn't reply and I wished I hadn't said it. Things had become tense and I didn't like it. I wanted it to be fun. A time for him to think back on and treasure.

'Who's Reginald Jackson?' I asked, lightening the mood.

Scott chuckled. 'Where did you hear that name?'

'Leanne said you were acting like Reginald Jackson. I didn't know what she meant.'

Scott rolled his eyes. 'He's a movie character from the sixties. The 2060s that is. He's basically a superhero. But more Indiana Jones than Superman. He's just a normal guy who has this compulsion to save people. The more he survives these daring feats that give him fame and fortune, the more hooked he gets. It's not really serious.'

'Is it a major blockbuster?' I asked.

'They made four movies and it became this mega franchise. Anyway, I shouldn't be telling you this. You know how Seb hates spoilers.'

I laughed. 'I think he calls it "need to know".'

'Him and his rules. Where's the excitement in that?'

I smirked and then a worry pulled at my chest. Something Scott had said earlier was bothering me. Something he needed to know.

'I have to tell you something,' I said.

'What is it?' He put his arms around me. Our legs and arms became intermingled and our noses were just centimetres apart.

'I didn't really know much about The Beatles before I met you,' I confessed. 'In fact, *Eight Days a Week* was about the only song I could recall when you came out of those disabled toilets. And that was a bit of a miracle.'

Scott laughed. 'I'm well aware, Pepps.'

'But you said you knew the perfect woman for you would love The Beatles.'

'And don't you?'

I shrugged. 'I suppose I've grown to like them. But that's because of you. Your passion for them is infectious.' I hadn't really been a fan of any particular artist before I'd met Scott. I'd much preferred reading or watching telly rather than listening to music. But he'd opened my eyes to a whole new world.

He smiled. 'When I first met you, you knew who The Beatles were. That was a great start. Don't forget, I was born ninety years after The Beatles grew to fame.'

'Surely any girl of my time would know The Beatles.'

'But you humoured my love of them. How many times have I played *Abbey Road* for us?'

'It's your favourite album.'

'You never tire of it, though.'

I shrugged again. 'I quite like it too.'

'See! And you have a favourite song now. And a favourite album.'

I smiled as I recalled the most special night we'd had together.

'It wasn't me that insisted on listening to *Sgt. Pepper* over and over,' Scott said.

'I love that song *A Day in the Life*. It's so different. I could listen to it all day.'

'I've never seen anyone dance to it quite like you did that night,' Scott laughed.

'We'd had like two bottles of wine.'

'I knew then and there you were my Pepper Pot. It was the best night of my life. In any time.'

I kissed him and for a brief second I felt utterly contented. That was until irrational jealousy once again prickled at my skin. I'd believed everything that Scott had told me, but I couldn't shake my insecurities.

'Does Leanne like The Beatles?' I asked, as casually as I could.

'Not especially, I don't think.'

'Have you ever played *Abbey Road* for her?' Again, I was ever so casual, running circles around Scott's chest with my finger as if I really wasn't bothered one way or another. I was totally chilled.

'Pepps, other than that one date, I've not spent a lot of time with Leanne out of work. Yeah we have our team dinners, but that's a group social event. Everyone's there.'

'Oh right.' I stopped playing with his chest and I regarded him more seriously. 'There's something else I need to tell you. It probably doesn't matter. I mean I hope it doesn't. But I did say I'd tell you.'

'What is it?'

'As I was leaving to time travel back here... in the module room.' I hesitated.

'Yes.'

'Leanne raced in and told me to pass on a message.'

'Right.' Scott watched me, waiting for me to elaborate, but the words wouldn't easily form. 'What did she say, Pepps?'

'She wanted me to tell you how much she loved you. She was basically declaring her undying love. She said I was to tell you that she would have come back but she wasn't allowed to and that she loved you.'

'Okay.'

I shrugged. 'I said I'd tell you and now I have.'

'You know, you're going to have to get used to this.'

I scanned Scott's face, trying to work out what he was talking about, and then that sly smile of his curled up on his lips.

'I'm utterly irresistible,' he said. 'I can't help it. It's my curse. The ladies love me. If you're going to be with me then you're going to have to get used to girls throwing themselves at me from every angle. That's just life for Scott Lacey.'

'Is it now,' I said, trying to suppress my smirk.

'But you need to remember that it doesn't matter. Even if every single female in the world is swooning over me-'

'Swooning?' I said as I started to giggle.

'Oh, they swoon badly over me. But it doesn't matter. Because from the minute I laid my eyes on you, no other woman was ever going to stand a chance. I love you so much. So those girls can swoon as much as they like, but I'm only ever going to have eyes for you. I promise.'

I sniggered, half through how ridiculous he was and half because I loved what he'd just said.

'Utterly irresistible?' I asked.

'To all women. It's very frustrating.'

'Even Gloria?'

'Oh, she's the worst. That's a very bad case of Scott Lacey loving.'

I burst out laughing.

'But remember, not one of them compares to you,' he said.

'You're just saying that.'

He sighed. 'You're right. You got me. I just want another shag.'

He kissed me deeply as he pulled me on top of him. This time the sex was more lighthearted. We laughed and enjoyed each other and tried out different positions on the tiny space that was his bed.

I watched Scott's face as we made love and I imprinted the image on my brain. I didn't know when or if we'd ever be together again and I wanted to remember being this close to him. He looked down at me and I could see the love in his eyes.

After another intense orgasm, we curled up again in each other's arms and fell silent.

I couldn't fight sleep anymore. It had been a very emotional few days.

I didn't sleep well, luckily, and the night was mixed with chatting and dozing, and trying to delay the inevitable for as long as we could.

But finally Scott looked at the CPG still on my wrist and we could delay it no longer. It was four forty-five.

'You'd better go soon,' he said. 'You have to be gone by five.'

A sickening sadness punched me in the stomach. I didn't want to go but there was literally no way I could stay.

'Where's your CP... G thingy?' I asked. 'And what does CPG stand for?'

'Chronoperengrinator,' Scott said, the word just slipping off his tongue.

'Chro... Perry... What?'

'Chronoperengrinator,' Scott repeated with a curl to his lips that told me I'd amused him.

'No wonder you call it a CPG.'

'It literally means one who travels about time.'

'Why not just call it a TTD?'

'A TTD?' Scott asked, confused.

'A Time Travel Device.'

'That's not quite as elegant is it.'

'Oh, I didn't realise you police lot needed to be all elegant.'

'It was actually Earl who named it, and he's a civilian. He liked using old language to describe a modern device that could take us into history.'

'I think it's over complicated,' I stated with a smile. 'I'm going to start calling it a TTD. So where is your TTD?'

'My *CPG* is in safe-keeping somewhere. They took it off me when I was first arrested.'

'Didn't they wonder what it was?'

'I guess they thought it was just some new fandangled smart watch. I'll get it back when I leave, but who knows when that will be.'

I felt the weight of the conversation again. Any humour was never going to last long in such a horrid situation. 'Are you going to be okay?'

'Of course I am. Don't worry about me. You just get Theo looking into what the hell is going on. That would be helping me loads.'

'You know I'll be on the case,' I assured him.

'I know you will. And I'll see you before you know it.'

'I really hope so.'

'Come on, you'd better get dressed.'

We kissed one more time before untangling ourselves out of the bed. We both put our clothes back on and I went over to pick up the silver box proofer thing.

'Don't,' Scott said as I reached down.

'What?'

'Please leave it. Let me have it.'

I went to argue, momentarily forgetting what mattered. Then I stopped myself. 'Of course.'

Scott came over towards me. He wrapped his arms around me.

'I'm going to love you forever, Pepper Pot,' he said, kissing me.

'I'll always love you too.'

'I mean it,' he said, very seriously. 'Whatever happens, I

will always love you.'

'Why are you saying it like that?'

Scott picked up my wrist to check the time again, but I couldn't bear to look.

'We'll be together one day.'

'I know we will.'

'Have faith, Pepps. And don't forget I love you.'

He kissed me quickly and then everything went instantly black.

I started to panic. Where had he gone?

He'd sent me back?

I hadn't had a chance to say goodbye. Had I? It wasn't long enough.

As I stood there in the darkness all I could feel was a horrible sense of loss.

'Chloe?' I heard Theo say. 'Are you back?'

TWENTY-THREE

'I'm back,' I said with absolutely no enthusiasm.

The door opened and the brightness of the room hurt my eyes. I stepped out, squinting, trying to adjust. Slowly the room came into view and I was halted. Every member of Scott's team was glaring at me.

'Where the hell have you been?' Leanne snarled as Theo took the CPG from my wrist.

'You know where I've been,' I replied, defensively.

'It took six hours to ask him a question?'

'It's been six hours?' I asked, feigning confusion. It hadn't occurred to me how it would appear to Scott's team.

'What did you learn?' Gloria asked.

'It's not good. Apart from the fact that Scott is half the man he was when we all last saw him, he's under the firm belief that he saved the man. According to him nobody died and he's just been charged with arson.'

Theo shook his head. 'That makes no sense. The timelines might be messed up, but it couldn't be clearer that Scott is charged with murder.'

'I asked him about that. I asked him to run through the events. See, we had a lot to talk about! But he said he can't remember anything. He can remember getting to the room to help the trapped man and then it's all blurry.'

Theo shook his head. He turned to Seb, but no one said anything.

'What happens to him?' I asked.

'I'm still not sure,' Theo said, walking back over to his monitor. 'But at least now I know what I'm reading is different to Scott's version of events. Or at least what he can remember. Let me see what I can work out. Something is affecting things somewhere. And if we know it's affecting Scott's present then we know for sure it's far more than a computer glitch.'

Theo was right back on the case, shooting his hands around the screen again.

'Right, I think we all need to get some sleep,' Gloria said. 'It's been a tough day and we need to be on the ball tomorrow. Theo, I don't want you working past midnight. Get as far as you can for now and then give it a rest. You'll work smarter with some sleep and that will be far more beneficial to Scott.'

Theo nodded but his eyes didn't leave his monitor.

'Will you come with me?' Seb said to me quietly, so that no one else could hear.

'Of course,' I nodded.

I followed Seb, quickly glancing at the concerned faces of Scott's colleagues as I passed them. Bradley, in particular, looked very worried. It made me even more nervous about Scott's future.

We walked down multiple green corridors until I knew exactly where we were heading. Seb was taking me back to my room. He could have at least said.

I immediately assumed that I was in trouble for staying away for six hours. I wanted to explain, but I wasn't sure what I could say. No convincing arguments were popping into my head.

We approached the door of my room and I was desperately trying to think of a defence as fast as I could, when Seb didn't stop. We walked right past it and then up some stairs at the end of the corridor. We came to a new section that I'd not seen before with just four doors.

He stopped outside one.

'Do you know where we are?' he asked.

I shook my head. I had no idea.

He fiddled with his black box thing and the door popped open.

'Go inside,' he said.

I stepped in and I immediately knew where we were. The room was bigger than mine with more furniture and a huge bed, but they weren't the reasons why it looked so different. What stood out the most were the mountains of Beatles memorabilia.

'This is Scott's room?' I asked.

Seb smirked. 'How did you guess?'

I scanned every inch of it. There were posters and pictures and books all over the place. Albums – proper vinyl albums – were stacked in the corner, and he even had a record player.

'He says you can only truly appreciate *Abbey Road* on vinyl,' Seb said and I wanted to cry. He'd said the same thing to me, but little had I known that he would go home seventy years in the future and listen to the album on his very own record player. It must have been a proper antique in 2086.

'Scott's always had an obsession with the twentieth century,' Seb explained. 'He's a good man with a strong set of morals, but I'm under no illusion that this job appealed to him mostly because it meant he could see the twentieth century for real.'

'It's not just The Beatles he's obsessed with then?'

'I know. It's hard to believe.'

'Look at that,' Seb said, pointing to a particular framed picture on the wall. It was a slightly blurry black and white photo. It had to have been of The Beatles but they looked very young. Across it were two signatures.

'When you first join Shape the Future you're given a lot of training,' Seb continued. 'The most important part is that we prepare individuals for the culture shock that can come with time travel. You could be sent anywhere at any time so we like to ease people in gently. To help, every new recruit gets to go on three pleasure trips.'

'That sounds incredibly dodgy,' I stated with a smirk.

Seb smiled. 'They can choose any three dates in history to go and visit. They can stay there for a maximum of two days, depending on how we can slot them into that time undisturbed.'

'I'm guessing Scott went back to the twentieth century. Probably the 1960s?'

'Most people just say a year or general period, but Scott said Sunday 19th August 1962.'

'That's very precise.'

'I was shocked. I thought it was maybe the date of his Great Grandmother's birth or something. But it turns out it was the first ever gig at the Cavern Club that Ringo Starr had played. If you know what the Cavern Club is and who Ringo Starr is?'

'I do,' I said, smiling. 'You're not... friends with Scott without knowing such things. So he actually saw them play there?'

'It was all he wanted. He prepared himself fully before the trip. He printed off that photo - he'd found it somewhere on our systems - and he stayed overnight in a little guest house. He did his research and just happened to bump into Paul McCartney and John Lennon the next day. That's their autographs. I know he would have liked all four Beatles, but just to get those was quite an achievement for Scott.'

I stared at the picture for ages. It had to be his most prized possession.

'For his second trip he asked to go back to 30th January 1969.'

'What did the Beatles do then?' I asked with a grin.

'That was their last ever live performance. He must have told you about it, on the roof?'

'He was there?' I asked with astonishment.

'He only travelled for a few hours that day. He just happened to be walking by when they started playing. He couldn't wipe the smile off his face for days after that. I remember it well.'

'What about his third trip then?' I asked. 'What Beatles inspired journey did he make then?'

The smile dropped from Seb's face. 'His third trip surprised me even more. That's when I knew he was going to be a star in this branch.'

'Where did he go?'

'He went to late 1940. To central London.'

'World War Two?' I checked.

'He said he wanted to know first hand what it was like in the Blitz. He felt sure it had been romanticised through time and it must have been purely horrific. He spent a day walking around and then at night he stayed in the Clapham South underground shelter.'

'My God. He wanted to do that?'

'Scott's always found the twentieth century fascinating. Decade after decade, there's so much that happened. The world changed drastically in just a relatively small period of time and it's always sparked his interest.'

'But to go back to the Blitz? I'm not sure many people would be as brave as him.'

'He wasn't smiling when he came back from that trip, that's for sure. He's never really spoken about it but he was certainly more focused after the experience.'

'He's incredible.'

'He's got a good heart.'

'A very good heart.'

'And that's why you love him.' It was a statement, not a question, and I didn't know how to respond. 'And I'm starting to see why Scott loves you in return,' Seb added.

'I don't know what you mean,' I mumbled.

'Scott went back to 2018 as a troubled man that first time. I could tell the job was getting to him and I could certainly see how Leanne was testing his patience on a daily basis.' As soon as Seb had uttered those words, I felt the last shreds of my insecurity fade away. Scott really did love me.

'I was very concerned that we were going to lose him,' Seb continued. 'He's by far the best Inspector we've ever had, but his love for the job had clearly dwindled.'

'So what happened?' I asked.

'We only expected him to be gone for forty-eight hours on that first trip to 2018, but he didn't return for a week. It's not unheard of for Inspectors to spend longer away. Things aren't always as smooth-sailing as we hope. However, on this occasion I was very worried. He'd left for 2018 in a dark mood and his disappearance definitely gave me cause for concern. I was straight there the second Theo reported his return and I expected a distressed man to step from the module. But it was like a transformation. There was a spring in his step and his face was beaming.'

'Oh right,' I said. That's all I could say. I wanted to jump for joy but I knew I had to contain myself.

'Something in 2018 had changed him. I could practically see him counting down the days to another trip back, and he was coming up with wild and wonderful reasons as to why he needed longer away. Donna was proving to be more difficult than we'd imagined, apparently. At first I thought maybe he'd fallen in love with her. To be honest, I wasn't quite sure what was going on. Until you appeared in the module. Then everything fell into place.'

I opened my mouth to say something but I didn't know what words to use.

'Scott's a lucky man,' Seb stated. 'I know he wouldn't have risked everything for someone he didn't truly love. And I'm very pleased to see how much you love him in return. I was quite taken aback by your determination to fight for him earlier. I knew you'd be the only person he'd want to see today.'

'I thought you were going to send Leanne back?' I countered.

'The thought never even crossed my mind.' Seb grinned and I rolled my eyes.

'And now you can be together,' he said.

'How?' I asked with hopeful excitement.

'He's back in your time. Well thereabouts. By the time he gets out of prison you'll be free to be together. I'll make sure you are. You won't have to wait too long, I'm sure.'

'What?' I was horrified by what I thought Seb was suggesting.

'This really is a blessing in disguise. Against all the odds you'll get to be together.'

'After Scott's served time in prison? For something he didn't do?'

'It's a small price to pay, surely.'

'He shouldn't have to pay any price.'

'Why aren't you happy?'

'Because Scott's in prison and it sounds like you're quite content to leave him there. We need to get him out.'

'This is the best outcome for everyone. You must see that?'

'How? How can this be for the best?'

'I don't understand,' Seb said, puzzled. 'Didn't Scott explain?'

'Explain what?'

'You don't know, do you?'

'Know what?'

Seb sighed. 'Take a seat.' I hesitated, nervous about what else was going to come my way. Not feeling at all ready for any more bad news, I reluctantly sat on Scott's bed and Seb joined me.

'I wanted you to see his room so you could get to know the real him,' he began. 'I thought it would be good for you to see before you started your life together. I was trying to be kind.'

'I don't get how you're being kind.'

'I'm being exceptionally kind.'

Jabs of rage cut through me at Seb's words.

'You do appreciate that Scott has broken the law, don't you?' Seb asked.

'He has not! He didn't light that fire. And he saved the man's life. Something no one else was willing to do.'

'Scott's messed with time. You have to follow orders. You're not supposed to interfere with anything unless it's strictly part of your assignment. The ethics committee is dedicated to making sure that each job only has a positive impact on the world. If they're not sure, we can't go.'

'But he saved a man's life.'

'I'm not talking about that. Yes, that's going to raise a lot of questions, but that's not his crime.'

'Crime? What are you talking about?' My heart began to pound as a stark realisation dawned on me.

'When Scott met you, he interfered with time unnecessarily,' Seb explained. 'It's a criminal offence. It's absolutely forbidden and Scott knew it. Even if we bring him back, he'll face a custodial sentence anyway.'

'What? No! He just fell in love. That's crazy!'

'He was supposed to be a professional.'

'He's given up his whole life for this stupid job. Surely that's got to mean something? Surely he's allowed to be human?'

'I'm not blaming him. I can see how it happened and I know you've been good for him. But the law is the law.'

'It's a ridiculous law!'

'It's not.'

'Anyway, what harm has there been? You said it yourself, Scott's been happier since he met me.'

'I know. I'm not arguing with you. But the consequences of his actions are out of my hands.'

'Whose hands are they in? Are you talking about Earl? Well how is he ever going to know? Send me back to 2018. He'll never know. Scott can just get on with his life as if we'd never met. Nothing has happened. No one needs to know.'

Seb shook his head regretfully. 'It's too late for that.'

'What have you done? How can it be too late?'

'You just spent six hours with Scott to ask him a few simple questions. The murmurs have already begun. Everyone's started putting two and two together.'

'His team would drop him in it?'

'No, they'd never do that. Scott's dropped himself in it. He's done this all to himself. He's got himself trapped back in time and I can only delay what will inevitably be a thorough investigation. As soon as they start looking into Scott they'll find out the truth. It won't be hard. The best thing is to not fight it and let Scott serve his time. I'll persuade Earl to let Scott stay there. He'll face charges whatever happens, so it shouldn't be hard to convince Earl that this will be the safest and easiest option. Then we can work out a long term plan whereby he can stay with you without impacting history too much.'

'How can you be so flippant about it?'

'I'm trying to do what's best for you and Scott. Can't you see I'm trying to help?'

'No!'

'Think about it. You'll get to grow old with him.'

'After he's suffered unnecessarily. After he's been punished for years when all he's ever done is sacrifice his own life to help others. For one moment he put himself first. Just one fleeting moment. And this is how you treat him. Surely after all the good he's done, you can be lenient?'

'It's not my call.'

'I don't believe that.'

'I'm doing everything I can for you. Earl knows nothing about Scott being trapped back in time yet. I'm keeping it covered for as long as I can. I've given you the chance to go and visit him and I've brought you here to see his room. I won't let Earl find out until you're safely back in your own time and you're able to visit Scott on your own terms.'

I was utterly flabbergasted. 'I cannot believe you're saying this to me, as if somehow you're the huge hero and we should both be eternally grateful. You should be ashamed of yourself.'

Seb turned away from me and put his finger to his ear. 'What is it?' He was on his phone thing and I was glad of a few minutes to catch my breath. But it was a short lived break. 'We're on our way,' he said. He looked back at me. 'Theo has an update.'

TWENTY-FOUR

I followed Seb back to the module room where Theo was still flicking away like there was no tomorrow. I couldn't help but think how his arms must really ache at the end of each day.

Gloria was already there and Leanne appeared just seconds after us.

'What's the news?' Seb asked.

'The timelines aren't just a mess. Time is changing,' Theo said. He looked exhausted. 'It's literally changing around Scott. It took me a while but I found a trace that he did save that man and then everything changed.'

'How can that be possible?' Seb said.

'We know exactly how that's possible,' Theo stated.

'What do you mean?'

'It was the only logical reasoning I could come up with so I cross-examined it with data from our own assignments. The patterns match. Someone is affecting time. Someone is changing time. In the way that we do.'

'What?'

'Who?' Gloria asked.

'I have no idea.'

'Someone's crept back in time unnoticed?' I asked.

'I can't see how that's possible,' Theo replied. 'You can only travel with a CPG and I can track every journey.'

'Who would do such a thing?' Gloria said.

'What if it was someone from a hundred years in the future and they've invented some other way to time travel?' I asked, desperately trying to be helpful.

'It wouldn't matter if it was a thousand years in the future. It's not possible to travel through time without leaving a footprint. That's just physics. But I can't see anyone other than people from this branch - with journeys all accounted for - that have travelled to that time.'

'Why would someone want to hurt Scott?' I asked, coming at it from a different angle.

'Whoever it is, my guess is that they were the ones who planted the documents in that office,' Theo said. 'This is definitely personal.'

Seb regarded me with sorrow. 'We have no choice now. I need to tell HQ. We need their help.'

Full of panic, I searched my brain for something to say. I was terrified that as soon as HQ knew about this then Scott was going to prison for definite. Whether it was in this time or in my time, he was facing criminal prosecution and I couldn't let that happen. There had to be something I could say; some sort of a clue that I could give them as to what was going on. Things don't just weirdly happen. If spending years working with data had taught me anything, it's that things always add up. I just had to find the logic.

I worked my way through Scott's team in my mind. They were the first obvious culprits, so at the very least I had to either find a reason to suspect their guilt or definitely eliminate them.

But I knew so little about them. All I could do was work with the snippets of information I had and hope for the best.

Leanne first. I really couldn't believe that Leanne was a threat to Scott, other than wanting to marry him, so I quickly brushed her aside.

Next Barbara. What about Barbara? She seemed to adore him, but...

Gloria perhaps? She was stern and scary. Did that make someone guilty? I don't know.

Bradley?

Instantly my mind flagged up Bradley's recent actions.

'Bradley!' I shouted out.

'What about him?' Seb asked as he was about to leave.

'Bradley. When he returned from 2014 he was acting oddly.'

'We all were,' Leanne stated. 'Scott hadn't come back.'

'No, before that. He came out of his module and barely moved. Then he disappeared really quickly.'

'So?' Leanne said.

'Earlier tonight too, when he was standing in this room, he had a ghostly look on his face. I'm telling you, there's something he knows. I've stood back and watched all of you for days, and I know there's something up with him.'

'Are you clutching at straws?' Seb asked me.

'You tell me,' I said, far too assertively. 'You've known Bradley a lot longer than I have. Do you think he's seemed himself today?'

'None of us have been ourselves today,' Leanne argued. 'How could we be?' I fought the urge to slap her.

'I had assumed it was related to concern for Scott,' Gloria interjected, 'but I can't deny that Bradley's been off his game today.'

'Fine,' Seb said. 'It's probably nothing but it can't hurt to ask.' He pressed his finger to his ear. 'Can you join us, please?'

How Seb knew he was dialling Bradley and then how Bradley just magically knew where we were was beyond me. This finger to ear communication was mystifying. It quickly passed through my mind that I still needed to ask Scott how it worked, and then I felt sick. What if I never got the chance again?

No. I will see him again. I had to believe we'd sort this

out.

Bradley appeared a couple of minutes later. 'Is there news?' he asked.

'What aren't you telling us?' Seb asked and Bradley immediately turned pale. It was obvious that he was guilty of something and I couldn't help but feel a little relieved.

'Nothing. What do you mean?'

'Why is Scott facing murder charges in 2014?'

Bradley's face became grave. He stood firm for a few seconds before he finally shook his head. 'I don't know the answer to that question. Honestly, I don't. But there is something I haven't told you. It just didn't make sense. It didn't want to bring it up as I couldn't be sure that I wasn't imagining it.'

'Let us be the judge of that,' Seb said.

Bradley took a deep breath. 'When we were back in 2014 I saw someone. She was standing at the end of the corridor. Just for a moment. I imagined it. I must have.'

'She?' Seb queried.

Bradley paused. 'My mother.'

'What?' Leanne gasped.

'Your mother was in 2014?' Seb asked, equally astonished.

'I don't know. Even if she was, it must have been an assignment. It's the only logical explanation.'

'It can't be,' Theo said. 'I'd have the data'.

'What has your mother got to do with this?' I asked.

Bradley glanced across at me. 'It's true about you, isn't it?' he said.

'Let's keep focused,' Seb ordered before he turned to me. 'Bradley's mother, Fiona, used to work here. She was one of the original Inspectors.'

'Well, can't you just ask her why she was there?'

Everyone glared at me as if I'd asked the most heartless question imaginable.

'She died last year,' Seb explained.

'Oh. I'm very sorry to hear that,' I said.

'Don't be,' Bradley replied quite harshly.

'I've got something!' Theo blurted out. He seemed wired.

'Fiona?' Seb asked.

'No, I set it to alert me when anything in Scott's timeline stabilised. Something just has.'

'What is it?' Seb nudged.

'We have a court date. Actually it looks like everything is starting to stabilise. It goes to the Crown Court.'

'What happens to him?' I asked, full of agitation.

Theo scanned his monitor. 'I can't get a track on that yet. It could take hours before I get all the readings through. But whoever's been changing time, it's like they've finally settled. Whatever happens now is what happens.'

'Is he found innocent?' Seb asked.

'I only have data as far as when the date was set. As there's been so much fluctuation, it's going to take time for the system to process.'

'Is there any way you can speed it up?' Seb asked, revealing just a small hint of being discomposed; something I could tell was unusual for him.

Theo shook his head, evidently feeling the weight of the stress. He flicked his hands around his monitor. 'There's so much to process.' He flicked around some more. 'Hang on, hang on,' he said and my heart started to pound. 'Dates. I've got more dates. No details but the outline of everything that happened.'

'Excellent,' Seb said.

'What does that tell us?' I asked.

'Nothing,' Seb told me. 'But it does mean we can speed up the process of finding things out.'

'How?'

'We'll attend the court case ourselves. If he's found innocent... when he's found innocent, we'll be able to bring him straight back.'

'I'll go,' Leanne said.

'No,' Seb replied. 'I'm going this time. I need to see it

for myself and Scott needs to know how seriously we're taking this.'

'Can I come too?' Leanne asked.

'We have a very limited resource. We can't waste it. Theo, let Logistics know we're on our way.'

'We?' Leanne asked with hope.

'Me and Chloe,' Seb said, quite to the point.

'Chloe?' she bellowed. 'I thought you had limited resource?'

'We'll both be travelling on the same CPG.'

'Won't you need that to bring Scott back?' she yelled.

'I'll send an alarm if we need to bring him back and you can come then.'

'But... Of all the people that Scott will want to see, it's me. He'll need to see me!'

'Leanne, I've made up my mind.'

'But you aren't thinking it through-'

'Inspector Donnington,' Gloria snapped. 'Have some self-respect. Are you really that stupid that you can't see what's going on?'

My mouth dropped open. I hadn't expected that at all.

Leanne scowled at me. Her face was burning red. I thought she was going to explode. She darted out of the room like a school girl with a temper.

'Theo, what date are we going back to?' Seb asked, carrying on as if nothing had just happened.

'12th February 2015,' he said.

'2015?' I queried.

'Yes,' Theo said.

'But aren't we going back to see Scott?'

'Yes.'

'But Scott's in 2014.'

'His court case was February 2015.'

'No! He said his court case was next week. That's what he said. He's just told me.'

'It went to the Crown Court. That takes a lot longer.'

'He's been in prison for a year?' I asked as the sickness

burrowed through me.

There was a small pause before Theo said, very quietly, 'Yes.'

TWENTY-FIVE

'We have to get back to see him now!' I demanded.

'We're going,' Seb said.

We paced over to Logistics to pick up our fresh early twenty-first century fashion – or just normal clothes as I called them – and we headed back to the module room.

Theo had the CPG ready. 'I'm sending you back just before the jury announces its verdict.'

'Verdict?' I queried. 'So literally the last breath of his case?'

'Yes. The outcome.'

'That's all we need to know for now,' Seb agreed.

'Be invisible,' Theo said. 'There's an outside chance that if someone connects you to Scott then it could cause complications.'

'How?' I asked.

'Because he's a mystery,' Seb informed me. 'His anonymity will have undoubtedly caused a lot of issues. It's best we avoid encouraging questions that we can't answer.'

'So we won't get to see Scott?' I asked.

'Of course we will,' Seb replied. 'It's his trial.'

That's not exactly what I meant and I'm sure they knew it. There was something cold and efficient about their behaviour and it really riled me.

Seb wrapped the CPG around his wrist. 'I want you tracking Fiona when we're gone. Let's not lose time.'

'It's all I'll be doing,' Theo replied.

'Get Archie to help.'

'I'll call him the second you're gone.'

Seb stepped over to the module and I followed him. 'We both get in the same one?' I asked.

'We have no choice.'

I squeezed in first and Seb joined me. We were flat against each other and it was most uncomfortable.

'Just hold my CPG in your hand,' Seb said, pushing his arm in front of him. I shifted my hand forward and found the CPG. I wrapped all my fingers around it tightly.

'Ready?' Theo asked.

'Yes,' I replied and Seb nodded. He closed the door and it all went black. I could barely breathe.

A few seconds went by and all I could hear were my own erratic attempts at breathing. Seb was so still and controlled.

It instantly became light. Thankfully it wasn't too bright, just a bit of sun, but it was very cold. I shivered all over, feeling grateful for the thick jumper and coat that I'd been given. I stepped away from Seb as he checked his CPG. 'It's this way,' he said.

I followed his brisk walk around the corner to where we saw the grand building of the court. I'd never been in a court before and just the idea of it made my legs shake.

We swiftly walked in and located the right place to go. It was impressively formal inside and had the whiff of authority about it. I actually found it quite intimidating, but then I guessed that was deliberate.

Not surprisingly, the timing was perfect. We took our seats just seconds before Scott was brought into the dock.

My breath immediately extinguished as soon as I saw him. He looked haggard. He'd been less than himself before, but a year on and he was crushed. I couldn't believe the man before me was actually my Scott.

He hadn't looked around. We were facing his back and I knew there was no way he'd see us. His eyes had barely shifted from the floor. I wanted him to know I was there, though. He had to know we were still fighting for him.

It wasn't like I could call out his name in the silent court, and Theo's warning of being invisible echoed in my mind. But it was so important that he knew we were there. I had to grab his attention.

I scanned my brain for what sort of silent signal I could use. There had to be something I could do.

I knew I didn't have long before my chance would be gone and I forced my brain to think more quickly.

Banging, falling, whistling, coughing. They were all rubbish ideas.

No, hang on. Coughing. The word triggered something in my head. Anyone could cough and no one would care. The same if someone were to sneeze. Only I had a special sneeze; one that Scott would instantly recognise.

I suddenly felt so grateful for my weirdness.

I took a steadying breath and then I launched into the loudest pretend sneeze imaginable, making sure that I properly maximised my strange horsiness.

As I'd hoped, Scott immediately spun his head around (as did most of the court) and he fixed his eyes on me.

The sadness across his face lifted for just a second as he took me in. I smiled without taking my eyes off him. I had to let him know that it would be all right. We were there.

I wanted to run over and hug him. I knew he'd need a hug more than ever. But all we could do was casually glance at one another. I felt utterly useless.

If only I could have read what was going through his mind. Everything about him seemed different and I wanted to understand what he'd been through. If the man I'd been chatting to a few hours before was a bit departed from his normal self, the man in that dock was like a distant relative from the other side of the world. It was heartbreaking.

Scott turned back to face his future and I wanted to

throw up. I couldn't believe he was having to go through this. It was so horrifically unfair.

The jury returned and my heart was throbbing. They had to set him free. If he could just step free then we could get him back. No one would care if he disappeared after that.

The scuffling stopped as the jury settled, and then the judge addressed them. 'On the charge of arson, how does the jury find the defendant?' he said.

It had to be good news. There was no evidence. How could they convict a man with only circumstantial evidence?

'Guilty,' the woman replied.

I couldn't believe it. It was ridiculous. I fought for breath as I waited for the next verdict.

'On the charge of murder, how does the jury find the defendant?'

The head juror paused ever so slightly. All I became aware of was my tunnel vision on her and my ears waiting for her words.

'Guilty.'

No!

The fear and dread punched me hard inside. It couldn't be happening. How could they find him guilty?

I closed my eyes as I fought the urge to cry. I couldn't let myself fall apart. I took a deep breath and focused on Scott. He didn't even appear to flinch. He was keeping his composure perfectly. How was he so brave?

Seb clasped his hand over mine. It made me suddenly aware that my whole body was clenched tightly. My nails were digging into my palms and my muscles began aching from how firmly I was holding myself. But all that mattered was wishing for the judge to be lenient. Maybe it wouldn't be so bad. Surely there was still hope? Maybe Scott would be out in six months? Maybe he'd have served most of his sentence already?

The hope I was trying to give myself didn't resonate with my body, though. Tears were already trickling down my face.

Seb handed me a tissue. As I took it from him with trembling fingers, I noticed a slight shake to his head.

He was right. I had to keep it together. I needed to be better than a quivering, snivelling wreck. It wasn't going to help anyone.

I tried to control my emotions as the judge addressed Scott directly.

'This was a very serious crime. To willingly burn down a building with no care for who may be inside... I feel I'm left with no alternative but to cast the most severe penalty.'

I stopped breathing. He couldn't face life in prison. We couldn't let that happen. It was already taking him to breaking point. Any more time would ruin him completely.

I didn't take another breath as I waited for the judge to continue.

'You are hereby sentenced to death by hanging. You will remain in custody until such time. I can see no other option.'

The world stopped. It just stopped around me.

I didn't move. I couldn't move. Tears were rolling down my face but every other part of me was paralysed.

My eyes focused on Scott. He looked back at me, as white as a ghost. He was terrified and I couldn't do anything about it. I didn't even know where to start offering comfort.

This couldn't be happening.

My breathing returned, and now it was flowing fast. I was starting to feel dizzy and I couldn't stop it.

The death penalty didn't exist anymore. Not in the UK. How could he be sentenced to death? What was going on?

I watched as Scott was led away. I was choking on my grief, finding it hard to function, and the world was getting darker and darker around me. All I could see were Scott's eyes on me. All we could do was watch each other. In every other way I was helpless.

He disappeared out of sight and I nearly collapsed.

Seb grabbed me and helped me to my feet. He supported me as we fled straight out into the sharp winter air.

'Keep it together,' he said as I leaned up against the wall.

'You need to keep it together. Falling apart does not help Scott.'

I tried to control my breathing as Seb's words hit home.

'How do we help him?' I asked.

'I don't know. But we have to find a way.' His voice was shaking and I could tell he was only just about keeping it together himself. 'We have to get him home.'

'Well, let's do it then,' I said, standing up straight. I don't know how my trembling legs were supporting me. It was nothing but pure determination that was getting me through it. 'Let's go and get him.'

'We can't. Not like that.'

'But it's okay for him to be sentenced to death?' It was louder than I'd expected and it drew much unwanted attention.

Seb addressed the faces around us with a "mind your own business" glare and then he turned back to me. 'We need to get out of here.'

'But Scott...'

'I'm not leaving him, Chloe. But we can't do anything here and now. We need to get back and do this properly. I won't let him die. You have to know that. He will not die while I have anything to do with it.'

I took a deep breath and nodded. For the first time I believed that he cared and it helped to calm me down. I followed Seb away from the court.

'Let me go and see him,' I said as we turned the corner.

'I wish I could.'

'Of course you can. You're in charge.'

'We have budgets.'

'Oh bullshit! This is different. This is your best Inspector's life that we're talking about. Surely there has to be contingency plans for disasters such as this?'

Seb sighed. 'Contingency plans are one thing, but there aren't pockets of money floating about for you to go and comfort a man. That's all you'll be doing after all.'

'You self-centred arsehole,' I yelled. It was so loud it

echoed around the street. 'He didn't even want to go on that mission. Don't you see? Scott's life is ruined. He's all alone, probably frightened, with no clue what's going on. The least you can do is provide a bit of comfort for one of your men. Isn't that your duty of care as his boss? Aren't you supposed to protect your workforce? Because what we just saw was not a man under the protection of his employer. It was a man who had been thrown to the wolves when things got a bit tricky. So I'm going to ask you again, and you'd better give me the right answer this time, can I go and see him?'

Seb didn't flinch. He stared at me forcefully, telling me I'd crossed the line, but I refused to back down. Scott's welfare was all that mattered as far as I could see.

'Hold my wrist,' he said. It wasn't a polite request. I stood tall for a minute, reluctant to just give in. But then I conceded that standing on the pavement and arguing was going to get me precisely nowhere. I wrapped my hand around his CPG and blackness instantly surrounded us.

He opened the module door and we practically fell out.

'What happened?' Theo asked.

'Get the team in here now,' Seb ordered.

Theo did his finger to ear bit, summoning everyone.

'I'm guessing from the looks on your faces Scott wasn't found innocent?' Gloria asked as soon as everyone had joined us.

'No,' Seb replied. I could see him trying to be confident but the wobble in his voice gave away his humanity. It was a relief to see he had some. 'Scott was found guilty and he's been sentenced to death.'

A shocking silence engulfed the room. Not even Leanne could react.

I scanned the faces of Scott's colleagues, taking in their upset, disbelief and anger. It took a few minutes before anyone could process Seb's words enough to speak.

'There was no death penalty in 2015,' Barbara finally uttered; the fear in her voice sending chills through me. It was an obvious point, but one that needed to be said.

Theo was the first to move. He sat at his monitor and began flicking through information. We all watched him, no one daring to say a word.

He stopped, quite abruptly, and his whole body instantly tensed. Slowly his head turned towards us, his face haunted.

He went to speak but no words came out.

'What is it?' Seb asked.

Theo just shook his head.

'What is it?' Gloria insisted.

'It's like... it's broken,' he uttered.

'The system?' Gloria asked when he didn't elaborate.

Theo shook his head again.

'What's broken?' Seb pushed.

'It wasn't like this,' Theo mumbled. 'It's... I don't know where it's come from.'

'What is it?' I asked, not even trying to hide my jittery state.

'Time.' That's all Theo said in response.

'Time is broken?' I asked.

'What do you mean time is broken?' Gloria demanded.

'Issues are shooting up all over the place,' he explained. He seemed quite upset. 'More than I can keep up with. It's not just the death penalty; it's everything. Things we've corrected are reverting back and new problems that never happened are now popping up all over time. It's like a virus has been set free in history and it's eating away at all the good.'

That eerie silence grasped the room once more. What could we say to that?

'Do we have anything more on Fiona?' Seb finally asked.

'No,' Theo replied. 'I can't find any trace of her back when the team was there. I've also run a trace on every CPG journey ever taken, just to be sure. There's nothing. Everything is accounted for.'

'It's time to elevate it,' Seb said, addressing everyone in the room. 'We have to involve HQ. I think it's best I go over there. In the meantime, Chloe is going back to visit

Scott. He needs our support more than ever now.' I glanced at Seb, gobsmacked. He didn't acknowledge me in return, though. 'Theo,' he said instead, 'please find the first possible time that Scott's alone after the sentencing and get Chloe back there.'

'Doing it now.'

'Dom, can you get another proofer from Logistics.'

'On it,' Dom said as he shot off out the room.

Finally Seb turned to me and, with no glimmer of humour, he said, 'I'm assuming you forgot to bring the last one back?'

'Yeah,' I replied. I wasn't sure whether I'd get into trouble or not if he knew the truth. At this stage it was seeming anything was possible.

'I want you to tell Scott that we're all working on this,' Seb said. I'd never seen him so serious. 'We will not let him suffer and we won't rest until this is sorted out. Do I make myself clear?'

'Yes sir,' I replied.

'The rest of you,' Seb continued, once again addressing the team, 'I want you supporting Theo and Archie. Let's start building some facts. What do we know and where are there holes? Are there any patterns?'

Everyone responded with their understanding and people darted off in all directions getting busy.

Theo handed me a CPG. 'Scott's in a single cell,' he said. 'I'm sending you there that night, just a few hours after the sentencing. You'll land at twenty-three fifteen, same as before.' Theo looked me straight in the eye. 'I don't expect you back for six hours. Do you hear me?'

I tried to smile. Theo was nice. 'I'll be there for him.'

I had no clue what the time actually was in my own timeline. I didn't know how these Inspectors did it. I felt exhausted yet I was pumped with adrenaline. The day was going on forever and there seemed to be no end in sight, but at the same time I was far from ready for it to end.

'Here,' Dom said, reappearing in the room, breathlessly.

He handed me the silver cube that was the soundproofing thing.

'Thanks,' I said.

I slipped off my coat, knowing I wouldn't need it, and handed it to Theo. I then strapped the CPG around my wrist and I headed back into the module.

'Are you ready?' Theo asked.

'Yes,' I said quickly, before I had a chance to dwell on how I was actually feeling. That would have been far too dangerous.

He closed the door and I waited. Within seconds the light changed and I was in Scott's cell again.

TWENTY-SIX

'Chloe!' Scott said in a whisper, immediately looking up at me. He was lying on his back, wide awake. He jumped to his feet and threw his arms around me.

My skin prickled at the feel of him. He was so much thinner and noticeably weaker. I touched his cheek with my hand and scanned his face. His eyes were weary with huge bags under them. Their characteristic glisten was like a distant memory.

I let him hug me for as long as he wanted. I squeezed him in my arms, holding back the tears. I had to stay strong for him. I knew I'd probably cry for months after this was all over with, but for now I had to stay in control.

I slowly pulled away. I needed to give us some privacy. I held up the proofer cube to show him and a relieved smile edged up on his lips.

I placed the cube down near the door. This cell was narrower than his last one, but not too different.

I glanced up at him for approval and he nodded.

'Perfect. Just like before.'

'Do you still have the proofer I left?' I asked.

'I kept it for six months. Until a supposedly random cell search. They really hate me here.'

'They took it off you? What did they think it was?'

'I told them it was a lucky charm. They laughed at me and threw it out. I got the piss taken out of me for a few weeks after that.' He shrugged as if to say he didn't care, but I could see the pain in his eyes.

'Right,' I said, holding out the CPG on my wrist. 'Do your fiddly bit. You're coming back with me.'

'What?' He seemed genuinely taken aback.

'Come on. I'm not letting you go through this anymore. It's meaningless and ridiculous, and I have the power to make it all end. So do your bit. Get us back.'

'Oh Chloe.' His face showed a combination of sorrow, regret and the warmth of being loved. It was both adorable and heart-breaking to witness. 'I can't.'

'You'd rather stay here? You'd rather go through the agony of being sentenced to death? It's ludicrous.'

'I'd rather be anywhere but here, believe me. But I have no choice. I have to stay.'

'Of course you have a choice. I'm offering you that choice.' I waved my CPG in his face, demonstrating how easy it would be.

'Okay then, I choose to stay.'

'What?' I screamed this so loudly, I was worried it would break through the proofer's power. But Scott didn't bat an eyelid. Instead he just took my hand and led me to the bed.

We sat down and I noticed how his usual, ready for anything, animated mannerisms were non-existent. He was hunched over, as if the heavy load of his anguish was crippling him.

'If I leave with you and vanish from my locked cell in the middle of the night, how's that going to look?'

'Why do you care?'

'It won't be forgotten about. My face will be everywhere. There will be a huge man hunt. They'll not only want to bring the dangerous criminal – as I've been labelled – back into custody, but they'll also be desperate to know how I escaped. If word gets around that someone can escape from a locked cell, it's not good for the system.'

'But again, why do you care? You'll be seventy years in the future. What will it matter?'

'I won't be though, will I?'

'What are you talking about?'

'It's 2015. In three years' time I meet you. In three years' time I meet Donna. What if I'm casually having lunch with you or Donna one day and my face gets spotted? It could be from something as simple as CCTV. I'll be arrested. It might be three years on from this point in time but it's actually eighteen months ago in my past. I'm not going to have a clue what they're talking about. Then it means I won't go back to my future, I won't go on the assignment to set fire to that building, I won't try to save that man and I won't be sitting in this cell.'

'Isn't that a good thing?'

'It will rip a hole in time. Can't you see that?'

This silenced me.

'If I leave with you now I could cause a contradiction in time,' Scott explained. 'I could potentially be stopping myself from doing the thing that sends me here in the first place. It would cause a time paradox. The results could be catastrophic.'

'So you really can't leave?'

Scott shook his head. 'It would also mean that I'll never see you again. How can I travel back freely to this time if I'm a wanted man? I don't know how we're ever going to find a way to be together, but at least at the moment there's hope. Isn't there?'

His question was like a desperate plea and I knew my answer had to be positive. However unsure I was myself about what lay ahead, he needed my optimism. 'Of course there's hope. More than hope. If we love each other then we'll make it work. I don't know how, but we'll find a way. We will. And that begins with making all of this nonsense go away. You're not going to stay here. I'm not going to stand by and let this happen. If you won't travel back with me then I'll find another way. You mark my words, I'll find a way.'

'I know you'll try,' he said, putting his arms around me.

'I'm going to do more than try.'

He held me firmly and I could tell he was holding back tears.

'How about we snuggle up for a while?' I said.

This set his tears free. He was an absolute mess. It wasn't the man I knew at all.

I tried very hard to control my own emotions. My face was stinging with the urge to cry but I refused to give in to it. He needed my strength. He didn't need my pity.

We tucked ourselves up under his blanket and we wrapped our bodies around each other.

'How can I be facing death?' he asked through his reluctant sniffles. 'I don't even remember killing anyone. In my memory the man lived. They were telling me things as fact that I couldn't remember happening at all. Have you any idea what's going on?'

'We're working on it,' I said. 'Theo said time's changing all over the place. I think you've just got caught up in the middle of lots of stuff. But Seb's over with HQ now. They'll get to the bottom of it. He told me to tell you they're not going to rest until they sort it all out. And they bloody well won't be resting. I'll be making sure of that.'

Scott held me close against him.

'You know, when I was last in your cell it was just a few hours ago to me,' I said, trying to think of something else to say. 'This time travel thing really messes with your head.'

'It messes with your whole life.'

'It's been nearly a year for you?' I asked, cautiously.

'I didn't expect to see you again. Not even in court. I thought you might pop up in 2018, but not before that.'

'Why 2018?' I asked, innocently.

'I was hoping you might come and visit me when you got back to your own time. Would you have done?'

'You know I would have done. But that's all irrelevant.

You're not staying here.'

I felt Scott's whole body tense. 'You know, if you can sort out this capital punishment crap... it might be best for me to stay here. I don't really want to, but it might work out for the best.'

'How can it be for the best?' I felt angry at the mere suggestion.

Scott hesitated. 'I might not be guilty of arson or murder, but I'm far from an innocent man.'

'I'm not listening to that.'

'Travelling through time is great, but it comes with strict rules. Rules that have severe penalties should you break them.'

'They're stupid rules.'

'They're rules put in place for a reason. To protect everybody. I really shouldn't have done what I did.'

'I know you're talking about me.'

'I don't regret it. Six months with you is worth anything.'

'They can't stop you having a life.'

'I was supposed to be working.'

'Twenty-four hours a day? Weeks at a time? No one can ask that much of you.'

'They can ask me to protect the timelines. They can expect me to be professional.'

'But you were just dropping me off home. I'm Donna's friend, nothing else. How is that unprofessional?'

'Come on, Pepps,' Scott sighed. 'Putting aside any suspicions that Seb may or may not have had when you turned up in 2086, I'm guessing my secret was properly out when it took you six hours to ask me a few questions.'

'You knew that would raise alarm bells?' I asked. 'But you were the one who convinced me to stay.'

'It didn't matter. I'd got myself arrested. I would have had to go through an internal investigation anyway. It wouldn't have taken them long to find out about you. I might as well have got a night of incredible sex out of it.' He tried to smirk but his sadness was too dominant. 'Besides, now they know and I'm serving my time aren't I? I knew Seb would talk them into letting me stay in this period. We can be together...' He stopped himself. 'This is our best chance to be together. Our only chance. It might be a blessing in disguise.'

'A blessing?' I bellowed. I couldn't believe what he was saying.

'Do you see another way for us to be together?'

'No, but I also see that me coming to 2086 was nothing short of a miracle, so I've got faith that somehow something else will work out for us. In a future where you don't have a criminal record. For anything. Because falling in love certainly does not make you a criminal.'

Scott hugged me tightly again. I nestled my head against his chest. I didn't want him to see my furious face. I was seething just thinking about the stupid law that made the best man I knew a convict.

After a while of us not speaking, my guilt started screaming at me. What was I doing? I was supposed to be offering him comfort, not feeling sorry for myself.

'I haven't even asked, how have things been?' I said, trying to be a better girlfriend. 'Has time really dragged? I can't believe it's been a year. I'm so sorry.'

'It's fine. It is what it is.'

'Have you made any friends?'

Scott didn't answer.

'Surely there must be a few people around here you could get along with?'

'Pepps, I'm a policeman. I've dedicated my life to fighting against the very people that I now have to eat breakfast with every day. I have no desire to be making friends with anyone. I'm keeping my head down and minding my own business. That's the best thing I can do.'

'But that's so lonely.'

'It's survival.'

'Is there no one who's nice? Maybe another person who's innocent like you?'

Scott scoffed. 'Are you saying the system I believe in is flawed? That in every prison there's likely to be innocent people?'

I could tell I was riling him and it was the last thing I wanted to do.

'No, not at all,' I insisted. 'But things happen. You're innocent.'

'I'm not.'

'Of course you are.'

'If it wasn't for me and my team that building wouldn't have burned down and that man would be alive.'

'But you didn't do anything. You didn't want to be involved.'

'It doesn't change anything.'

'And before you open your mouth, I don't want to hear a single word about you being guilty of having an affair in history. I will not let you defend that ridiculous law.'

Scott sighed heavily again and I knew I had to stop. Things were getting tense and it was totally wrong. He was going through hell and my ranting was only making it worse. I had to get a grip.

I took a breath to calm myself and I tried to think of something more lighthearted to talk about.

'Seb showed me your room,' I said.

'Did he?'

'Yeah. I hope you don't mind.'

'When was that?'

'About three minutes after I last saw you. Which was about an hour before we went to the court, which was just minutes before I got here. It's been one hell of a day.'

'I bet you don't even know what time it is,' Scott said.

'I don't even know what day it is!' I smirked.

'I've been there. You leave one place at two in the afternoon and it's three in the morning at home just seconds later.'

'You must have been... well, jet lagged quite a lot.'

'You do get used to it.'

'Is that another reason why you get sent on those... what did Seb call them? Pleasure trips?'

'Did you see my Beatles signed photo?' he asked as his eyes brightened for the first time.

'Yes. I took a guess that it's was your most prized possession.'

'Of course.'

'You've met Paul McCartney and John Lennon?'

Scott smiled. It was lovely to see. 'I've wanted to tell you so many times. It was very brief, but yeah, I met both of them.'

'That's amazing! What were they like?'

'Friendly, I suppose. I don't know. It all happened really quickly.'

'I bet!'

'I know how lucky I am.'

'I didn't know you had so many records, either. There were dozens of them.'

'Shh,' Scott said with a grin. 'I'm not supposed to. You rarely find a vinyl in my time, so I had to free them of their own time on my travels. I could have got into serious trouble. I knew Seb wouldn't mind, but Earl would go mad if he ever found out.'

'They're so fixated on idiotic rules. What would it matter?'

'It's about being professional.'

'But you're also human. Surely you're allowed a moment of indulgence every now and then?' I noticed I was bringing down the mood again. I had to keep it light. 'I want to know where you got the record player from!'

Scott chuckled. 'You should have seen the look on Theo's face when I appeared with that in the module. I couldn't really hide it.'

'You got it from the twentieth century?'

'The late 1980s if I remember rightly. It was there in a shop window as I was passing, calling out my name. I didn't really have a choice.'

'Will you play *Abbey Road* for me sometime on it?'

This silenced Scott momentarily. 'I'd really like that,' he said with a choke.

'I won't allow them to leave you here to serve a prison sentence,' I told him with a very firm voice.

Scott edged up on his elbow so he could address me properly. 'Who are you?' he asked. 'Because you certainly look like my girlfriend, but she was never quite so bossy.'

I looked down at his chest, feeling sheepish. 'This whole experience has really rocked me,' I muttered. 'I've never been so angry or sad or indignant or bewildered. It's like an emotional tornado is ripping through me.' I hesitated as the truth of it all became apparent. 'I think it's making me stronger.'

'I'll say.'

'You know, I might take a more angry approach from now on,' I said, feeling my confidence blooming. 'It's like I've had a taste of sticking up for myself and I've really enjoyed it. I called Seb an arsehole earlier. An arsehole! He's like the most senior person there and I yelled his head off.'

This made Scott laugh again. It was such a lovely sound. 'Oh I wish I'd been there,' he said.

'It doesn't put you off me, does it?'

Scott shook his head. 'You're joking, aren't you? Quite the contrary. I've always loved your shy innocence, but I used to get really frustrated when you'd tell me about how people had walked all over you. They treat you like crap at your job. It's despicable.'

I considered his words for a second. 'You're right. You're totally right. I've always been too afraid to say anything. But when it came to witnessing people treating you badly, it sent shockwaves through me. I've been like a new woman, bossing all your colleagues around. They don't know what's hit them.'

'I'm glad to hear it. Especially if I'm not there. Someone needs to keep them in line.'

'I don't want to go back to who I was,' I admitted. 'I

don't want that life anymore. I want to be the person I am when I'm with you.' My voice faded away.

We kissed but it was nowhere near as passionate as it had been a few hours before. Now it just felt needed.

I snuggled in against his chest again and we lay in silence for ages.

We dozed for a bit and then awoke to share silly memories of our past, before dozing some more. It was far more sombre than my previous visit and I found it all ten times more difficult.

By the time ten to five came around, I was utterly drained. Drained of everything: my hope, my faith, my belief in goodness, and all of my strength.

The strongest, bravest and most considerate man that I had ever met was like a frail, teary shell in front of me. How could life do that to anyone? Let alone such a good person. It was cruelty beyond measure.

'You'd better go,' he said, looking at my CPG.

'It won't be another year. I promise. All of the team is on the case. Nothing else is mattering. It's all about you and getting you free. Trust us.'

We got out of bed and he held me one more time. 'I still love you. I've thought about you every day. You're the only thing keeping me going.'

'I love you too. Know that I won't rest until you're free. You have my word.'

'Thanks, Pepper. My lovely Pepper Pot.'

'Shall I leave the proofer again?'

'Please.'

'I think it's the least that crappy branch can do for you. For its star.'

'I don't feel much like a star at the moment.'

'You don't need to burn brightly to be important.'

'I'm not going to die in here, am I?' Scott said, fighting to keep some composure. He looked broken to bits.

'No,' I said. This time I was the one to cup his face. 'No. I'm not going to let that happen. Are you going to trust me?'

He nodded.

'Say it.'

'I trust you.'

'Mean it.'

'I trust you.'

'Well, there you go. You'll be out of here before you know it. Just a little while longer. Just hang on.'

'I'll try.'

I picked up my wrist to show him my CPG. 'Do you still remember how to do it?' I asked.

'How could I forget.' He placed his hands gently on the device.

'I love you,' I said, kissing him one last time.

'I love you too. Thanks for coming to see me.'

'I'll see you again. Very soon.'

'I really hope so.' His voice was quivery and I could see the tears fill up in his eyes, and then everything went instantly black.

I didn't move. I needed to catch my breath. That had been heart-breaking. In a few seconds I'd have to be back in that room, ensuring everyone was focused on freeing the man I loved. I just needed a minute in the darkness to find some strength.

'Chloe? Are you back?' Theo said, opening the door.

As soon as the light hit me, I snapped into action. I had no choice.

I stepped out and all of Scott's team watched me with anticipation. Everyone was there except Seb.

'How is he?' Gloria asked.

I shook my head. 'Not a speck of the man we all know him to be. You've ruined him.'

'We'll get him out of there,' Gloria said.

'No we won't,' I said as a surge of confidence took charge.

'What do you mean we won't?'

'We're not getting him out of there because he won't be going in there in the first place. Do you understand? This is a bloody time machine,' I said, pointing to the CPG around my wrist. 'Let's make it so it never happened at all.'

TWENTY-SEVEN

'Come on then, let's start making a plan,' I ordered. The adrenaline was coursing through me.

Nobody said a word. Everyone just glared at me.

'If you could see him,' I said, 'you wouldn't just be standing there gaping at me. He's in sheer hell. We need to stop picking at this mess. We need to go back and figure out how we can sort it once and for all.'

Gloria put her finger to her ear. 'Yes. We're all in the module room. Very good.' She addressed the room. 'Seb's back.'

'He's been at HQ all this time?' I asked, to which Gloria nodded in reply.

'How is he?' Seb asked me, appearing in the doorway.

'He's a wreck. What is HQ doing about it?'

'They're working through things. They hadn't been aware of the re-emergence of capital punishment, so Earl said that's going to be their primary target.'

'How does that help Scott?' I asked.

'I think that's obvious.' Seb moved towards the centre of the room to address the whole team. 'Earl and I had a very detailed discussion about Scott and this unfortunate situation and we've both agreed that it would be best if we, as a team, step away from the case. We're too close to it. Therefore we're going to leave HQ to handle things.'

I shook my head. As if that was ever going to happen.

'What about all the work we've done so far?' Theo asked.

'If you send me a progress report then I'll pass it directly on to Earl. Anything we've got so far is going to be of great use, I'm sure. But then we need to leave it to them.'

I couldn't believe what I was hearing. There was no way things were being left to HQ. Not only because I was dubious about how good HQ actually was, but also because I knew that if they got involved then Scott was definitely going to have to serve time in prison. Serve time because he fell in love with me. I absolutely could not let that happen.

'What is the progress?' I asked Theo. 'Did you manage to find out anything else while I was gone?' I walked over to Theo's monitor but he didn't say a word. All he did was remove the CPG from my wrist.

'I know it's hard, but the best thing we can do is stand back,' Seb said, joining us.

'No,' I replied, extremely firmly.

'Excuse me?' Seb was clearly not impressed by my defiance, but nothing was going to stop me from helping Scott.

It wasn't good enough just to stop Scott dying. We had to make sure that this nightmare never happened in the first place, and the power lay at all of our fingers. All they had to do was start thinking for themselves.

'Scott needs us,' I insisted. 'He needs every brain in this place working on a way to free him.'

'I know you're-'

'Is everyone else happy with just taking a step back?' I asked, staring around at the faces in the room. All I got was stunned silence in return, though. Their muteness was very irritating.

'Am I the only one who thinks it's irrelevant what Earl wants and all that matters is Scott?'

'Earl is doing what he thinks is best,' Seb said. 'And I

agree with him.'

'But you're Inspectors and Superintendents. He's not even from the police force. Surely you're the ones trained to detect stuff and follow clues. How can Earl be better than you?'

'Being part of the force means you work as a team and you follow the chain of command.'

'Even when one of your own has been sentenced to death for something he didn't do? Are you really just going to sit back and let people who can't even figure out a so-called computer glitch take charge?'

'This branch is built on trust and I won't have that trust broken.'

I exhaled loudly. I'd made a promise to Scott and I was adamant that the only steps back we'd be taking were ones in time to rescue him.

I took another breath as I considered what I could say or do. This chain of command stuff was all great in theory, but I couldn't possibly see how it was right that the people who cared the most were being side-lined.

Something began niggling at my mind. I'd said they couldn't figure out the computer glitch. Or the so-called glitch. Something somewhere wasn't adding up, and it clearly hadn't added up for a long time. I recalled Scott challenging Earl, but he'd refused to engage in conversation. He'd just been sweaty and awkward.

I realised it might be a loophole that I could exploit.

'Okay, I understand,' I said, hoping everyone would believe my sudden capitulation. 'If we can't proactively be involved, can we at least be given progress updates? For example, let's say this computer glitch was related. HQ is working on that, isn't it? Could we find out any information? Like how close they are to a resolution? We don't need the details, just a quick overview. Where's the harm in us knowing that? Do you speak with the HQ team?'

'I speak to them all the time about assignments,' Theo replied.

'So there must be someone you know that you can ask. Even if it's just a percentage, surely they can give us an indication of how close they are to sorting it out. If it's eighty percent then we can all relax, can't we?'

My suspicions were that it would be closer to zero percent and it might actually shock the team into action.

Theo glanced over at Seb who didn't move for a moment. Finally he nodded to give the green light.

Theo started swiping at his computer again and I figured this was more of an online chat than the usual finger to ear stuff. We all waited in silence.

'What?' Theo gasped, sitting back.

'What is it?' Seb asked.

'Do they have news?' I asked.

'This can't be right,' Theo said, shaking his head.

'What is it?' I pushed.

'Earl told his team that we were working on a solution. Apparently the computer glitch is with us. Earl said I'm a problem-solving expert so they should leave it with me. My mate's just asked *me* for a progress update.'

'What about Scott? What do they know about Scott?' I pushed.

Theo consulted Seb again who just nodded for him to proceed.

Theo swiped his fingers across his monitor some more, his expression becoming increasingly graver. I glanced across at Scott's team. They all seemed equally as concerned.

'What the hell is going on?' Theo virtually shouted, almost making me jump.

'Tell us,' Seb ordered.

'They're not investigating anything. My mate doesn't know anything about what's happened to Scott. He didn't even know about the assignment to set fire to that building.'

'Maybe only a selected few knew,' Seb suggested.

'He's pretty senior over there,' Theo replied. 'Why would he not know? Besides, even if he didn't know at the time, you're telling me Earl hasn't got all of his team working on the re-emergence of capital punishment?'

'You did just say that was their primary focus,' I stated, directly towards Seb.

'He's protecting her, isn't he,' Bradley uttered.

All eyes turned to him.

'Let's not make assumptions,' Seb said.

'Protecting who?' I asked.

'Her,' Bradley said in a deeply venomous tone.

'Fiona,' Seb clarified. 'Bradley's mother.'

'There is no rational reason for her to have been there,' Bradley said. 'And when you throw in all the weird things that have happened since I saw her... well, it's obvious isn't it.'

'But why would she cause so much trouble?' I asked.

'Fiona had a lot of issues,' Seb explained. 'She became disillusioned with the job. She left shortly before her death, questioning the whole morality of what we do. She seemed to believe that we were in fact ruining people's lives and not saving them. She caused the whole team a great deal of distress. It was a very unpleasant time.'

'She took her own life,' Bradley stated, without any emotion. 'It was the only good thing she ever did.' I was stunned.

I shivered against the icy tension as the major hole in what they were saying troubled my mind. I had to ask. I needed to ask. I spoke very delicately. 'How can this all be happening if she's dead?'

'You didn't know her,' Bradley virtually hissed. 'She probably put something into play just before she died that's now contaminating everything it touches. Even death doesn't rid the world of her poison.'

I didn't know what to think. I'd never seen anyone feel so much hatred towards their own flesh and blood.

'Whatever's happening, if Earl is covering for her, then he must have his reasons,' Seb said.

'She doesn't deserve it,' Bradley seethed.

'Whether that's the case or not, it's evident that this

whole situation runs far deeper than we can understand,' Seb said. 'We have to leave it to Earl.'

'Are you joking?' I snapped.

'There are things at play here out of our control.'

'Clearly!'

'And if we start to meddle we may make things worse.'

'Or Scott will be hanged for a crime he didn't commit.'

'I'm sure Earl is working on the best outcome for everyone.'

'How? How exactly? It appears no one is working on it. The HQ team is completely in the dark and we've been told to stand back.'

'I'm sure-'

'As far as I can see, with every passing second this problem escalates. It's got to a highly dangerous level and we need to get Scott out of there.'

'It's important we work as a team-'

'Precisely! And that's exactly what Earl is trying to stop us doing. Can't you see that?'

'I'm sure there are very good reasons-'

'Yeah, to protect that bitch,' Bradley interjected. 'She's twisted his mind, like she always did. Even dead she still has her grips on him. Chloe's right, he's protecting her and he can't see the damage it's doing elsewhere.'

'Damage that we have to correct,' I finished.

'Scott was also right,' Gloria said, finally breaking her reticence. 'Since when have we ever been asked to sacrifice someone's life for the greater good? We've always been about upholding the law, not about making judgements on whose life is more important. Earl should never have asked us to do that.'

'He had his reasons,' Seb countered.

'And as for leaving Scott there to help him – which I know is exactly what's been running through your mind – I want to make it clear, I am dead against that happening.'

Seb addressed Gloria directly. 'I only have Scott's best interests at heart.'

'Then you're severely misguided. Whatever Scott may or may not have done back in time...' Her eyes glanced across at me for just a second. 'He's a good man. A very good man. Who here would have acted differently in the same circumstance? In fact, you know what, I celebrate his decision. He's the only one of us around here who's had anything to smile about for years.'

'Gloria, it's not that simple-'

'She's right,' Barbara joined in. 'Nobody would ever agree that leaving Scott back there was the right decision. Not even those who are closest to him.'

All eyes turned to me and I felt myself blush.

'Scott is the best Inspector that this branch has ever seen,' Barbara continued. 'I've learnt so much from him. We all have. When he takes the lead on an assignment we relax because we know it will be a success. We know we can trust him. And now it's our turn. Now he needs us.'

'He needs us more than ever,' I said as the relief of the team finally coming around washed through me. 'Surely you can see that, Seb? If Earl has taken his eye off the ball to protect this Fiona, then we're Scott's only hope. Do you really want to risk him dying when we could have helped?'

The room stiffened with apprehension as we all watched Seb churn through his thoughts.

'I don't like assuming that Earl is in the wrong here,' he said. I felt my palms clench. 'But I concede that we don't actually know what's going on and Earl's behaviour is unusual. However, if we start to meddle without properly appreciating the situation, we may make things worse for Scott.'

'But that's-'

Seb put his hand up to silence my argument. 'Therefore, I suggest that we try to find out what's actually going on.'

I didn't move. Had he really just said that?

'And I can see the only way for us to do that is to find out from Fiona herself.'

Bradley shook his head in both annoyance and disbelief,

but I was now all pro-Seb.

'So we're going to go back to the fire to find out what she was doing there?' I asked.

'No.' Leanne tutted like I was an idiot.

'Why not?' I asked.

'Because we're already there,' she replied. 'We can't take the risk of running into our other selves. That could have disastrous results.'

'We can't interfere with what we've already done,' Theo said. 'That assignment was a success. As ludicrous as that sounds. If we go back there we may make things worse.'

'So what do we do?'

'We need to find her before that night,' Seb stated. 'Theo?'

'I've been checking,' Theo replied. 'I've checked across a few weeks. There's no trace of her.'

'She's there somewhere,' Seb said.

'Could Earl hide her? Can you hide a time traveller?' I asked.

'No,' Theo replied. 'As I said, anyone who travels through time leaves a footprint and I'd find it. There isn't a single unaccounted footprint anywhere around that time.'

'Then think outside the box,' I said as the hours I'd spent poring over difficult spreadsheets flashed through my mind. 'If you know something's wrong then there has to be an explanation.'

'Obviously,' Theo retorted.

'If you can't find where's she's come from, it just means you haven't looked in the right place yet.'

'How far across 2014 did you look?' Seb asked.

'Six weeks before,' Theo replied.

'How long to scan a year?' Seb asked.

Theo shrugged his shoulders. 'I suppose we'll have to.' Theo started to do his thing again and we all waited. He looked across at the team's anxious faces. 'This could take hours.'

'Right, let's get this thing moving,' Seb ordered. 'Gloria,

can you take the lead on this? I can give you one journey. That's it. So how can we optimise it to help Scott?'

'I don't want him going to prison at all,' I said.

Seb regarded me with surprise. 'You're calling the shots now are you?'

For the smallest of moments I felt hesitant, and then I recalled Scott's teary eyes and my resolve returned. 'I'm just protecting the man I love,' I said. 'Who has done absolutely nothing to deserve a prison sentence. In this time or any time.'

I caught Leanne's scowl from across the room, but she didn't say a word.

'I told the team before you got here,' I said to Seb. 'We're not getting Scott out of jail, we're making sure he never goes there in the first place. Is that clear?'

I couldn't read Seb's expression and my instincts were telling me to back down and apologise, but I stood strong. He finally spoke with a firm and measured voice. 'I agree that's the best course of action. The man in that court was not the man from this team. We need him back as he was and there's only one way we're going to achieve that.'

I nodded, trying not to show my surprise and desperate relief. At last things were moving forward!

'You're an extraordinary lady,' Seb added, more softly. 'Far from a criminal offence.'

'Do the rest of us have a role?' Leanne whined.

'Gloria?' Seb said.

'Leanne, Barbara, you can help me,' Gloria instructed. 'We'll run some scenarios. Bradley, I want you working with Theo and Archie. Find something useful. Dom, get Logistics prepped please. Francesca, I want you to analyse all the intelligence gathered for the 2014 job. What do we know and is there anything odd about it?'

Everyone nodded and took up their roles.

'What about me?' I asked.

Gloria studied me. 'What time is it?' she asked quite firmly.

I tried to think but I hadn't got a clue. I didn't even know what day it was.

'I'm not sure,' I said.

'Do you know how long you've been awake for?' she said.

'I dozed for a bit with Scott.'

'I need you to get some rest,' she said.

'I don't think-'

'It's not a request. You've now been on the go for around twenty-four hours. It's seven ten and you look absolutely shattered.'

'Seven ten in the morning?' I asked with a gasp.

'Seven ten on Monday 10th June 2086.'

'Monday?'

'No doubt you're feeling a little disorientated?'

That didn't even come close to how I was feeling but I didn't want to confirm it. I wanted to make out that I was totally fine with time travel.

Just twenty-four hours before, I'd been waiting for Scott to appear at my door. I couldn't believe how much had been packed into just one day.

I'd literally gone through a year of Scott's life in one day.

Time travel was utter madness. I really didn't know how any of them could sustain it in the long term.

'Do you see why I think you need a short rest?' Gloria said. I really didn't know how I was going to get any rest knowing that Scott's life was at risk, but I couldn't deny how drained I felt.

'Okay. But will you let me know the second something happens?'

'Of course,' she said. 'I promise.'

'Thank you.'

I went to head off when she stopped me. 'Scott's a very lucky man,' she said and it nearly brought tears to my eyes. All I could do was nod.

I paced back to my room, trying to keep it together.

As soon as I got there, I sat down on my bed and wept.

My eyes were sore and tired, and I felt thoroughly wretched.

I lay back but my head was spinning at a hundred miles an hour. How would I ever get any sleep?

The banging on my door woke me up with a jump. I looked at the clock next to the bed to find it was half past eleven. I was relieved to see I'd got some sleep, although it hadn't been pleasant. I'd been having the most awful nightmare about Scott dying.

I stood up, feeling very groggy, and opened the door. It was Dom.

'Is there news?' I asked.

'Yes.'

'What is it?' My heart was pounding again.

'I think Theo should explain.'

TWENTY-EIGHT

We walked quickly back to the module room where all of the team had already convened. Dom led me straight over to Theo.

'What's the news?' I asked, far too urgently.

'We couldn't find any trace of Fiona travelling in 2014,' Seb said, joining us.

'But we obviously knew for a fact she was there,' Theo added. 'So I spread the search out a bit.'

'And?' I encouraged.

'We found her. We found the trace. I don't know how she did it as I couldn't match a CPG journey, but I tracked down an unidentified footprint and I've been able to link it to her. She entered the timeline at the end of 2013. The 29th December to be precise. Then she waited it out.'

'That's great!'

'There's more,' Seb said.

'I cross-examined this journey with Fiona's known timelines to work out when exactly she'd made the trip and something very strange emerged,' Theo explained. 'There are no gaps that aren't accounted for. She was here working most days and she died just a couple of months after leaving the branch. Yet she was in 2014 for at least five months.'

'So? It is time travel,' I argued. 'She could easily have been moving around without anyone noticing.'

'That's exactly what she must have been doing. And repeatedly.'

'What do you mean?'

'Her timelines are all over the place,' Theo replied. 'They're so mangled I can't make any sense of them. The only thing I've become sure of is that she's definitely at the heart of everything that's going wrong. It's too intricate to be a coincidence.'

'What are you talking about? What's a mangled timeline?' I asked.

Theo paused to consider his answer. 'Time isn't linear.'

'You said that before, but I don't know what that means.'

'It means that whatever happens to you, will always have happened to you. When we go back to help people, we don't wipe what originally happened out of existence. That's why we can remember it. We just put them on a different time pathway.'

'Why can't they remember it?'

'Because they're not aware that any of it has changed. As they know no different, their consciousness just accepts it.'

'Where does mangled fit in?'

'If we go back and change things then my system will show two distinct timelines.' He pointed to his monitor as if the complex data I was looking at perfectly explained what he meant. 'The original history is a dimmed line and the new pathway is solid.'

'Right,' I nodded, staring at the vibrant colours on his screen as if I understood. 'So you track timelines?'

'Yes. And when I started to examine Fiona, I found she had multiple timelines for hundreds of individual events. I've never seen anything like it. This pattern occurs over several years. The latter part of her life has been changed over and over.'

'So she's gone back and changed her own life?' I asked with surprise. 'Like again and again and again? As in the same events have been changed repeatedly?'

'Yes.'

'What about the event with Scott? Does that have mangled timelines?' I asked.

Theo reluctantly nodded. 'More than I can track. It would appear that Fiona has been manipulating the whole event. Whatever Scott originally did is long forgotten about.'

A chill prickled my skin. 'Did he really die?'

Theo stared blankly at his screen. 'Yes.'

'Why save him only to then execute him? That makes no sense.'

'Believe me, none of this makes sense.'

'Is that why Scott's memories are all over the place?'

Theo consulted Seb. 'That's a good point. If she's changing Scott's time pathways, how is he aware of it?'

'The only rational answer is that he's somehow involved,' Seb said.

'He's not involved!' I insisted. 'He's a victim. I've seen him. This is ruining him. Why is she doing this to him?'

'Because she hates everything that we stand for,' Bradley stated from the back of the room.

'But why Scott?'

'He's the best,' Seb suggested. 'Bring down the star Inspector, bring it all down.'

'We need to stop this happening!' I almost shouted. 'We need to go back and stop all of this.'

'We can't,' Theo said.

'Why not?' I asked, dreading the answer.

'Because that fire has to take place,' Seb explained. 'It's the only way to protect this facility.'

'Well can't we go back and prevent Scott from going? You didn't need him to start the fire.'

'We can't interfere with our own timelines,' Theo said. 'We also have to consider that there are multiple changes around that one single event. There's a very good risk that changing anything else could rupture a hole in the timelines.'

'You mean like a time paradox?' I asked.

'Yes,' Theo replied, clearly surprised.

'Scott told me about that.'

'That fire and what we did is at the epicentre of everything. It's too dangerous to even attempt to alter it.'

'Then how do we save Scott?' I asked with desperation. 'Are you saying he's trapped?'

'One thing at a time,' Gloria said. 'Let's find out what Fiona's doing there, and then we can start to unpick it.'

I scanned the faces in the room. 'Is there a way to save him?'

'Keep your focus,' Seb said. 'We have a plan.'

'To save Scott?'

'We can't do anything until we get some answers,' Seb said.

'Okay. How do we do that, then?'

'We need your help.'

'What can I do?'

'Fiona knows all of us,' Gloria said. 'There's no way she'll talk to any of us, but she's the only person who can give us answers.'

'Our only option therefore is to use our secret weapon,' Seb said, looking directly at me.

'What's that?' I asked.

'You. We need you to go back to early 2014 and interact with Fiona. You're the only one who can find out what she's been up to.'

My jaw dropped open.

'You're Scott's best hope,' Gloria said, reading my reaction.

'How?' I asked, not even remotely attempting to mask the panic in my voice.

'You're going to spend the rest of today getting trained up,' Gloria said.

'I'm very sorry to do this to you,' Seb added. 'Normally team members work up the ranks and have months of training. You've got the rest of today. At nine hundred hours tomorrow we have to send you back. We have no time to lose. We can't predict what she's going to do next.'

'At least you have the advantage of knowing the time period,' Theo added. 'Acclimatising is half of the problem. You'll have all of that nailed.'

I appreciated his positive spin but I was utterly terrified. I was about to go on my own assignment. A week ago I didn't even know such a thing existed. A week ago I thought my boyfriend was a hotel consultant. Now I was expected to travel back seventy years – or four years in my own life – and speak to a vile woman who had framed my boyfriend for arson and murder and then had somehow managed to bring back the death penalty to kill him. It was lunacy.

The whole idea petrified me to the core. So much could go wrong. I could cost Scott absolutely everything.

But I also realised that I had no choice.

'I don't even know where to start,' I admitted.

'You will do,' Gloria said. 'Only the best get picked for the Shape the Future programme, so you're literally going to be trained by the best. Albeit squeezed into a very short space of time.'

'Do you think I can do this?' I asked. My voice was actually shaking.

'Yes. Absolutely,' Gloria said. 'And we're all going to be helping you. Everything else is on hold.'

'What could go wrong?' I asked.

'Nothing,' Seb said. 'Nothing can go wrong. At the very worst you don't succeed in getting any useful information and we go back to the drawing board.'

'What if she gets suspicious? Can I make things worse?'

'How do you think this can get any worse?' Gloria asked. 'Scott's still alive isn't he?'

'Scott would have faith in you,' Theo said from his seat. 'I think we're all starting to see things through his eyes.'

Theo's words warmed me. It was very kind of him to say.

'We need to get on with this,' Leanne demanded. 'You can come with me first.' Her tone made my heart pound.

She was the last person I wanted to be alone with. 'I'll run scenarios with you.'

I turned back to Gloria and she smiled sweetly, although I could sense an edge of caution peeking through her grin.

'Just one hour, Leanne,' Gloria said. 'Don't overwhelm her. We'll have a working lunch at thirteen hundred and I'll run through the strategy.'

'I'll get your CPG prepped,' Theo said. 'I suggest at sixteen hundred you spend some time with me. We'll need to get you confident using it. You're going to have to communicate with us from 2014.'

My brain was starting to melt from the enormity of the task ahead of me and the little time I had to get prepared, but I also felt a buzz. For the first time in my life I was doing something that really mattered. For the first time in my life I didn't want to hide behind a desk or my computer, I wanted to get involved. For the first time ever Chloe Noble was thrusting herself forward and making a stand.

It felt bloody good!

TWENTY-NINE

'Come with me,' Leanne said. It wasn't a polite request but I had no desire to argue with her.

She led me silently to Scott's office, which actually thinking about it was probably the "Inspectors' Office". She pulled over a chair and we both sat in front of her monitor.

The colours on it were vibrant and everything on the screen seemed to move at a very swift pace. I found it hard to understand any of the information in front of me.

'We don't have a lot of options,' she told me. 'Theo was only able to find Fiona three times in the target period.'

She scanned through the data at a pace that made Theo seem slow. I had no hope of keeping up with her at all. But part of me suspected that was the point.

'What do you mean three times?'

'He positively identified her three times in 2014.'

'I thought Theo couldn't find her in 2014?'

'He couldn't find where she'd entered the year, no.'

'Well, what else did he find?'

Leanne was clearly irritated by my lack of understanding. 'He found her through digital photo footage.'

I was too afraid to ask this time, but my face gave away my confusion.

'Photos uploaded through social media,' Leanne explained. 'That sort of thing.'

'Oh right. Really? Couldn't he have just done that in the first place?'

Leanne rolled her eyes – she actually rolled her eyes. 'Just pick one day; any day in 2014. How many photos do you think were taken?'

I shrugged my shoulders.

'Theo was only able to get us any intelligence at all because he knew exactly where she landed and at what time. Thankfully there are quite a few tourists in London.'

'She was in London the whole time?' I asked.

'Yes. And other than being caught just three times in other people's photos, she was completely anonymous. She was a very good Inspector.'

'Just not a very nice person.'

'You didn't know her.'

'I'm learning about her.'

'I'd like to learn about you. Who are you exactly?'

I hesitated.

'And when did you start sleeping with my boyfriend?'

I don't know how she did it, but in those few words she made me feel completely insignificant. Even though I knew that Scott wasn't her boyfriend, it was like she still had a power over me.

'I...' I was totally lost for words. 'What makes you...'

'You're from 2018 aren't you?' she said, like it was a horrible disease.

All I could do was nod.

'He does these things,' she said, flippantly. 'Time travel's difficult. He gets distracted. It's totally illegal, you know; shagging around in the past. Although I doubt you're the first. Not that he'd tell me. I'm just the one he comes back to.'

I kept in my mind all the things that both Scott and Seb had told me. She was dangerously close to properly rattling me but I was determined not to let her.

'In this time, I'm the one that he sleeps with,' she added.

I took a deep breath. I had the upper hand, why was I letting her get to me? 'Yes, I know all about how he fell asleep on your bed,' I replied, very nicely.

She flashed me a dirty look. 'I'm not mad at him. But you need to understand: girls like you come and go; I'm his forever. I don't want to see you get hurt.'

I sat back. Scott was right, she was delusional. It was obvious that she genuinely believed Scott was going to spend the rest of his life with her.

Poor, sad girl.

'Thank you, I'll keep that in mind,' I said. 'Shall we crack on with these scenario things?'

Leanne didn't take her eyes off me. I tried to smile but it was incredibly awkward. Finally she turned her attention back to her monitor.

'We've got Fiona either walking near Westminster, getting on a bus, or entering a café,' she said.

'Right, so you input the data and the system tells you the best thing to do?' I asked.

'We could do that, or we could use our brains.'

She'd done it again: made me feel small and stupid.

'On the bus or street you could easily lose her,' she told me. 'The best chance you have of connecting with her is in the café. It's common sense.'

'Okay. Is that it then? Do we still need to run scenarios?'

'Yes,' she said like I was an idiot. 'We've only identified a location. What are you going to do next?'

'I don't know. Isn't that what you're supposed to be helping me with?'

'Yes. So you need to listen.'

I felt the urge to write notes, although how this was accomplished in 2086 I had no clue. I opened my mouth to ask but quickly halted. I was worried that if she made me feel any smaller then an ant could have squashed me. It was a safer option to rely on my memory.

'Get to know her first,' Leanne stated. 'You need to start

building a relationship as quickly as you can. Then follow her. You'll need to keep tabs on her at all times. A good move would be to find out where she's living.'

'Where she's living? Keep tabs? I thought I was just going to have a chat with her.'

'Yeah, what am I thinking? A chat would work. All you have to do is ask the person who's plotting to bring down a government organisation and execute one of the staff a question and they'll definitely give you a straight answer. You'll probably know everything in ten minutes.'

'Okay, I don't know,' I said, defensively.

'This is an assignment. It will take time.'

'How long are we talking about?' I asked, now feeling both belittled and overwhelmed.

'You have until the day of the fire,' she said, flicking through the monitor. 'So, seven weeks.'

'Seven weeks?' I gasped. 'Seven weeks? What am I supposed to do with myself for seven weeks?'

'That's what Logistics will help you with. It's fine. We all do this every day. You need to focus on finding out everything you can about Fiona, and Logistics will take care of everything else. I'm sure Scott will be very grateful. We both are.'

I wanted to slap her around the face. I wasn't doing a good job of not letting her rattle me.

I survived her less than enthusiastic help for the next hour. She succeeded in scaring me more than anything, but at least I had a feel for what was involved through my task and an idea of how to break it down.

At precisely twelve fifty-seven, she led me to the canteen for lunch, making sure we arrived, as planned, at thirteen hundred hours.

The whole team had lunch together and Leanne explained that we'd found the café to be the best play and I was then going to follow Fiona and attempt to integrate myself in her life.

Theo had put together a character profile and he talked

me through every inch of Fiona's known life. By all accounts she'd been a lousy mother. I began to see why Bradley hated her so much. She was neglectful and manipulative. It was like no one ever knew where they stood with her. The stories about her were elaborate and dark, and it appeared that although she was a part of their team, she kept her distance. It must have been very different to the family feel that now surrounded them all.

Next I spent two hours with Gloria who talked me through some of the problems I could encounter and how to get around them. For example, if Fiona refused to engage with me or if she became suspicious about my interest in her. Gloria's advice was mostly common sense, and all of it, with no exception, required me to take my time.

Seven weeks both felt like forever and no time at all, considering how high the stakes were.

After that I was whisked along to Logistics where I was given clothes, money, documents, details of suitable accommodation, and just about everything else a person needed to set up a temporary life somewhere. It was maddening.

Part of me wished that I could just go back to my flat. I lived in London in 2014. But Seb's words of warning about interacting with myself or anyone else I knew in that time were sobering.

Luckily, the café and bus that Fiona had been getting on were in Notting Hill, so that's where we all assumed she was staying, and that was nowhere near where I lived. It wasn't an area I knew well at all. But at least I knew London etiquette in 2014, so that put me ahead of everyone else. I felt quite chuffed with that.

The final couple of hours of my day were spent with Theo who trained me up on how to properly use a CPG.

Leanne hadn't even attempted to hide her sniggers at my inability to grasp flick-switch technology. Apparently it was something even babies could handle. But it confused the hell out of me. You had to do five things at once and I really wanted to use both hands, although I couldn't as I'd been warned never to take the CPG off my wrist.

'What about when I have a shower?' I asked when it was finally just me and Theo. 'Is it okay to get it wet?'

'Of course,' Theo replied as he watched me practice the technique. 'It's waterproof. In fact it's pretty much everything proof,'

'Oh.'

He regarded me. 'You mean why did Scott take his off?'

'Yes. Why would he have done?'

Theo sighed, thoughtfully. 'There are two massive coincidences that led you here, Chloe. Two things that beat the odds immensely.' This halted my practice. He had my full attention. 'Firstly, we have never had an issue with any CPG ever, except for just before the last time that Scott made that trip to 2018. Barbara had returned from an assignment working with life guards and after multiple soakings in the water she'd noticed a small delay in the performance of her device. So I asked them all to take their CPGs off when under water for a few days until we could investigate. Just in case. It turns out it was a small defect in the lining of the upgraded versions and was quickly sorted out.'

I thought about the real reason as to why I'd been messing with Scott's watch and I realised that at any other time I wouldn't have had the opportunity.

'The other oddity,' Theo continued, 'is that you managed to work out how to use it. I mean look at you now. I'm showing you what to do and you're struggling. Flick-switch technology is so well used today because of its security. There's about a forty billion to one chance that you could get the combination right and travel on someone else's CPG.'

'I didn't know what it was. I was just looking at it,' I said.

'And I'm very pleased you did. In doing so, you may have saved Scott's life.'

'Haven't I also sent him to prison?' I noted.

Theo paused as my words sank in. 'I guess we'll find out,' he said.

By midnight I was absolutely shattered and as ready as I could be in the limited time available.

I flopped on to my bed and lay staring at the ceiling. In just a few hours I would be a time travelling policewoman on a mission to save the man I loved. It was mind-boggling.

Things like that never happened to me. Yet, after what Theo had told me, I couldn't help but think that maybe it was my destiny after all.

I turned to double check my alarm clock. Theo had set it for me. It also used a form of flick-switch technology but I was flick-switched out. I couldn't see my generation ever coming to terms with it.

It was set for six thirty and I knew that all I had to do now was get some sleep. I took a deep breath and snuggled under the duvet.

I was jittery with nerves at the prospect of what lay ahead but nothing was going to stop me.

Fiona, I'm coming to get you, I thought. *Scott, just hang on in there. The end's in sight now.*

I really hope I don't let you down.

THIRTY

I was awake well before my alarm went off the next morning. Even though I'd desperately needed a good night's sleep, my brain just wouldn't switch off. I knew this was probably going to be the biggest day of my life.

I had a refreshing shower, dressed myself in the jeans and jumper that Logistics had given me, and I made my way to the canteen to get some breakfast. They'd provided me with a rather large jumper that had huge chunky sleeves, as it was the best way to cover up my CPG. Apparently, covering up a CPG was normal practice for those who ventured to a time before the mid-1970s, where the public might be a bit curious about something that looked like a digital watch. And we all agreed it was probably wise to do the same when going back to meet an old Inspector who wasn't to know that I was from the Shape the Future branch.

Although it was obviously the right decision, the jumper was incredibly warm. I'd only had it on for a few minutes and I was already sweating buckets. I knew I'd have to get used to it though, I had a suitcase packed full of them. I was disappearing off for seven weeks and I had to make sure my CPG was covered up the whole time.

I was so very grateful that I was going back to winter.

I selected a light breakfast and I sat on my own in the corner of the busy canteen. I picked at a bit of fruit but I really didn't have much of an appetite.

By half past eight I was with all of the team in the module room, being given mountains of last minute information, none of which I could absorb. The voices around me were becoming so overwhelming that I had to actively block them out. Although I was sure their advice was invaluable, my brain couldn't take any more. All I could do was breathe slowly, keep myself calm and tell myself that no one can expect more than my best shot. At least I was giving it a go.

Theo took the training CPG off me and I was given a real one. It was now starting to get real all over.

After lots of good lucks being thrown my way, I stepped in the module.

I instinctively held my breath. This wasn't a trip to see Scott, this was a trip to the unknown. A trip to visit a woman who had been described as the closest thing to evil that existed. And I was about to integrate myself in her life.

How did any of them do this all the time? It made me admire Scott all the more.

'Are you ready?' Theo called in through the closed door.

'As I'll ever be,' I said back. "Yes" seemed like too much of a lie.

I waited patiently for the blackness to disappear. The anticipation was unbearable. I felt dizzy. I didn't know if I could do it. What was I thinking?

Daylight struck me. Despite the fact that there was no one around, I could hear the background noise of traffic and I could smell the city air. I knew I was back in London. London 2014.

I'd been dropped off down a small side street that Theo said was normally quiet at this time of day. And it really was.

I took a calming breath and noted how I already felt better. I'd got here. That was a good start.

The next step was to track down that café.

I'd had maps drummed into me so I made the short journey, relying totally on my memory, dragging my suitcase behind. I was both delighted and relieved when I saw it.

It was a small cosy café just off the main road. I peered in and could see straight away that Fiona was sitting at a table on her own. I'd been given multiple pictures of her to study, so even though I couldn't see all of her face – she was resting it in her hands – I knew without a doubt that it was her.

She looked vulnerable. She didn't look anywhere near as scary as I'd been expecting. After all the stories I'd heard, I'd been expecting a witch.

I entered the little rustic I and took a seat at the slightly rocky table next to her. It was a simple place but it smelt lovely. I was convinced that the food would be good.

I'd practiced conversation starters a hundred times with Gloria. However, now I had to actually do it, it seemed impossibly hard.

'What can I get for you?' a man with a foreign accent asked me. (Perhaps east European?)

'A cup of tea, please,' I said.

'Will a pot be all right?' he confirmed.

'Yes, thank you.'

I scanned the room, making out that I was interested in everything and anything, until my eyes rested on Fiona; as if for no special reason at all.

I was immediately taken aback when I saw that she was crying. It wasn't obvious, she was hiding it well, but I could see the redness in her eyes and she was dabbing her cheek very gently with her serviette.

'Are you okay?' I asked, taking my chance.

She didn't look at me. She completely ignored me. I had to try again, though. This wasn't something I'd expected based on any of the information I'd been given about her.

'You seem very upset,' I said, joining her at her table. 'I'm a good listener, if I can help.'

'I'm fine,' she said quietly.

'I don't mean to overstep but you really don't look fine.'

She pulled her hand away from her face and I got my first proper look at her. She had greying straggly hair and a long face. She may have once been very pretty but she looked worn now and exhausted.

'It's...' I could see that she wanted to tell me something. In fact she looked like she desperately wanted to tell me something and I was getting quite excited.

I stayed quiet, heeding Gloria's advice of letting Fiona speak. *Always let her fill the gaps.*

'Do you ever...?' she started.

'Yes?' I asked after she didn't continue.

She shook her head and covered her face up again with her hand.

I wanted to yank her arm. She needed to tell me.

'Thank you,' she said, placing down a ten pound note and heading off. She was so quick to get to her feet, it took a second for my brain to catch up that I needed to follow her.

'Actually, forget about the tea,' I shouted to the waiter as I grabbed my case. But I was abruptly halted when a voice told me to sit down.

It was so firm I almost did exactly as she ordered, until I snapped back into gear and realised that Scott's only chance of living was now getting away. I had to follow Fiona.

'I'm sorry, I have to go,' I said to the lady, trying to push past, but she didn't budge.

'I asked you to sit down,' she said again, quite firmly. 'I want to know why you've been following me and you're going to give me answers.'

This stopped me completely. I looked at the woman and I couldn't believe it. It was Fiona. She was wearing different clothes and looked more jaded than the woman I'd just seen crying, but it was definitely Fiona.

'We'll still have that tea,' she said to the waiter behind the counter. 'Make it a pot for two..

THIRTY-ONE

I sat back down at the table where the other Fiona had just left, and the new Fiona joined me.

I had about a thousand questions to ask but my mouth wouldn't work. We just silently studied one another until the pot of tea arrived.

'Thank you,' Fiona said to the waiter before she poured the tea for both of us.

'Thanks,' I said, grabbing the little jug of milk. This was refinedness at its most tense and I didn't like one bit of it.

She stirred sugar into her tea before taking her first sip, not once moving her eyes from me. It was highly unnerving.

'Who are you?' she finally said. Her voice was stern, demanding an answer.

I tried to find words, but I didn't even know where to begin.

'I'll ask again. Who are you?'

All I could manage was a shake of my head. What was I supposed to say? My one day of training hadn't even come close to preparing me for this.

She sighed and placed down her tea cup. 'How about I make it easier for you? I'll tell you what I know and you can fill in the gaps.'

She was still staring at me with her drained eyes. She seemed incredibly tired. Her firm tone was totally at odds with her weary frame.

'I know your name is Chloe and you have a CPG under that sleeve; and I know it's an official one. You've been following me but I can't work out why.'

My brain scrambled, trying to make sense of what she was telling me.

'I've only just come to this I,' I replied. 'I've only just met you.'

'But you're about to spend the next few weeks following me, trying desperately to integrate yourself in my life. Only you're incredibly bad at it. I can't work it out. That CPG tells me you're from the Shape the Future branch, but everything else tells me you've never done a day's surveillance work in your life.'

I let her words settle in my mind.

'I followed you?' I asked. It was all I could muster up.

'Yes,' she exhaled.

'For weeks?'

'I've been watching you watching me. I can't imagine you stole the CPG. Not just because they're heavily guarded, but because I can't believe you'd have the skill set to pull off such a feat.'

Her criticism of my abilities was starting to hurt. After having just one day to learn a job that most people spend months training for, I knew I was never going to nail it, but I at least thought I'd show some flair. I guessed not.

'You've been watching me?' I asked.

'Why is this so difficult for you to comprehend? You follow me out of this café and then turn up pretty much everywhere I go, pretending that it's all a terrible coincidence. It was highly suspicious. So I evaded you one day and followed you as you tried to find me. I saw you consult your CPG. I know you're from Shape the Future but I haven't been able to determine exactly why you are following me. So I thought I'd travel back and ask.'

'Doesn't that contradict time?' I said as my head tried to fathom the logic.

'What are you talking about?'

'You've stopped me following you so now you'll never know that I was following you and so you won't know to return back here to question me.'

The ridicule on her face was alarming. I thought I'd made a clever observation.

'Do you even understand time travel?'

I chose not to answer that question.

'Surely you understand time pathways?'

'Why does that not contradict time?' I asked, remembering what Scott had told me. I was desperate to grasp on to any loophole.

'How on earth would that contradict time?' she said, taking a sip of her tea. There was a slight shake to her head and I felt my face flush. This was genuinely complicated. Surely anyone from my time would have found this confusing.

'Why did you come back to this I?' I asked, eager to move the conversation on. 'Why not just stop me in the street when I was following you?'

'It seemed safer. I don't know what intelligence you've been gathering on me. I don't know why you're here.'

'But in travelling back haven't you left one of those travelling footprint things? Theo will know.'

'Theo? So you know Theo? You are from the branch then. Although, again, "travelling footprint things"? You show absolutely no acumen for time travel and undercover work at all. Why on earth would you be sent back to follow me? What's Earl playing at?'

'Earl doesn't know I'm here.'

For the smallest of moments I wondered if that had been a good thing to say, but her whole demeanour instantly appeared to relax. She sat back in her chair like she'd been set free from a terrible burden.

'Are you an Inspector?' she asked me.

'I'm a consultant.'

'A consultant?' she asked with total surprise. 'Do you know who I am?'

'You're Fiona.'

'Yes,' she said, expecting more.

I paused. I didn't want to tell her what I knew about her. 'Bradley's mum,' I finished, hoping that would be enough.

'You know Bradley too?' She leaned forward with a concern only a mother could have. 'How is he?'

'He's good. I think.'

'Did he send you back?' Her face was full of hope.

Despite the rocky start, nothing about this woman matched the descriptions I'd been given before I'd left. She was a little scary but I could see it was more out of desperation than malice. She certainly didn't seem self-centred or manipulative. She could have tried any number of tricks to find out who I was, but here she was instead just asking me directly.

'I'm here to help Scott,' I said, trying to sound confident.

'The star Inspector?' she asked, her eyes aglow with curiosity. 'And why would he need your help?'

'Because of what you've done to him.'

'Is it because I don't know you?' she asked, totally brushing aside what I'd just said. 'Have they outsourced in an attempt to fool me?'

I sat on the fence about what my next move should be. Could there be any harm in me admitting Scott's "illegal activity"? Maybe it would tug at her heart strings?

All I could think was that she wasn't going to confess all believing that they'd sent some hopeless novice out to spy on her. No one would admit everything if they felt unimportant. I didn't need time travelling cop skills to know that.

Maybe my honesty would encourage her honesty. Like proper girl talk.

'I haven't been outsourced,' I said. 'The truth is a bit more complicated.'

'I really hope it is. Otherwise it would appear that the branch has vastly lowered its standards.'

Her insulting descriptions of my undercover attempts were making me angry now. I'm sure I'd been trying my best. Not many girls could get thrust into such a situation and stay intact. My boyfriend – a time travelling Police Inspector born sixty years after me – was facing death by hanging, and the whole vast revelation of these events had happened in less than a week. I was much better than she was giving me credit for. And I needed to tell her!

'It depends what standards you're talking about,' I stated. 'Because Scott certainly thinks a lot of me. I'm his girlfriend. Only we should never have met. I was born in 1989 and we met in 2018 when he was on an assignment. He told me he was a hotel consultant who travelled a lot for work.' I stopped. I realised how rose-tinted my view of Scott had been. I absolutely adored him but I hadn't seen him at all for who he truly was. I was so grateful that I'd been given the chance to get to know him properly.

I glanced over at Fiona. Her eyes were fixed on me again, waiting for me to continue.

'That's not important,' I said. I needed to get to the point. 'All you need to know is that one day when he was in the shower, I accidentally swiped his CPG. It looked like some sort of smart watch. I didn't know. Anyway, by pure coincidence I managed to flick-switch myself into 2086.'

I paused, ready for her response, but she sat very still and quiet.

'I've got to wait three weeks before I can go back to 2018 so I've been stuck in 2086. I've been spending time with the team and that's when I saw an assignment go badly wrong. No thanks to you. So I'm back here to find out what you're up to so I can stop my boyfriend from getting arrested and being sentenced to death, and stop you causing any more hurt. Not so amateurish after all, is it?'

Fiona didn't move. She watched me, like she was taking me in; absorbing my words and my flesh at the same time.

It was extremely creepy.

'Scott would never take off his CPG,' she said. It was clearly a challenge but she said it softly.

'Not normally, no. But a small defect when under water had been noted, so Theo asked the Inspectors not to get their CPGs wet until he could fix it.'

Her head tilted and her eyes pinched as if I was a strange mathematical problem that needed solving. 'Earl doesn't know you're here?'

'No,' I replied.

'Has no clue that you're from the past?' she asked, with the smallest of smiles.

I hesitated. 'No.'

'He thinks you're a consultant?'

I just nodded.

Instantly a huge smile broadened on her face and her eyes twinkled with what had to be tears. 'You're my miracle,' she said.

THIRTY-TWO

'Miracle?' I asked, utterly bewildered by the huge beaming grin that now dominated her round face.

'We have no time to lose. How long has it been since you arrived in 2086?'

I shrugged. 'A week. I think.'

She nodded, sympathetically. 'Time travel does that. I don't think I ever got used to it. That's why I'm sorry for what I have to do. But you need to know the truth.'

The truth was all I wanted to know, although the gravity in her voice told me I was going to get far more than I expected.

She pulled up the sleeve of her black cardigan to reveal a strange device.

'This is my CPG,' she said. It looked nothing like the one wrapped around my wrist. It looked like a sports watch that had lots of bits stuck to it. 'It's a tad rudimentary,' she said. 'But it's all mine.'

'What do you mean all yours?' I asked.

'Just that. Not property of the British government but property of Fiona Stainthorpe.'

'You stole it?'

She tutted and shook her head. 'Of course not. There's

so much you have to learn. I'm over the moon you're here. I've been praying for a miracle and here you are!'

All I could do was look at her. I had no clue how I could respond. I felt like answers were on their way but I was getting more and more nervous about what those answers might be.

'Are you ready?' she asked me.

'Ready for what?'

'Just promise me you'll open your mind.'

I couldn't promise anything. I was stunned by the change in her. Her whole essence appeared more energised.

She fiddled with her rough-looking CPG and then she touched my hand that was wrapped around my tea cup.

'Good luck,' she said and instantly everything around me became dark.

I was still sitting, but I couldn't quite make out my new surroundings. Suddenly a door flew open and it became clear that I was in a cupboard.

In walked Fiona, but this time she was younger. Quite a few years younger than the Fiona in the cafe. This was getting more confusing by the second. This was the third Fiona I'd met in a matter of minutes.

She clocked her eyes on me and jumped.

'Oh, I'm terribly sorry,' she said, clearly agitated.

'It's fine,' I said, feeling rather foolish that I was sitting on a shelf in what looked like a food storage cupboard.

'Do you work in the kitchens?' she asked. 'Am I disturbing you?'

'Yes,' I said, happy to go along with her logic. 'I mean yes I work in the kitchens.' *Must think quickly. What can I say?* 'I'm a chef.'

She regarded me strangely and I felt the urge to tell her all about how I liked to be at one with my food or something like that, but I quickly stopped myself. I recalled Gloria's advice of how sometimes being vague was best. 'Let others fill the gaps,' she'd said.

'Can I help you?' I asked instead, as confidently as I

could; as if sitting in a cupboard was normal practice for a chef.

Fiona opened her mouth to speak but stopped herself too. I hopped down to the floor and stood next to her. She looked very weary and stressed, no different to the other Fionas I'd met.

'Are you okay?' I asked.

'Do you know many people that work here?'

'Not a soul,' I said, which was no word of a lie. 'I'm very new. This is my first day. Hence why I'm lost in the cupboard.' *Nailed it!*

'Oh right,' she said backing away. 'It's just... it's my husband. I don't know what to do. You have to... I need...'

'What is it?' I asked. She was becoming increasingly distressed.

'He's controlling it all,' she whispered. 'I know he is. I know it. I can't remember of course, but nothing else makes any sense. They all hate me but it makes no sense. Do you see?'

'Who's he?' I asked, getting a horrible feeling that there was far more to this than any of us had realised.

'I can't. I can't. He'll get to you too.'

'No he won't. I promise he won't. I can help.'

'You can't. You won't remember. He'll know. I don't know how he's doing it. I need to find out how he's doing it.'

'Doing what?'

There was a bang from outside and Fiona nearly jumped out of her skin. She was such a mess.

'I can't. Please don't say a word. You haven't seen me. Trust me, it's for the best.' She darted out of the cupboard.

'Not as simple as you thought, is it?' a voice said right in my ear. This time it was me who jumped. It was older Fiona again. 'Ready?'

Bright lights hit me and I had to cover my eyes for a second to adjust.

'Go in there,' older Fiona instructed. I saw a white door

ahead of me with frosted glass panes. Fiona vanished and I stepped forward with a deep breath.

I opened the door to find myself in some sort of waiting room. I scanned my very white surroundings and I saw an even younger Fiona sitting in a chair with a young boy. He was sitting on her lap and she was giggling with him.

I sat down just a few seats away so I could listen to their conversation.

'Daddy will be here soon,' she said, putting her finger to her lips. 'Let's not tell him. He'll say it's a naughty joke. He doesn't like me telling you naughty jokes.'

They both sniggered and I casually glanced over. It was Bradley, I was sure of it. He was just a young boy, perhaps five at the most, but he still had the same pretty face.

'I like it,' he beamed. 'I love it! Monkey sick!' They both laughed quite hysterically and it was beautiful to watch. They had a lovely relationship and clearly adored one another. It was a far cry from the hatred I'd seen in Bradley's eyes the day before.

'Will you stop it,' a male voice said with no humour at all. He entered the room through a virtually hidden door right next to me.

'We're just making each other laugh,' Fiona replied. She placed Bradley down on the floor and he ran off to play in the corner. There was a little table set up with a few toys on it.

The man turned around to watch Bradley and I got my first look at his face. I knew him! He was a lot younger with more hair and a slimmer belly, but it was definitely Earl.

'It makes such a scene,' he said, glaring back at Fiona. 'You'll make a laughing stock out of me.'

'No one cares,' Fiona argued and I could sense the tension between them.

'Well, it's going to have to stop when you start working here.'

Fiona's face lit up. 'I got the job?'

'Of course.'

Fiona threw her arms around him. She seemed far happier than he did.

'Thank you. Thank you so much,' she said. 'Do they know I'm not from the police force?'

'No one needs to know anything. All that matters is that I can finally keep an eye on you.'

Fiona backed away. 'You can't know where I am all the time.'

'I can when I get you in a CPG. I'll be tracking your every move.'

'Don't be creepy.'

I had to agree with her, Earl was indeed sounding very creepy.

'You're my wife, it's only right that I know where you are. I always tell you where I am.'

I didn't catch Fiona's response as I was too busy being shocked. Earl was Fiona's husband? Earl is Bradley's father?

Why am I only just learning this? This is a fundamental piece of information! Why did everyone keep it from me?

'Can I help you?' Earl said, looking down at my gaping face.

'No,' I meekly replied. 'I'm just waiting.'

'Waiting for whom?'

Panic struck as I realised that I didn't even know where I was, let alone who I could credibly be waiting for. What could I say that would suffice?

What would Earl absolutely not be interested in?

'My boyfriend,' I muttered. 'He knows I'm here. At least I think he said wait here. I don't know, we haven't been together very long. I'm sure he'll be here soon.'

Earl sighed, thankfully losing interest in me, and grabbed Fiona's hand. 'Let's go home,' he said. He practically dragged her out of the place, picking up Bradley on the way. I couldn't believe it.

No wonder he didn't want us investigating Fiona. He was obviously caught up right in the middle of it somewhere. Why had no one else seen that?

'There are just a few more things that I need you to see,' the voice of older Fiona said in my ear as the world instantly changed around me again.

I was standing before a monitor in what looked very much like Scott's office. It could have in fact been Scott's office. The monitor flicked on and it showed me Fiona and Earl in the module room. They were alone.

'It has to stop,' she said. She seemed deeply upset. 'You can't behave like this anymore. Don't you have a sense of decency?'

'Don't marriage vows matter to you at all?' Earl replied. 'I'm just trying to abide by them.'

'I don't want to be with you anymore,' she pleaded. 'You have to let me go.'

He shook his head. His whole persona was eerily controlled compared to Fiona's obvious distress. 'Never. You're Bradley's mother, my wife. This is where you belong. You won't be leaving.'

'It is you, isn't it? I know I packed. I packed seven times, yet seven times everything unpacked itself. How are you doing it?'

'I don't know what you mean.'

'And why can't I tell anyone? What are you doing to me?'

'I'm standing by my wife who's going through a tough time. You're clearly unwell.'

'You bastard!'

Fiona grabbed his wrist. She pulled up the sleeve of his suit to reveal a CPG, but it looked homemade, just like the one the older Fiona had.

'You bastard!' She started to cry and my heart broke for her.

Suddenly the screen changed. I took a seat on the chair next to me, totally engrossed.

This time Earl was sitting with Bradley on a sofa somewhere. Their surroundings were a calming pale blue colour and Bradley was a young adult.

'She's been altering time,' Earl said. 'I've tried to stop

her. I didn't want you to know, but it's wrong of me to lie to you. We need to forgive her, though. She's ill. She doesn't mean to.'

'She's trying to stop me from being born?' Bradley asked.

Earl hesitated, before nodding. 'She's been trying to prevent your conception. But don't worry, I'm not going to let her succeed.'

'Why?' Bradley said, utterly distraught. 'Why would she do that?'

'I don't know. She told me you were an accident that needed correcting. You know she's got this obsession with correcting things in time, but her brain's getting very confused. She doesn't know what's right or wrong anymore. You weren't an accident. You have to know that. What she's saying is simply not true. We planned for ages to have you. If she tells you she regrets having you, just ignore her. She'll tell you all about her regrets, but just ignore her. Something's happened to her. She isn't the woman we once knew.'

'She won't speak to me. Every time I try she just blanks me. It's like she's always got somewhere better to be.'

'I know. I wouldn't use the word hate, that's far too strong. She's just going through a change in her life. We have to love her still. We have to be the strong ones. She may have turned her back on us, but we have to be there for her if we can.'

I couldn't believe it. That was not the Fiona I'd met. What was Earl playing at?

The screen flicked again. This time it was Scott and Earl. They were in an office that I didn't recognise.

'Fiona's been to see me,' Scott said. He didn't look happy.

'Has she?' Earl replied and I noted a dash of tension across his face.

'Yes, and I think we need to talk.'

'When did she come to see you?'

'Earlier today.'

'I think you'll find she's out of the country.'

'No, she's just been to see me.'

Earl pressed his finger to his ear and summoned someone in. It was a tall, skinny man.

'Where's Fiona at the moment?' Earl asked the man.

'She's in France, training. Why?'

'Scott was just curious,' Earl said to the man. 'You can leave.'

'How can she be in France?' Scott said. 'I've just seen her.'

'What did you want to talk about?' Earl asked.

Scott glared at Earl. I could see his brain working but he didn't say a word.

'Truth be told, I had to send her to France,' Earl explained. 'She's been upsetting some of the other Inspectors and I needed to give her a break. Did you know she disagrees with this branch's ethics? She's been spouting out that we're causing harm. Between you and me, she's been taking illegal trips to undo a lot of our good work and it's cost me a great deal in damage control. Maybe that's where your confusion is coming from.'

Scott eyed Earl suspiciously. 'That doesn't sound like Fiona.'

'Ask Bradley.'

Scott stood firm. 'Why can't I remember why I came to see you?'

'You've had some tough assignments of late, they're sure to take their toll. Maybe it would be best for you to also take a break. I'll clear it with Seb.'

'I'm fine.'

'It's not a request, Inspector Lacey.'

'Three times I tried to speak to Scott,' old Fiona said from next to me. I nearly fell off my seat it shocked me so much. The screen in front of me went blank and she pulled her chair closer to me.

'What was all that about?' I asked.

'I'd say that's why Scott's in trouble,' she said.

'What?'
'Scott was the only one who could save us all.'

'What?'
'Scott was the only one who could save us all.'

THIRTY-THREE

'What are you talking about?' I asked with horror.

'I knew I'd be able to get to him. Scott could have broken through. Scott could have seen what Earl was doing.'

'What were you just showing me?'

Fiona sat up straight. 'Earl is a bully. He treated me appallingly for years, as I think you've just seen. I finally got the guts up to leave him, but I couldn't. I mean I literally couldn't.'

'What has that got to do with Scott?'

'What you saw on Earl's wrist was the original CPG mock up before money was put in to get them professionally made. It was supposed to be locked up in Earl's office for safe-keeping, but when he realised he could use it off the radar, the power went to his head. He's been travelling around unnoticed for years. Sometimes it's been for pleasure, but mostly to control the world in a very scary way. He's abused just about everything in the system that he worked so hard to create.'

I wanted to say I couldn't believe it, but from everything I'd learnt about Earl, even from my first encounter with him, I knew it was absolutely true.

'He came home one day to find my bags packed,' Fiona continued. 'He obviously didn't like it so he used his secret CPG to change time. He unpacked everything I packed. It all changed around me. I tried seven times in one night to leave him but he kept stopping me.'

'What?'

'He watched my every move and anything that didn't suit him, he'd go back in time and change it. It got severely out of hand. I was nothing more than his puppet at the end. I couldn't remember what my life was like.'

'How did he fund all that time travel?'

'Oh,' Fiona exhaled, shaking her head angrily. 'That's just more of his controlling nonsense. How can time travel be expensive? It's shifting physics; it's free! But if Earl pretends that budgets are tight and people have limits then it stops them from behaving in the way that he has.'

'Oh, right. Well there must have been something you could do.'

'I told every single person in the branch what he was up to, but every conversation became erased from time. He was manipulating every minute of my life to the point where I had no free choice at all.'

'That's awful.'

'Until Scott. It took me a while to realise. Let's face it, I wasn't exactly living a normal reality. But I finally came to see that Scott was my out.'

'How?'

'Because he can remember different timelines. He's the only person I've ever met who can do it. He was my first miracle. Someone who's able to detect that time has changed.'

'But the branch changes things all the time and the Inspectors remember it.'

'We can all remember things that we've actively changed ourselves because we're conscious of the original history. But Scott can recall things that have been changed around him, when he really should have no awareness of the original history at all.'

'Why can he do that?'

'I have no idea. But it doesn't really matter why, what matters is that he can. He could remember things that Earl had tried to change. You saw it yourself. There was no detail, but he knew enough to suspect foul play.'

I took a breath as Fiona's words rested in my head. 'That's why he's being sentenced to death?'

'You said that before. What exactly do you mean sentenced to death?'

'Just that. He's in prison in 2015 and for a reason that no one can explain he's facing the death penalty.'

Fiona didn't move. The blood drained from her face. 'Why are you here?' she asked.

'To save Scott.'

'But why? Why now? How did you know how to find me? Oh God. What happens?' All the energy she had was completely extinguished.

'Earl sent Scott and his team back to burn down a building. He said there were documents listing all the names of those in the team and they needed to protect the future. However, there was a man trapped there. He would have died and Scott knew that wasn't right. He went to save the man and that's when he got arrested. At least that's one version of events.'

'Let me guess, it was Douglas Atkinson's office at Hobson Pierce?'

'Yes. You were there. Bradley saw you. That's why we linked this all back to you.'

A small, warm smile touched Fiona's lips before gloom crossed her face once more. 'There were no names. The documents were evidence that Earl has been manipulating me and the system. I had a plan; a grand plan. I was going to plant the evidence in Leanne's great-grandfather's office and then send a ransom note to Earl. I figured I couldn't lose. Either Earl did nothing and the truth got out via Leanne's family, or Earl would send Scott back – because I knew he'd send the best – and I could get to speak to Scott. I thought I could manage the whole situation.'

Something Scott had said pinged into my mind. 'You did speak to Scott!'

'I did?'

'Yes. He said someone was there when he tried to save that man. Someone he was shocked to see. That must have been you! But he couldn't remember the details. Why couldn't he remember?'

Fiona sighed. 'Tell me about this man that died.'

'He got trapped beneath a bookcase. The Security Guard alone couldn't save him, so Scott knew he had to help.'

'Security Guard? So Earl found a way to distract attention to get you in.'

'Are you saying Earl was responsible for the man being trapped?'

'Of course he was. But I bet he didn't count on Scott's attempted heroics.' Fiona paused. 'Although I would have done. How else would I have spoken to him away from the team?'

'But he can't remember what actually happened. He thinks he saved the man but he's been charged with murder.'

'This reeks of Earl. There must be a time pathway where I spoke to Scott and he got a message back that I was alive. Earl must have reacted. God knows how many times he's been back and forth, ensuring that the outcome would end in his favour. The outcome always ends in his favour. Don't you see, even though you know the truth, as soon as you go back and tell the team, Earl will find a way to change it. He has ultimate control. There's no way around it.'

'If he's going back and forth all time, isn't he leaving a footprint thing? Isn't that a way to catch him?'

'We always leave footprints, but the system doesn't have to reveal them. Earl's in control of everything. He owns the whole system. There's a setting on his CPG that can conceal his movements. I know I have it too, I just haven't figured out how to use it yet. It was on the original mock up but

Earl insisted that the feature was removed from the final product. But this gem,' she said, holding up her CPG to show me, 'is an exact replica of the original design. Just about the only thing I could do off the radar was build my own device. When I was quiet and alone and seemingly doing nothing, it was the only time he left me alone.' A small smile caught her lips as she shrugged. 'I guess he still should have been watching me. But it's a very small win and so far it hasn't helped me at all.'

'Are you off the radar now? Theo couldn't find a gap in your timeline.'

'What do you mean?'

'Do you nip back every now and then to show your face? How are you doing this?'

'I'm not following you.'

'Where are we at in your life?'

Fiona sat back. 'Do you mean before my death?'

I remained silent. That was a very difficult question to answer, not least because it was far too bizarre.

'Do you still think I died?' she asked.

I still couldn't answer. After what felt like the longest pause on the planet, I managed a short nod.

'No! Oh no! I faked my death. I realised it was the only way to be truly free of Earl. I thought you knew.'

'You faked your death?' I asked, gobsmacked. 'No, none of us knew. We couldn't figure out where this version of you fitted into everything.'

'I had it all planned. My own CPG, how I was going to get my evidence, what I was going to do. It's taken me a couple of years to get this far, but at least I've had some control.'

'I can't believe you had to die. Earl really does have unstoppable power, doesn't he.' I scanned my brain for any way to help her. It was all so sad and awful.

I thought through all the events that had led me to be sitting with her and the computer glitch stood out as a major issue. Could that be useful?

'What about Earl's timelines? Theo saw yours. Couldn't that help them catch him?'

'He's been doing this for a long, long time. Fifteen, twenty years. He's hidden a lot. There's so much that no one has any clue about.'

'But they're starting to have a clue. He's blaming a computer glitch, but things are obviously going wrong. There are issues all over the place. They must be caused by him.'

'No doubt. That's the problem when you keep hiding things, there's a point when the secrets start bursting at the seams. I knew the day would come when questions would be asked, but no one will ever be able to point a finger in Earl's direction. He has all the control. Someone else will take the fall and he'll just carry on. It's what happened to me. It's what's happening to Scott. Think about it: if Scott dies then he has no way of defending himself. Not only will Earl be free of a threat, but he'll be able to pin everything on the one person that everyone used to look up to. I tell you, if we don't do something, not only will Scott's life be gone, but his whole reputation and everything he stood for will be in tatters.'

'Then we need to do something!'

'But what?'

I scanned my brain again.

'You have a CPG that's off the radar,' I said. 'Couldn't you meet up with Scott somewhere else in time?'

'I wish, but he's a time traveller. I have no way of knowing where or when he's going to be. And I can hardly hang around the branch waiting for his arrival. If Earl so much as suspected I'd been there, everything would be lost. That's why I planned to orchestrate this whole hidden document thing.'

'I know exactly where Scott is now. Couldn't you speak to him in prison?'

'What good would that do? Who's he going to tell trapped in a prison cell?'

'I could get people to go back and see him?'

'Earl will stop it happening. I've tried. I've tried so many times. Earl controls everything. One way or another he knows everything about everything and he changes time until the outcome suits him.'

'He doesn't know everything,' I said.

'What do you mean?'

'He doesn't know about me. He thinks I'm a consultant. I know it won't take long for everything to come out when they start to investigate Scott, but as it stands at the minute I'm just your average consultant paying the branch a visit.'

Fiona's eyes lit up. 'Of course!'

'I guess it's a good thing?'

'You really are a miracle!'

'How?'

'Because not only does Earl have no idea that you're a threat, but you're Scott's girlfriend. You're a trusted ally. Does the whole team know who you are?'

'Yes, I think so. They put two and two together when I visited Scott in prison.'

'And not one person has told Earl. They won't, of course they won't. That team's a family. Everyone is going to protect you and no one is going to stab Scott in the back, no matter how illegal his actions may have been.'

I felt myself flush. I hated being a reason why Scott was in such a mess.

'I still don't get how that helps.'

'You can get to Bradley. Don't you see? The team will trust you. They must do. You're back here. But Earl doesn't know that. He thinks you're a third party consultant with no ties to anyone. You can get Bradley to come back. If I can show Bradley the truth and show him how his father has spoken to me, it will shock him into remembering. I'm sure of it. If I force him to accept that his timelines have been messed with then he might at least start to question the history he remembers. It has to unlock things.'

'Haven't you tried to do that before, though?'

'Yes, but when I was alive my every move was monitored and now I'm "dead" I can't get to him. Like Scott, he could be anywhere at any time. But you can help me trap him.'

'How?'

'Get him back here. Use your CPG to bring him back. He won't be able to leave until he listens to me, and Earl will have absolutely no clue until it's too late.'

'Back here? Where are we? When are we?'

'In 2059. We're in the Shape the Future building two days before it opened. It was the only place I could think of that I knew would have a working computer.'

'Won't you get detected?' I asked, feeling panicked.

'Not in here. Not now. It's one of the safest places we can be. Believe me, it's where I've done a lot of prep work.'

'Right. So I bring him back here?'

'Yes. I'll wait here. Make him listen. You're out of time completely. He'll have to listen to you.'

'I'll try my best.'

'It's the only way to save Scott. Scott is going to die. There's no way around it at the moment. He's going to die an agonising death by hanging and he'll be utterly terrified. Don't let that happen.'

I felt a chill race through me. She certainly knew how to motivate.

'I'll get him back here,' I said, determined.

'Give me your CPG,' she said. 'I'm going to send you back to the night before you left 2086. I'm sending you to Bradley's room and I'm setting it so all you have to do is flick and switch holding his hand and you'll both appear back here. Do you understand?'

I hesitated. Did I understand that? 'Yes,' I said, feeling more nervous than ever. I wanted to cry. Scott was going to die. Earl was going to kill him. This was literally all the hope we had.

I had never felt so much pressure. I wanted to collapse.

As quick as a heartbeat, I appeared in a room. It was just

like Scott's room but with fewer pictures on the walls.
I looked down and saw Bradley sleeping.
Everything rested on that moment.

THIRTY-FOUR

I stood over Bradley. What was I going to say? I didn't move as I desperately tried to gather my thoughts. Everything was happening so quickly. I needed my head to catch up.

It was fine. There was nothing stopping me from taking a few minutes to think through a plan.

Oh yes there was: Bradley suddenly awoke with a jump. 'Chloe?'

I realised how creepy it was me standing over him in the dark, behind a locked door, in the middle of the night.

'Sorry,' I said, awkwardly.

'What are you doing? How did you get in my room?' He sat up and flicked on his bedside lamp, illuminating my embarrassment.

I knew I couldn't just tell him what I was about to do. There was no way he'd voluntarily let me take him to see his mother. His hatred for her was palpable. And I felt very uneasy about grabbing his hand out of nowhere. I wasn't adept enough at flick-switch technology to do it swiftly. He'd see through what I was trying to do faster than I could do it.

I needed a way around it.

'Are you all right?' Bradley asked, watching me watching him. It was getting creepier by the second, and he looked quite disturbed.

I hurriedly urged my brain to come up with a reason as to why I would be weirdly standing in his room. What could I say?

'Sorry for the intrusion,' I said. *Think of something. Quick!* 'I need some friendly advice.'

'Okay, but how did you get in my room?'

I stood very still. There had to be a convincing reason. *Oh I know!*

'Scott sent me.' I waved my wrist in the air, showing my CPG. 'These are magical things. He said you'd be the best person to speak to.'

'Oh right,' Bradley replied, a little relieved but still obviously uncomfortable. 'How can I help?'

He watched me, eagerly waiting for me to explain why Scott had sent me to see him, but I was stumped again.

I stepped forward slowly and purposefully, using any sort of delaying tactic to give me time to think.

I studied my CPG, as if I was looking at something very important.

Then thankfully something came to me.

'How can two people travel on one CPG?' I asked.

'You can't bring him back, Chloe.'

'I know. I've tried that already, but Scott told me all about the paradox it would cause.' I paused. Now was my time to ask. 'How does a time contradiction differ to a time pathway?' It wasn't really relevant, but I was eager to explore any avenues that could help to save Scott.

Bradley sighed. 'Theo's already run the scenario. It doesn't work. The contradiction comes from the fact that his past self is in the same time period doing an assignment.'

'But why is that not just a time pathway thing?'

'If we go back and change someone else's life, we set them off on a different pathway. If you see life as having many different roads, it makes it a lot easier to understand.

But a contradiction is where you prevent something from happening in the first place that needs to have happened. Like putting a blockage in the road. It unravels time. If Scott gets arrested six months before he commits the crime, it prevents him from ever being able to commit that crime. So he'll be arrested for something he can't then actually do. It's not a new pathway, it's a complete mess. Does that make sense?'

'I think so.'

'It's really only ever a concern if you mess with your own time, or you do something really stupid. That's why my dad has always insisted that the ethics committee has full control over all our work. It's too tempting to go back and alter your own life.'

I couldn't stop myself from scoffing.

'What's the matter?' Bradley asked.

Suddenly my CPG beeped, flashing up a message that ran across the centre of the screen.

I'm getting strange readings. Did you mean to come back?

It must have been Theo. I forgot he'd be tracking my movements. I just ignored it. I had to get on with this.

'I have a plan to save Scott,' I said, knowing Bradley wouldn't argue with that. 'But the first thing I need to do is understand how two people can travel on one device.'

'And you're not attempting to bring Scott back?'

'No. I'll explain all if you explain how this bloomin' thing works.'

'Okay. Firstly you have to set it to transport two people. Do you know how to do that?'

'Yes,' I lied as convincingly as I could. 'Is this right?'

I sat down on the bed next to him and showed him my CPG. He glanced at it quickly before nodding. 'Yes. You have a two in the corner when it's set to carry two people. You've done it right.'

I looked at the CPG on my wrist and saw the "2" nestled

in the corner, surrounded by dozens of other symbols and statistics.

Another message popped up in the middle of the screen.

Please confirm you're okay.

I shook my head and exhaled with slight panic.

'What is it?' Bradley asked.

'Nothing,' I said, looking back at him. I had to get him to Fiona now. Why couldn't Theo just leave me alone?

'What's this all about?' he asked.

'Then we have to touch. Is that right?'

'Yes, you have to be touching.'

I nodded. 'So I could just hold someone's hand. Like this?' I said, grabbing Bradley's hand. 'And then I'd just fiddle, like so,' I continued, making out that I was just pretending when actually I was really doing the flick-switch thing. I'd spent hours practising it, but it wasn't easy. All I could do was pray that I really was a miracle worker.

We both hit the floor with a smack as we landed back with Fiona. There was no bed at this end and it bloody hurt.

'Bradley!' Fiona said.

'What have you done?' he asked, quickly scrambling to his feet and backing away from her. 'She's got to you?' he asked me. 'You can't believe her.'

'I don't believe her,' I said. 'I believe what I saw with my own eyes. I believe what is the truth. You need to see it for yourself.'

'I won't be drawn into this.'

'I'm sorry, Bradley,' Fiona said with obvious deep regret. 'I think it's time for this to all end. You have no way to leave and no one knows you're here except for us.'

Another message beeped from my wrist.

What are you doing in 2059? Please let us know what's going on.

I felt a small respite from my panic as it dawned on me

that I could message Theo back through my CPG to say I'm fine. I could just say that this was all part of my tracking Fiona plan.

I brought my right hand up, all ready to start typing away, when my mind went blank. Theo had shown me so many things, how was I supposed to remember them all?

'What are you going to do with me?' Bradley asked, the terror in his voice snapping me back to my surroundings. He looked so helpless backed against the wall in his pyjamas.

'Trust her,' I said. 'She's not going to hurt you.'

'She already has.'

'This is going to end and it's going to end now,' Fiona said. She stepped towards Bradley. 'We'll be back in a minute,' she said to me, before grabbing Bradley's arm and disappearing with him. They both vanished so quickly I barely had time to process it.

I looked at my CPG and another message popped up.

I see that you're in our building, but the wrong year. Do you need me to bring you back to the present?

My levels of panicking rose again. The present? I was losing track of what the present was to me. Life as a time travelling police person was most disorienting.

All I had to do was send him a message. I tried to fiddle with the CPG but I couldn't remember what to do. I worked through the steps he'd shown me but the more I panicked the more I forgot.

I didn't want to leave. I needed to stay here. I couldn't leave until I was sure that Bradley knew the truth. Fiona needed my help. Bradley needed my help. Scott needed my help.

Why couldn't I remember what to do!

I'd been so worried about the flick-switch stuff that I'd not really been concentrating on anything else. It all seemed so easy in comparison but now it was nowhere in my head.

If you don't want us to bring you back, send me an alarm.

My heart started to thud loudly as I saw this new message.

I took a deep breath. An alarm. That was easy. Surely I could remember that. That was the five times thing. Just press the button five times.

Which button?

I closed my eyes to remember what Theo had said and I recalled it was the button at the bottom.

Great!

I pressed it five times but nothing happened. Why had nothing happened?

He'd definitely said five times.

I was struggling to breathe now, I was so desperate. My head had reached such a saturation point that information was leaking out of it at a rapid pace. I couldn't remember anything. All I knew was that I wanted to stay put.

I pressed the button five times again, knowing it was the right button. Then, like a welcome spark in my mind, his other words came back to me. Press it five times in a pattern. Slow, slow, fast, slow, slow. Or something like that.

Bradley appeared again with Fiona in front of me. He was shouting at her and she was pleading with him, tears streaming down her face.

I reached out my hand to offer help when everything went black.

Why had it gone black?

Oh God, I was back in 2086.

THIRTY-FIVE

'Send me back!' I shouted, knocking open the door to the module.

The faces of Scott's colleagues all glared at me aghast. Everyone was there except for Bradley.

'Where's Bradley?' I asked, checking to see what reality I was in. My head was spinning.

'We don't know,' Gloria answered. 'He wasn't here earlier. But this must be hard for him.'

'You've got to send me back,' I said. 'You have to. Scott's going to die.'

'What happened?' Leanne asked.

'Why have you been travelling so much? Did you mean to come back here?' Theo asked.

'No!' I insisted and then I stopped. I didn't want to explain any more. They all believed that Fiona was evil and so I figured it was best not to say anything until I had proof. 'You just need to send me back. I was following Fiona. I was on to something good. It's the only chance we have of saving Scott.'

'What is going on?' Earl's voice boomed at the door.

My breath extinguished.

'Good morning, Earl,' Seb said, sheepishly. His usual

commanding tone had vanished. 'Please excuse our kerfuffle. Scott's situation is putting a strain on the team, as you'd expect.'

'What are you up to?' Earl asked, clearly displeased. 'I've been alerted to a number of unauthorised CPG journeys from this team.'

Everyone stood stock still and I realised that Fiona's plan was in grave danger. Earl was not going to like any answers that he got, I knew that for sure. I needed to buy us time. Fiona needed time with Bradley if we were going to have any hope of defeating this awful man.

'Somebody has travelled to 2014, then to last night, and then to 2059, all in a very short space of time,' he stated. 'We haven't got the budget for this sort of activity. I want to know what's going on.'

I started to burn with fury as I listened to his blatant lies.

In the corner of my eye I noticed Seb open his mouth to explain, but I knew I couldn't let him talk. He didn't understand the severity of the situation. I had to take control if Fiona was going to have any chance.

'It's my fault,' I said, cutting in quickly. 'Sorry.'

'Your fault?' Earl queried. 'And who are you?'

'I'm no one. Just a visiting consultant.'

'And what exactly are you consulting on?'

I hesitated. 'The early twenty-first century,' I replied, keeping to Seb's story as best I could. Earl went to say something more, but I knew I couldn't let him. If I was going to give Fiona more time then I had to pad this out.

'I know some of the team from my days on the force,' I continued. 'But since leaving the force... due to injury... I've become a historian. I injured my leg. It was very painful. It meant I couldn't carry on as a policewoman. But that's the job, isn't it. Sometimes we get hurt. But I like being a historian instead. I'm now utilising a great passion of mine. I like all things... early twenty-first century...ish.' I could feel my cheeks flushing at the utter rubbish that was coming out of my mouth.

Earl turned to Seb. 'This wasn't approved.'

'No, it wouldn't be,' I responded. 'I'm doing it as a favour. Completely off the radar. My boss has no idea that I'm here. If he found out I'd be in big trouble. He's a tough boss. But I'm willing to do anything to help out my lovely friends. My old work mates from the force. Yes, I was in the police force. As I said. Before becoming a historian.'

Every pair of eyes in the room was glaring at me with absolute confusion, although thankfully none of them attempted to stop my endless, nonsensical babble. It might be waffle, but every extra word I could fit in bought me a few more seconds.

Earl turned to Seb for clarification and I found myself holding my breath.

'Yes,' Seb said after a short pause. 'I didn't see how I could turn down such invaluable and free advice, and from someone all the team thinks so highly of. I thought it best to keep it quiet, however. I didn't want to alert the other teams to such a useful resource. As Miss Noble said, she doesn't have a lot of time to spare so this short period she's spending with us really is going to be a one off.'

Seb was so good at thinking on his feet. That all sounded completely plausible. And he said it so concisely.

'Very well,' Earl said.

'It's been a total pleasure,' I added. 'Such fine people here. Really, really, really, really fine people.'

'That still does not explain why unauthorised journeys have been made. I need to know what's going on.'

'As I said, my fault,' I replied very quickly.

Earl exhaled sharply. I was clearly irritating him. 'You still haven't explained how.'

'No. I never quite got to that, did I. Right.'

I took a deep breath. I needed a reason. A really good reason. I looked at the CPG on my wrist. Why would a historian consultant have a CPG on their wrist?

'I'm a nosey parker,' I replied, hoping I could get my rough idea to sound logical. 'Comes with the territory, I'm afraid. Us historians are all really nosey. But the eagerness to find out about other people's lives makes us the perfect fit for the job. Do you see?'

Earl exhaled sharply again before turning his attention fully to Seb. 'Chief-Superintendent Wiley, will you please explain to me why unauthorised CPG journeys have been made.'

'I just picked it up,' I continued, making sure that Seb wasn't allowed any room to speak. 'I saw it lying on Theo's...' I went to say desk, nearly forgetting that the whole concept of such a useful thing was eradicated in this time. 'Lap,' I finished. That was ridiculous. 'I mean hand. He had it in his hand. He was setting something and I asked if I could take a look. Before he knew it I'd swiped it from him and I was putting it on my wrist. Like this. Do you see?' I pointed to my CPG. 'Then I started to play with it and, despite all the odds, I managed to transport myself back to 2014. It was like being at home, I know that era so well. Then Theo sent me a few messages, trying to get me back, and that's when I accidentally got sent to 2059, and then Theo brought me back here. Or thereabouts. Basically that's what happened.'

Earl glared over at Theo. 'You let her take it from you?' he snarled.

'I think it's a blessing in disguise, don't you?' I said as a marvellous thought appeared in my head.

'And why is that?' Earl replied.

'Because you all thought that flick-switch technology was highly secure. I've demonstrated that it's possible to break the code and travel by accident. The first thing Theo said to me was that he was going to report that very thing to Head Office. He said that was a clear breakdown of security and it needed to be reviewed. I've done you a favour.'

No one said a word and I tried to calm myself. I'd been getting rather excited. Earl was incredibly scary. If it hadn't been for the fact that Scott's life was in danger, I would have run for the hills. But the thought of losing Scott was giving me a strength I didn't know I had.

'Whether the outcome was positive or not,' Earl stated, 'it is completely unacceptable that someone who is in this building without proper clearance has been allowed to get their hands so easily on a CPG and then travel off to an undeclared destination at the great expense of this facility. This is going to cost us greatly. There will be consequences, I assure you. The budget will be coming out of this team somewhere.'

I didn't know what to say. He was such a horrible man.

'This used to be a good team,' Earl continued, 'but now you've let one of your own get arrested and you're allowing unauthorised people to play around with highly sensitive equipment. Who knows what else you've been up to. I'm beginning to think that maybe these glitches in time all stem from the unprofessionalism of this department.'

I was gobsmacked. Fiona was right. He must have been looking for any way to pin all his mess onto someone else and I'd just gift wrapped it for him. Scott really was going to take the fall.

I couldn't let that happen.

'I'm going to be leading a full investigation into this matter,' Earl said. 'Including into you, Miss Noble. Until that's completed, you're all suspended. This team will cease working immediately and I'm giving you until tomorrow morning to vacate your rooms. I can't risk any of you being near this equipment.'

He was such a despicable control freak. He was as good as hanging Scott himself. I had to stop this. Where was Fiona? Would I ever hear from her again?

'Earl, this is really not necessary-' Seb started, but Earl cut him off.

'My decision is final. You're all suspended. And if you try to fight me, you'll all be permanently withdrawn from this programme. Do I make myself clear?'

I had to do something. He had far too much control.

Fiona getting through to Bradley was seeming like the only hope any of us had. I had to buy us more time. As soon as he left he could do anything. I wouldn't have put it past him planting evidence to set up the team. No, that's exactly what he'd do.

'Very well,' Seb said, his voice full of regret.

I had to think.

Earl was a control freak. Could I use that against him? There had to be a weakness in his strength.

I had to make him feel out of control. Just enough to make him wobble. Perhaps just for a few minutes. Just until Fiona was here. Surely she would come through soon.

'Hang on, we've met somewhere before,' I said. It just blurted out.

He immediately flicked his head across at me. 'What are you talking about?'

'You seem eerily familiar. We've definitely met before. I'm really good with faces.'

I saw a flash of concern dart across his eyes and I knew I was on the right track. He'd flitted across history with no care. He could have met me at any time. This could cost him dearly.

I became very conscious that all of Scott's colleagues were staring at me in astonishment. I could only hope that they'd put some faith in Scott's girlfriend.

'Where do I know you from?' I asked.

'No doubt when you were in the police force,' he said, attempting to brush me aside.

'But you weren't in the force.'

'No, but I have a close relationship.'

'No. I think it's after I left the force. Let me think.'

'You're clearly mistaken,' he said, and it came across as an order. He was so used to ordering everyone about, but I didn't have to listen to him.

'No, I'm definitely not.'

'I think it's time I leave,' Earl said.

'You can't!' I demanded. My hands had started to

tremble and I hid them behind my back. I needed to look confident although I felt anything but.

'I beg your pardon?' he said, his eyes burning into me.

'I've remembered where I know you from.' I deliberately didn't elaborate. He'd want to know. He'd have to know. I had to string this out for as long as I could.

Come on Fiona, I thought over and over. *Please say you're fixing things. Please give me a sign that you've fixed things.*

'Where?' he asked, again ordering a response.

I thought I saw something in the corner of my eye. For a second I hoped it was Scott. I was clinging on to a hope that maybe Fiona would fix it all and Scott would just reappear as if none of it had ever happened.

It was nothing, though. Just my imagination.

'Where?' Earl pushed.

'Yes,' I said nodding, as if confirming it to myself. That's all I could think to do.

'Where!' he bellowed.

'No, hang on.' I shook my head and pondered on nothing, as if I was doubting myself.

'I've had enough of this.'

'That's it!' I said.

'I'm leaving.'

'No!' I shouted. Part of me expected him to vanish and then everything around us would change. But I realised he couldn't do that. He couldn't because we'd all remember. We'd remember that something had changed because we'd be aware of it happening.

Oh, I was getting it! Time travel was getting easier to understand.

So, he couldn't just vanish, he had to be alone before he could travel to ensure that he raised no suspicions.

Suspicions. That's all anyone needed. Suspicions were exactly what Fiona was trying to give Bradley. If they started to question what they knew, she'd said it might unravel the truth. If I used Fiona's logic, all I had to do was leave a little thread for people to tug at. She'd never been able to do that because he controlled her whole life. But he knew absolutely nothing about me.

'I've really had enough now. Seb, you need to deal with her. Please escort her off these premises for good.'

Seb opened his mouth to speak but I had other plans.

'I know where I know you from,' I said as sternly as I could. 'You were playing with me.'

'Playing with you?' he asked, knitting his brow in a sinister manner.

'Yes. You were playing with me. And Scott. And everyone else. Everybody else.' I really emphasised the last bit. I could be sinister too.

'What are you talking about?'

'Theo, could your computer scan back to 2059, to two days before the branch opened, to see what was on the monitor in Scott's office? I mean the Inspectors' office.'

'What?' Theo asked. The whole team seemed utterly flabbergasted.

'Theo, can you do it or not?'

'I don't... Why would there be something on a monitor before this branch opened?'

'Theo!'

'You've gone too far,' Earl told me. 'You have no right to ask any of this team to do anything.'

'Theo!'

'You were back in 2059 and you're clearly a threat to this facility. Seb, I want her arrested.'

'I'm not sure what crime she's committed,' Seb stuttered. This was far too bizarre even for these time travellers.

'These glitches have escalated since she's been here and then we find out she's been travelling freely through time. We need to restrain her until we can investigate further.'

'I...' Seb didn't know what to do, but his stumbling for words gave me a chance to come up with another probably awful idea. But I was beyond desperate.

'Actually, I'm placing you under arrest,' I said with an obviously trembling voice.

'Chloe, what are you doing?' Seb asked in disbelief.

'I'm making a citizen's arrest. I'm entitled to.'

'Seb, sort this out,' Earl demanded.

'I've seen his timelines,' I said. 'I got access to them by pure chance back in 2059. He's been on dozens of pleasure trips. He's been travelling through time illegally. I've seen it. It's true.'

'This is nonsense,' Earl shouted. 'She's trying to deflect the truth.'

'Fiona showed me,' I said. 'So whether you believe me or not, we need to arrest him until you can investigate further. Because what if I'm right?'

'Seb, I'm warning you. Restrain her now.'

Seb glanced between me and Earl with total confusion.

'What if she is right?' Gloria said, to both my surprise and relief. 'Our job is to maintain law and order. It doesn't matter who it is, if we suspect foul play we're obliged to act upon it.'

'Gloria, please,' Seb said.

'Precisely,' Earl said, pointing to me. 'This woman is clearly guilty of something and I'm asking you as your boss to act upon it.'

'You're the one who's been lying to us,' Gloria said, directly back at Earl. 'We know that for a fact. And I want to know how you found out about Chloe's trips so fast. She was only in 2059 a few minutes ago. Even if the system immediately flagged up an unauthorised journey, it takes an hour to get here from HQ. And that's if you don't hit the London traffic.'

'I was on my way here anyway,' Earl countered.

'That may be so,' Gloria replied, 'but from where I'm standing things don't add up and it's our job to investigate further.'

'I agree,' Barbara said. It was working! 'Chloe has got too much to lose to be making false accusations. If she believes Earl is guilty then it's because she really believes it. The stakes couldn't be any higher.'

'You're all trying to cover it up,' Earl said. 'None of you will have a job by the morning and I'll be bringing my team over to find out exactly what you've all been up to. I'm sure it won't take us long to find the evidence of your deception.'

'See!' I said. 'He's trying to set you up. Remember this. He's guilty. You all know it.'

'Seb,' Gloria pushed. 'Are you going to let him get away with this?'

'I own this facility!' Earl boomed. 'I say what goes on here.'

'You don't own the law, though,' Gloria replied. 'Seb, arrest him.'

Seb hesitated. I could see how hard this was for him.

'I'm leaving now,' Earl said and he turned to walk away. He only had to get out of view and I knew it was all over with.

'No!' I shouted. I leapt towards him and yanked up his sleeve. 'Look everyone!'

He quickly pushed me away, but I saw it. Poking out from the sleeve of his shirt was his rough-looking CPG. The original mock up, not too dissimilar to the one that Fiona had.

'Chloe, you're going too far,' Seb warned.

'Did you see his wrist? He's got his own secret CPG. It was there. Check his wrist! There's your evidence! He's been using it to travel through time illegally.'

'Chloe, that's not possible,' Seb said. 'It's just a watch.'

'Why are you defending him?'

'You'll regret this,' Earl said as he vanished.

'No!' I gasped. What had I done?

'What was that?' Gloria asked.

'Remember this everybody!' I screamed. 'Remember!'

'What have you done?' Theo said.

Everything became blurry. The world had lines across it like a bad signal on an analogue TV and I clenched my fists as if I was trying to hold on to reality; as if somehow gripping on to time would make me remember.

But it was all fading away.

Clarity reappeared in an instant as Earl smacked down to the ground. 'Don't you dare,' Bradley said standing above him and then he smashed Earl's CPG with his fist.

I had to bend over, this was all far too overwhelming.

'This man is a criminal,' Bradley said, full of rage and anguish. 'He's been changing time all around us. We need to get hold of his timelines. He's manipulated us all and he's sent Scott to die.'

'Bradley, no-' Earl started.

'Don't you dare,' Bradley spat down at him. 'Don't you dare.'

THIRTY-SIX

'Theo?' I asked, desperate to bring all of this to a close as fast as humanly possible. 'Can you get to Earl's timelines?'

'No,' Theo replied. 'No one can.'

'I can.' It was Fiona. Just seeing her made me want to sit on the floor and sob. This had to be the end.

Fiona approached Theo's monitor. Everyone's wide eyes followed her and Theo stepped away, too bewildered to even as much as disagree with her.

She flew her hands around his computer and then stood back. 'This will give you all you need,' she said, calmly.

I couldn't believe she was so calm. I was a jittery mess and I'd only been involved for a few days. She'd had years of torture at the expense of that horrible man.

I looked down at him, pinned to the floor under Bradley's unforgiving stare.

'What the hell?' Theo said with a gasp.

'What?' Seb asked.

'Earl has the most complex timeline I've ever seen. I don't even know how it's possible.'

Most of the team circled around Theo's computer. Their shocked faces told me they understood.

'What have you been doing?' Seb asked Earl in utter

disbelief.

'I found out years ago,' Fiona explained. 'He's been travelling through time for his own advantage. I tried to tell you. I tried to tell you so many times. He's been controlling us all.'

'He changed time over and over to make it look like mum had been doing awful things when actually she was trying to warn us,' Bradley added. The sadness in his voice made me feel quite emotional. 'I've seen it all. I've seen...' Bradley turned to Fiona. 'I'm so sorry.'

'How can he have been doing this?' Seb asked.

'For starters, time travel costs nothing. It's just physics,' Fiona said. 'Every one of us has been a victim in his world of deceit.'

'Mum had to fake her death,' Bradley said. 'It was the only way for her to be free of him.'

'I'm sorry I lied to you all,' Fiona added.

No one knew how to respond. It was far too many major revelations in a very short space of time. At least I wasn't the only one overwhelmed for a change.

'It's all here,' Theo said, consulting his monitor. 'Earl has been crossing pinnacle points in time and changing countless events in history. The fallout is monumental. It explains why there were so many glitches in time. It's a mess.'

Earl slowly rose to his feet. He tried to compose himself and keep some dignity but he was met by nothing but disgusted glares.

'There it is,' Theo stated with a chill. 'He's been frequently travelling back to the early 1960s. It looks like he's been infiltrating Parliament, disrupting the campaign to end the death penalty. He's even prevented some high profile murders that gave weight to the abolishment of capital punishment. He's been actively ensuring its existence.'

'Why would you do that?' Seb asked Earl, horrified, but Earl didn't so much as blink.

'Scott was a threat to him,' Fiona said. 'He had suspicions and Earl needed to control it. But I'd say it got a bit out of hand.'

'Don't be ridiculous,' Earl declared. 'Scott is hardly that important. I'd started to put things in motion long before you all set fire to that building. Scott being eliminated was just a fortunate consequence.'

'But why?' Seb was determined to get answers.

'Because we weren't doing enough,' Earl asserted. 'We have the power to correct centuries of wrongs and we just tinker about preventing the odd murder or rape here and there. That was not my vision for this programme. The government hasn't got a clue. Our justice system was much stronger in the early twentieth century. You have to agree. It's been a shambles since. I was trying to bring about change for the better. That's what this branch was supposed to be all about.'

'What gives you the right to go around in history making changes just because you think it's for the best?' Seb roared. It was the first time I'd seen him really lose his temper. 'You're the one who set up the ethics committee to stop that very thing from happening. What's the point if you think you're God?'

'The ethics committee is to control the rest of us,' Fiona said.

'I founded this branch to improve the future for us all,' Earl justified. 'You don't realise half of the changes I've implemented that are now making our streets safer. Don't tell me your life wouldn't be easier if the prisons weren't so packed full or you knew vicious criminals wouldn't one day be set free. Why should they live after the hurt they've caused? We've met them. They take up valuable air that someone else has more right to breathe.'

'Do you really believe that?' Gloria asked, shocked. 'We all work here because we want to make a better world, but none of us have ever believed in killing. We believe in rehabilitation. Two wrongs do not make a right.'

'Rehabilitation is a fantasy,' Earl spat back. 'This branch is about correction. Change the past to shape the future and ensure a safer, brighter world for generations to come. There's no rehabilitation, it's all about correction.'

'And what is correction if it's not about pointing out someone's mistakes and then working with them to bring about a positive outcome,' Gloria seethed. 'Our job is all about rehabilitation.'

Seb pressed his finger to his ear and muttered something I couldn't make out.

'I've made your lives better,' Earl replied. 'You should be thanking me.'

Seb stepped towards Earl. 'No, Earl, you've broken the law. A law that is there to protect everyone and no man is above that. Not even someone as important as you.'

Two men appeared in the doorway and one was carrying handcuffs.

'Earl Stainthorpe,' Seb said, 'I'm arresting you on suspicion of breaching the Time Travel Act of 2058. You do not have to say anything, but it may harm your defence if you do not mention when questioned something which you later rely on in court. Anything you do say may be given in evidence.'

'You have no right to do this,' Earl said as his hands were constrained behind him.

'I think you'll find, Earl, this is exactly what you hired me to do.' Seb stood tall as if daring Earl to challenge him, but Earl said nothing. 'Take him to room six,' Seb instructed the arresting officers. 'I'll be there shortly.'

As Earl was led off he started mumbling under his breath, but he didn't fight too much. It wouldn't have surprised me if he believed he would actually get away with it all. It was quite shocking that he'd been in charge of such a powerful facility for so long.

There was a tense silence after he'd left as the truth sank in. But my mind could only focus on one thing.

'Scott still isn't with us,' I said.

'No, there are many outstanding issues,' Seb replied. 'Our first priority has to be to correct the glitches in time.'

'No, the first priority has to be to bring Scott back.'

'We must restore time as a matter of urgency,' Seb stated. 'We have no way of knowing what damage has been caused and will continue to be caused by Earl's actions. We have no time to lose.'

I knew Seb was right, but it didn't mean I had to agree with him. 'Surely having an extra pair of hands would be a massive help then?'

'I agree,' Gloria said. 'I think we should focus on Scott first. He's one of our own, we need to help him.'

'Our jobs are to help everyone.'

'And no one knows that more than Scott,' Gloria stated in her "don't mess with me" tone.

'So what do we do?' I asked, eager for action. 'Can't we just stop you going back to start the fire now?' I turned to Fiona. 'I've just thought, placing those documents in that office is in your future, isn't it? Does that mean Scott should just reappear?' I was full of hope.

'It's not that simple,' Theo said, regretfully. 'The fire is now deeply ingrained in time. It has to take place and there isn't a viable scenario where Scott isn't arrested.'

'No!' I yelled. How could we have been through all of that only for it to not have helped Scott at all? It wasn't right. It wasn't fair.

'We can't take the risk of causing any more damage to time,' Seb stated.

'Scott can't be arrested. He can't be! You didn't see him. He's trapped back there with no one to help him. He's a good man who doesn't deserve any of this.'

No one said a word. All eyes were on me, but no one knew what to say.

'You need to sort it out!' I insisted, frustrated by their lack of action.

'We will try everything-'

'No. Trying isn't good enough. We need to sort it once

and for all.'

'You know it's not that simple,' Seb replied and I could see his patience dwindling, but I'd had enough of their messing around.

'Why can't it be?'

'Go on then. You tell us,' Seb challenged. 'Tell us how simple it can be.'

I wasn't thinking at all now. Frantic words started leaping out of my mouth. 'Now that all this time changing madness is out the way, can't you all just go back to the room with the man in and help Scott save his life? That way you save the man and Scott. You could leave the Security Guard to take the injured man outside as you come back here. It will be weird that you disappeared, but you all know there's no CCTV in the room where the man gets trapped, so it will just be a strange event. There won't be anyone arrested.'

Again, silence gripped the room. They were all no doubt thinking how ridiculous my idea was, but at least it was an idea. More than they were coming up with.

'Theo?' Seb said, taking me completely by surprise.

'I'm running the scenario now.'

We all waited and I felt strangely uncomfortable. Had I accidentally come up with a brilliant idea? I fought an awkward smile.

'Yes, that could work,' Theo said. 'As long as Fiona still sees Bradley so that the original history stays intact, and as long as you steer clear of your original selves in that time, there's no reason why the plan can't work. It should work well, in fact. The sheer number of people helping speeds everything up quite substantially.'

'Won't they think we're all the arsonists though?' Leanne asked.

Theo shook his head. 'The likelihood is that with no evidence of anyone having been there, other than the Guard's confused statement, an electrical fault will be named as the cause, as per our original scenario. This could change everything.'

I don't think I'd ever felt so smug. I didn't want to ruin it by saying anything, though.

'Well done, Chloe,' Seb said, with a perfectly straight face. He turned to his team. 'I need to deal with Earl now. Gloria, can I leave you in charge?'

'Of course,' she replied. 'I'll keep you updated.'

Seb turned to leave, but before he did he approached me.

'Can I have a quick word outside?'

I nodded but my heart sank. He was obviously going to tell me off. I decided that whatever was coming my way, I was going to stand my ground.

We stepped into the room opposite. It had green walls and was virtually empty except for four chairs in the middle. Seb closed the door behind us.

'You never fail to surprise me, Miss Noble,' he said. 'Which is quite an achievement as very few people ever surprise me.'

I opened my mouth, ready to defend myself, but I wasn't sure whether this was in fact praise.

'I'd like to offer you a job.'

I think the world around me actually stopped when he said those words.

'This branch needs someone like you. I was thinking you could work with Theo. I've done my research. You're a data analyst, and a very good one at that. This team could use a brain like yours. That's not to mention it would mean you could be with Scott. What are your thoughts?'

The levels of excitement bursting through me gave me my answer. 'Yes! That would be amazing! Are you sure?'

'Absolutely.'

No more crappy job in 2018. No more back-stabbing from horrible colleagues. No more lonely, black and white life. I was now on the team of a secret, future, time travelling police force.

'I'm not a policeman. Or woman. Does that matter?' I

asked, searching for the inevitable problem in this superb idea.

'Of course not. You'll have to go through a lot of training, but you have a skill set we need. That matters more.'

'Thank you, thank you, thank you, thank you.' I didn't mean to, but I hugged Seb. As soon as I threw my arms around him it instantly felt wrong and awkward, but I was committed. I had to see it through.

He had a small, somewhat embarrassed smile as I pulled away.

'What shall I do, then?' I asked, ready to move on as fast as humanly possible.

'Are you happy to hit the ground running?'

'Always.'

'Then let's get you set up next to Theo.'

I didn't hear exactly what Seb said to Theo before he left to visit Earl, but Theo nodded warmly and enthusiastically and then Dom brought me a chair so that I could sit by Theo's very hard working monitor. Most of the other members of the team were elsewhere and it gave me a few quiet moments to absorb everything that was happening. I couldn't wait to tell Scott. We were finally going to be together!

'Technology has changed a lot since 2018, so why don't you just observe for now,' Theo said as I got comfortable. 'Get used to the speed of the system. I'll explain things as we go along.'

I took in the screen before me and I was immediately overwhelmed. Theo's monitor was like a rainbow of overly complex data. Boxes were dotted all over the screen full of graphs and charts, and rolling information popped up in random places. I didn't have time to read one thing before about twelve other bits of information were demanding my attention.

'You'll get used to it,' Theo said, spotting my fear.

'Are we ready?' Gloria said, entering the room with the rest of the team behind her.

'I intercepted Earl's incoming communication and found that Fiona had sent him a ransom note,' Theo said. 'That's how he knew about the documents and why he sent the team back to 2014. He never had any evidence that the documents were real, though. So that being the case, we knew we could skip a large proportion of Fiona's plan. She's back sending the ransom note now as per the original history, but this time there's no need to involve the documents at all.'

As if on cue, Fiona reappeared from the module.

'Step one is sorted,' she said.

Theo whizzed around his monitor. The text was so tiny and it moved so fast, I couldn't make out any of what he was doing.

'Yep, yep, we're all on track,' he said, as if the orange in front of him made perfect sense. I guess it did to him.

'The only thing you need to do now is ensure that Bradley sees you,' Gloria said to Fiona.

'I'm sending you back to five minutes before the team landed the first time, giving you the chance to get in place, under Bradley's guidance,' Theo said. 'You both have to get it right. It's the main catalyst to us understanding what happened.'

Just as I was trying to get my head around everything Theo was explaining, he pointed to the screen for my attention. 'This section here links to each individual CPG. It's all a coded system. I know you'll pick it up in no time. We work on a geographic coordinate system, with an addition at the end that deciphers things like floors of a building. It allows us to be precise with everything we do.'

My head was ready to explode.

'It's the perfect first example for you to see as all of the time travellers are going back. Even Gloria.'

'We need as many hands as we can get,' Gloria said.

'You'll be landing in the room ten seconds after the

phone call to the Security Guard,' Theo instructed everyone. 'That's twenty seconds earlier than you landed before, when you started the fire. So you'll be there before Scott.'

As Theo picked up the CPGs to hand them out, I gave up even trying to follow what was happening.

'One of you needs to ensure that you reset Scott's CPG so that he travels back to this time and not the original time. I don't need to tell you about the dangers of him travelling back to when he was supposed to return.'

'I'll do it!' Leanne bellowed eagerly.

'Good, thanks,' Theo said, before I saw him glance at me.

Let her have her moment, I thought.

The team headed into the modules and I instinctively held my breath.

I again wanted a sound or gush or something to tell me they'd gone, but nothing happened. They went in and then those of us left studied Theo's monitor.

Bands of colour swirled around his screen with text rolling up the side, like very detailed and very fast credits at the end of a movie. All I could do was sit back and admire how fantastic it looked, and hope that one day soon I'd understand it.

Within a few minutes a door opened. It was Bradley, with Fiona just a second behind him.

I sighed as they smiled and nodded. Their roles had clearly gone well. They headed over to look at whatever stats we were monitoring and we all waited eagerly for the man of the moment to return.

Another few minutes dragged on and I could feel myself getting shaky. I was both nervous about what else could go wrong and also over-excited about telling Scott the good news.

A door opened and I nearly collapsed. It was Barbara. Gloria appeared just milliseconds later.

We waited for the final two to arrive, but nothing happened.

'Theo?' Gloria said as it started to become concerning.

'They've returned,' Theo said, studying the gibberish on his screen. 'But they've landed somewhere else. They're in Leanne's room.'

I couldn't help my gasp. 'Can she do that? How can she do that?'

'You can land anywhere,' Theo replied. 'It's just best practice to land in the module. They could be leaving anywhere, from any situation, at any time, so it's good to know exactly what you'll get when you return.'

'Just not if you're with Leanne! Where's her room?' I demanded to know.

Theo turned to Gloria, but her eyes were already fixed on me. 'I think it's best we let them work through this together,' she said.

'But...' I didn't really have an argument. I wanted to run out of there and track down Leanne's room, but I didn't know what I'd say. Or do. Could I get away with slapping a colleague? It didn't seem like a very police person thing to do.

'Can someone tell me what's going on?' Scott said, appearing at the door of the module room. It was a wonderful sight. He looked far from impressed but he still oozed his long missed natural charisma. I wanted to hug him.

'Scott!' Leanne wailed, chasing after him. She appeared at his side. 'I told you, I'll fill you in on everything. Let's go for a drink.'

'Leanne, I think Seb should be the one to do the de-brief,' Gloria said. 'Don't you?'

'De-brief?' Scott asked. 'Why do I get the feeling I've missed a lot?' His eyes caught me, sitting next to Theo.

'Seb's with Earl,' Leanne whined. 'Scott needs some answers now. We'll just go for a quick drink. We have loads to catch up on.' She grabbed his arm.

'It's not the right time now, Leanne,' he said.

'Why not?'

'Because it's not.'

She tugged some more at his arm, growing in her insistence and annoyance. 'Come on. I've missed you.'

'Leanne, leave it,' Scott said.

'Surely you want to know what's happened to you?'

'Yes, and I'm going to find out in Seb's de-brief.'

'But we haven't had any proper time together lately.'

'Proper time together?' Scott asked. He glanced at her quickly before turning his attention to me, as if he was waiting to see my reaction.

'Don't look at her!' Leanne barked. 'We know the truth. We all know the truth.'

'What truth?' Scott asked, the conviction in his voice dwindling.

'I'm your real life, Scott. I'm the girl you come back to.'

I didn't know what to do. I was fascinated to see how this would play out. What was Leanne thinking?

'Not now, Leanne,' Scott said, quietly.

'We need to talk!'

He sighed. 'Maybe we do. But not now.'

'Chloe hasn't eaten in a while, Scott,' Gloria said. 'Perhaps you could escort her to the canteen.'

'Of course,' Scott replied.

I was so pleased with Gloria. I could see us being very good friends. I stood up as Leanne shouted, 'No! She doesn't need your help. She's been wandering about quite happily on her own since you've been gone.'

This halted Scott. 'What do you mean? How long have I been gone?' he asked.

'Two days,' Leanne said.

'Is that all?' I virtually spat. I couldn't help it.

'I've been gone for two days?' Scott asked, his shock almost mirroring my own.

'Come and have a drink with me. I can fill you in on bits,' Leanne said, tugging at Scott's arm again.

'Please leave me alone,' he practically begged.

'Why?' she whined. 'Why won't you come for a drink

with me?'

'Because I don't want to.'

'But why?'

'Because I don't.'

'Why? Give me one good reason.'

'Because I don't want to be with you!' he snapped.

There was an awkward silence before her eyes pierced. 'This is to do with her, isn't it. We all know, Scott. We all know you've been shagging around in the past.'

'I think that's enough,' Gloria ordered.

Scott turned to me as if he wanted to explain.

'Everyone knows everything,' I said confidently. 'But it doesn't matter. Seb's found a way for us to be together.' I glanced at Theo who smiled reassuringly. 'He's offered me a job. And I've accepted. I'm going to be working with Theo. How great is that!'

I wanted to jump around with excitement, but my feet didn't budge as I clocked Scott's fierce expression.

'What?' Scott stated.

'We're going to be working together,' I clarified.

'Absolutely not. Chloe, you are not taking a job here.

THIRTY-SEVEN

All I could do was breathe slowly in an attempt to halt my tears. It was heartbreaking.

'I think we need to talk,' Scott said.

I nodded. I couldn't look at anyone else. What a way to get dumped!

I stepped out the module room and headed straight into the green room opposite. I didn't want to delay this conversation a second longer.

'Why don't you want me to be with you?' I mumbled.

'I do. Of course I do.'

'You just said you didn't.'

'No, I didn't mean that. I meant I can't ask you to give up your life to join me here. I won't.'

'But you're not asking me. It's what I want to do.'

'Is it really, though? Because I know you'd regret it.'

'I would never regret being with you.'

'You'd regret never seeing your family again.'

'I could pop back.'

Scott shook his head. 'It couldn't work like that.'

'No, it could,' I replied, desperately wanting him to see. 'We found out that time travel doesn't cost anything. I could take journeys home whenever I wanted. Seb will tell you in the de-brief.'

Scott sighed. 'If you were to move to the future with me then you'd have to sacrifice your old life. There could be no other way. Think about it. How could it work if one moment you've seemingly vanished off the face of the planet and then the next day you pop up again out of the blue as if everything is normal? You live in a world of limitless communication. How are you going to explain that you're still around but you're never going to be in touch?'

'You did it.'

'It would never have lasted long term, and we both know it. Besides, one of the reasons you accepted it was because you knew no different with me. But I know how much you speak to your mum, and barely a day goes by when you're not swapping gossip with Freya. How are you going to explain that you're not going to be contactable anymore but you'll still see them infrequently?'

'I don't know.'

'Precisely.'

'I could tell them the truth,' I stated, only to meet the very insistent shake of Scott's head.

'If anyone was to find out that time travel is possible then it could potentially have huge implications,' Scott explained. 'It's dangerous enough you knowing.'

'We could trust my family,' I argued but Scott just shook his head again.

'Seb would never allow it.'

'Well, what else could I tell them?' I asked.

'That's the problem,' Scott replied. 'That's why you can't do this.'

I searched my brain for an answer but I couldn't think of any reasonable way to live in the future and still keep in touch with my home. There was no way to win. 'So I have to choose between you or my family?' I asked. 'There's no way around it?'

Scott suddenly put his finger to his ear. 'Yes, we're in room four.'

'Who's that?' I asked, but before he had a chance to answer, Seb walked in.

'I understand there's some tension here?' Seb said.

'Let me go back with her,' Scott said before I could even open my mouth. 'Let me go back to 2018.'

I was stunned. 'You're going to give up your life to be with me?'

Scott kept his eyes on Seb. 'I'm not happy. You know I haven't been happy for a while. The only thing that's given me anything to smile about in what seems like forever is Chloe. She's all I want.'

I felt my heart flutter at his words.

'I don't belong here,' he continued. 'The main reason I joined this branch is because I wanted to be back in time. So let me go back in time.'

Seb shook his head.

'You'd give all this up to start a life with me in 2018?' I asked Scott.

He nodded. 'With no question. I've thought about it a lot, ever since we first met; although I never thought it would be possible. But you being here has to have changed things.'

'But what about what you'd be sacrificing?' I asked.

'What would I be sacrificing? If I never saw my family again they probably wouldn't even notice. And my friends consist of my team. I'd be sad not to see them again but at least they'd know where I was. I've given up everything for this job, it's about time I got something in return.'

'I thought you loved your job.'

'He did,' Seb said. 'I know what you're saying, Scott. I've seen the change in you. I could see the job slowly eating away at you, and I saw the light in you return about six months ago, after that first trip to 2018. I understand. I do.'

'Then you'll allow me to go back?' Scott asked.

Seb shook his head, regretfully. 'I can't. I want to but I can't. It's against the law. One man has been arrested today for using time travel to his own advantage. I can't arrest him and then willingly allow you to do the same thing.'

'It's hardly the same thing!' I argued. 'Scott wants to set up a life in a different time not change the world because of his warped sense of right and wrong.'

'It's not my place to decide when the law counts and when it doesn't,' Seb replied. 'It's my job to uphold it, and I will do that.'

'But surely you can see-'

'Chloe, I've said my piece. That's officially where I stand.'

I stared down at the floor and took a deep breath. There had to be a happy ending somewhere!

'However,' Seb added giving me some hope. I flicked my head right back up. 'There are many things that go on without my knowledge. If one of my Inspectors disappears one day then that's just the way it is. What could I do? I've made it clear where I officially stand, but I can't be watching you twenty-four hours a day.'

I felt too nervous to smile. Was he really saying what I thought he was?

'I mean I'd have to start a full investigation,' he continued. 'I couldn't be in charge of this team and not investigate your sudden disappearance. You understand?'

Scott nodded.

'And the first place I'd have no choice but to look is 2018. The investigation will find out about your relationship. My job would be on the line if I tried to cover it up.'

'Wouldn't you just track my CPG journey?' Scott asked, a little confused.

'He can only track government issued devices,' I blurted out.

Scott looked at me and I could tell he wasn't following.

'I may have heard that other devices exist,' I shrugged.

'Yes, I heard that,' Seb added.

'Okay, but even if you can't track the journey, there will still be a footprint,' Scott said. 'You can't escape that.'

'No you can't,' Seb agreed. 'And the first place we'd search for your footprint is 2018.'

'And the second place?' I nudged.

'Well, if he wasn't in 2018 with you, then the next obvious place to look would be the twentieth century. You are a bit obsessed with it, Scott.'

'I wouldn't say obsessed,' Scott said.

'Oh I would,' Seb insisted. 'Totally infatuated. We'd have to search your room as part of the investigation. It would put the 1960s right at the top of the target list.'

'Definitely not 2019,' I said, remembering how Fiona had hidden her footsteps.

'How much of 2018 would Theo hypothetically scan?' Scott asked, catching up.

'I'd be surprised if he looked any further than six months after Chloe's return. Whenever that is.'

'Right,' Scott said. 'So not much of 2019 at all. Interesting. While I have you here, Seb, could I request some annual leave? After I've finished off my current cases, of course.'

'What cases do you need to finish?' I asked, worried that this might be a potential barrier.

Scott thought for a moment. 'I suppose the only outstanding one that I'd have to complete is Donna.'

'No you don't,' I said quickly. 'I'm doing that. I agreed with Seb.'

'You're completing my assignment?' Scott asked with astonishment.

'I made a deal with Seb. He let me go back in time to see you in prison if I agreed to finish your assignment and help the team.'

Scott stopped dead still. 'Prison?'

'We should probably go to my office for a de-brief,' Seb said. 'I can explain there too how Miss Noble will be finishing your assignment.'

Scott seemed as overwhelmed as I usually felt. 'Right. So it's all sorted?'

'I'm running through scenarios,' I said, desperate to sound like I knew what I was talking about. I saw a flash of a smirk through Scott's bewilderment. I was obviously amusing again, but it was nice.

'Shall we get on with the de-brief?' Seb said. 'Then we can arrange that time off for you.'

Scott nodded. It was so rare to see him lost for words. I didn't like it.

Scott and Seb headed off to his office and I headed back to my room. I felt tired. Extremely tired. I was more than ready for a lie down.

I didn't think I'd sleep. Not only was I still rattled from the enormity of recent events, but I was now overcome with joy, knowing that I was going to get to spend the rest of my life with the only man I'd ever truly loved. But, despite all that, as soon as my head hit the pillow I was out.

THIRTY-EIGHT

Scott had woken me up after his very long and revealing de-brief with Seb. We talked through everything that had happened. It had been a massive few days. But it had also brought us so much closer together.

We fell asleep that night in each other's arms, and awoke early the next day. There was so much we needed to do.

We spent the day working with Theo and Logistics to plan my assignment with Donna, and to secretly get Scott ready for his new life.

I was insistent that they find a way for Scott to still do a job he felt passionate about, although he'd have to keep a low profile as well. We were warned over and over about minimising our impact on time. That's when Theo came up with the idea of him becoming a private investigator. A low profile was a must with the job and he still got to use his skills. Scott was thrilled.

After running through many scenarios, it appeared that the only quick and easy way for Scott to build a brand new life for himself was to literally start from scratch. They said he was going to have to fake amnesia. I was going to "find him" on a bench and take him to hospital, where he'd have to get support from the authorities. No one would ever be able to find out who he was, but they'd have to support him anyway in starting again. It seemed the only logical way for Scott to just appear from nowhere with no plausible back story.

Next we had to tackle Donna. Theo's scenarios showed that if I told Donna Scott had been seeing both of us then she'd be devastated to the point of not trusting any man for a while. She'd had a rocky track record anyway, so this would push her to steer clear from men for the foreseeable future.

I was quite horrified by the idea but Scott assured me it was better than twenty years in prison for a crime she'd hadn't committed, and Theo added that it was her best chance of a happy ending.

I was dreading being the one to tell her, but I kept in my mind the positives and I knew I'd be able to do it.

Maybe I'd get Freya to help me.

After hours of preparation, Scott and I shared one final night in 2086 together; this time in his room. I helped him pack his records and a few sentimental pieces, and he told me dozens of stories about his time in the 1960s, working through the memorabilia across his walls. It was fascinating.

We fell asleep in his very comfortable bed and I dreamt of a brand new life. Everything from that moment was going to be different. And I couldn't wait.

The whole team was present in the module room as we arrived there ready to depart the next morning. I was teary as I watched each of them hug Scott, tell him lovely things and say their goodbyes. Even when Leanne grasped him tightly and declared her undying love, it didn't annoy me. Scott handled it beautifully, giving her just the right number of compliments so as to be kind but not return the sentiment.

'Thank you for all your help, Chloe,' Seb said, shaking my hand. 'I wish you the best of luck with Donna. We'll be checking things at our end and we can always come to your aid if we feel you need it.'

'She won't,' Scott chipped in, full of certainty. My mind flicked back to Fiona saying how dreadful I was at spy work and my stomach churned. But this was different. Definitely different. This was girl talk. I could manage that.

'It was good to work with you,' Theo said, giving me a hug. 'Scott's a lucky bloke.'

'Thank you for all your help,' I replied. 'Scott's lucky to have had all of you around him.'

'Are you ready?' Bradley asked. The plan was that Bradley would drop me back in my flat in the early hours, seconds after they'd collected Scott when I'd disappeared with his CPG. Then Bradley would return leaving me to get on with my life.

At the same time, Scott was going to be "doing maintenance work" on another module where he would strangely disappear without any of them having any clue where he could have gone.

Fiona couldn't have been happier to give him her CPG. I secretly suspected she'd just build another one anyway, but her support was still appreciated.

He was travelling straight to 1st May 2019 - a clear six months after my return - to land in the hotel where we met. Although he was leaving this room to instantly join me, I couldn't help the paranoia that something would go wrong.

I'd insisted that we meet at the hotel. Theo had confirmed that it was still very much open for business in May 2019, but he'd refused to tell me anything about my own life. Therefore I had no way to know if I was going to get kicked out of my flat before May, or I'd have to leave London for some unforeseen reason. I knew if that happened I might never find Scott. Therefore, to put my mind at rest, we agreed to meet outside the disabled toilets in the hotel in York where we'd met for the very first time. At least we both definitely knew it and we knew it would be there.

Over the past week, I'd been so close to losing Scott so many times, until we were actually together properly, I wasn't taking anything for granted.

'I'm ready,' I said. I hugged Scott tightly, as if it was the last time I'd ever see him. There was a part of me that really believed that could be the case. I knew it was silly. He was going now. He was leaving at the exact same time as I was. In reality, he should be the worried one as I'd have to wait six months to see him again. Anything could happen in six months.

I stopped myself from thinking any more.

'Don't worry, Pepps,' Scott said, kissing my forehead, reading my mind as usual. 'I'll see you soon. For me, I'll see you in about a minute.'

'I'm going to miss you so much,' I said, fighting tears. 'The next six months are going to be hell. You'll really be there, won't you?'

'I'm leaving with you now. What do you think's going to happen?'

'Is your CPG set properly?'

'Chloe, I've done this hundreds of times. Trust me, I'll be there.'

'I love you.'

'I love you, too. Now get back home, kick ass at work, get some good stuff in the fridge and I'll see you very soon.'

'Okay. See you soon.'

I kissed him passionately, making sure it was a kiss that neither of us would forget for a while, and then I nodded to Bradley.

I stepped in the module and Bradley followed me in, before Theo closed the door behind us.

'Are you in your module now?' I shouted out to Scott.

'Yes I am. I'm doing that maintenance work that Seb has asked me to do. Now stop worrying.'

'Okay. See you soon.'

'Don't worry, Chloe,' Bradley said. 'I've never seen Scott happier than when he's with you. He'll be there. I'd like to see something stop him.'

'Thank you.'

'Now grab my hand. I know you know how to do it,' he smirked.

I found his hand and clenched it tightly.

'Ready?' he asked.

'Take me home,' I said, feeling my heart pound erratically.

Not a second had gone by when my flat appeared around us. We were in my living room and it was exactly how I remembered it. I saw Scott had necked half the bottle of wine, but other than that nothing was different. Although I wasn't sure how it could be.

'This is a nice place,' Bradley said, scanning his surroundings.

'Thank you.'

'This is where Scott will be living then.'

'Yes. I guess.'

'Good to know. He'll be far happier here than he ever was at the branch. Keep that in mind.'

'I hope so.'

'I know so.'

Bradley hugged me. 'It's been good getting to know you, Chloe.' He paused and looked at the carpet. 'I'll always be grateful for how you helped my family. You...'

'It was my pleasure.'

'Thank you.'

'Look after yourself.'

'You too. And look after Scott. And don't worry about Donna. If you really hit problems, one of us can always come and help.'

I smiled. 'In the nicest possible way, I hope you don't have to. I have some pride, you know.'

'Yes, I know. Just don't worry whatever happens.'

'Thanks, Bradley.'

'I'll see you then.'

'See you. Take care.'

Bradley smiled at me one last time before he fiddled with his CPG and instantly vanished.

The emptiness quickly became unnerving. I sat on my sofa as if I was mourning a great loss.

Six months was a really long time.

I took a deep breath and told myself that this moment was the longest time until I saw Scott again and every minute that passed from now on was a minute closer to me seeing him. It would get easier, just as it always did.

But six months?

I stood up. I knew it was the early hours of the morning but I wasn't tired. It was mid-morning to me. This was going to be weird jetlag.

I took myself to bed to at least try to rest before I had to face work tomorrow, when I realised that after years of dreading every day I was actually feeling unusually confident about what lay ahead.

I'd been through so much over the past week, a bit of silly office politics suddenly seemed incredibly insignificant. For the first time, I wasn't feeling sick about going into work. I didn't feel the need to give myself a pep talk just to get through the day. I was actually feeling stronger than ever and it was a very welcome sensation.

Over the next few weeks I knew I was a different person. From the first second I stepped in the office, it dawned on me that "playing the game" wasn't the only way to get noticed.

I began my new approach by speaking my mind in a meeting. I didn't have an agenda, I wasn't trying to get one over anyone else, I just had an idea that I thought would be good for the company. And it turned out I helped to save them a bucket load of money.

After years of working at that wretched company, people were finally starting to know my name and my life was changing.

I'd met up with Freya during my first week back. I'd

needed to ask her to come to Harrogate with me to confront Scott's "other girlfriend". I couldn't do it alone, I knew that, but when I sat there with Freya I also realised that I couldn't have my best friend thinking badly of my boyfriend. Especially when he'd done nothing wrong.

So – knowing that I couldn't tell Freya the whole truth - I told her that I'd found out that Scott was actually an undercover agent who had been investigating Donna for links with a criminal underworld. Of course Freya thought I was nuts. It didn't even help when I said he was on one last assignment before setting up his own private detective agency so he could properly be with me. At that point I think she was actually pitying me.

As I tried to convince her, I realised I was making Scott out to be some sort of modern day *Dick Tracy*. But that was an easier picture to paint than a futuristic time travelling policeman. At least when Scott did start his private investigation company, Freya would have to believe me. I wouldn't be so pitiful then.

Whatever her beliefs, though, being the good friend that she was, she joined me on a jaunt to Harrogate the following weekend where we got Angela to introduce us to Donna.

Donna was attractive but stern looking, and her manners were quite brash. I wouldn't want to mess with her. She was completely different to me.

We went out for lunch and I forced myself to break the bad news to her that Scott was seeing both of us. I was terrified that she was going to punch me.

Of course at first she didn't believe me. I showed her texts from Scott to prove what I was saying, but I still faced hostility. It was only when I showed her a picture of the two of us arm in arm at the top of the London Eye, looking very much in love, that she eventually started to crack.

She shared her correspondence from Scott in return and told me how they were going to get married. She insisted that she knew Scott loved her.

Her hard exterior continued to crumble away as she

questioned over and over how such a genuine man could have been leading a double life.

She tried to get Scott on the phone then and there to have it out with him. But his phone just went to voicemail. She left him angry messages, sure that one day he'd call her back to explain, but I knew that phone was now in 2086 and it was never going to be answered. She was never going to hear from him again.

At first her reaction had made me uneasy with jealousy, but by the time we needed to leave, I just felt sorry for her.

To my great surprise, as we said our goodbyes, Donna hugged me. I was so relieved that she hadn't taken it out on me. I sobbed with her as we comforted each other. I knew she was going to keep calling Scott. I knew she was going to look for that explanation; for that closure. I also knew she was never going to get it.

There was no doubt it was going to be a long time before she'd be able to trust any man again. It was clear she wouldn't heal from this quickly.

As we headed back to the railway station, I felt awful. All I could do was remind myself that it would save Donna's life. Her heartache was better than a prison sentence. Surely if she could have chosen, she would have chosen this.

As the next few weeks rolled by, waiting for Scott became a little easier as I threw myself into my work. I needed to take proper control of my life. And it paid dividends. Just before Christmas I got my first ever promotion. It turned out being strong minded and being true to yourself was well worth it. I let the office politics bounce off me and I got on with my job without fear. And every time I wavered, I remembered how I'd called Seb an arsehole and I'd saved Scott from the death penalty. If I could do that, I could do anything.

Christmas was difficult as it should have been my first Christmas with Scott. To stop myself dwelling on it, I maximised my social life. I spent a lot of time with friends,

I attended my first work Christmas party, and I enjoyed lots of time with my family. By New Year I was exhausted, and then the January blues hit me hard, not least because I was very aware that I still had four months to go before I'd see Scott again.

And those four months really dragged by. The wait was torturous. By the time 1st May eventually came around, not only was I unbearably excited, but I'd also totally convinced myself that it was too good to be true and there was no way that Scott was actually going to be there.

I took a few days off work, as 1st May turned out to be a Wednesday, and I booked us a room at the hotel for the night.

I got the train up to York first thing and arrived an hour earlier than we were supposed to meet. I was lucky that I could check in to the room and I waited on the bed catching up on Facebook, feeling sure that time had stopped.

Eventually midday approached, our agreed meeting time, and I made my way down to the disabled toilets.

For a stupid moment I found myself wondering if he might have changed. But of course he would be in exactly the same state as the last time I saw him. I was six months older but he would be exactly the same. That was very strange to comprehend.

Had I changed? What if he didn't like me now?

I knew with the exception of a few trims of my hair, I was exactly the same too, but that didn't stop me fretting.

I was trembling by the time I reached the toilet door. It was vacant so I knew he wasn't in there. All I could do was wait. I took a deep breath and tried to calm myself.

I consulted my watch and saw it was bang on midday.

He wasn't there. That was it. He wasn't coming. I knew it.

Six months I'd waited. Six months I'd put my life on hold waiting for him. And now he wasn't even there.

I wanted to cry. What was I going to tell Freya and my parents? I'd said he'd been travelling for work but he'd finally handed in his notice and we could finally be together. I'd told them that I'd heard from him loads. And now I'd have to say we'd broken up.

He still wasn't there.

Nothing else could explain it. He was due to land at midday. It was now two minutes past.

I'd lost him forever.

'Long time no see,' Scott said, approaching me.

It was a choice between collapsing with relief or hugging him tightly. The latter was always going to win.

I threw my arms around him and held him closely to me.

'Where were you?' I asked, the panic evident in my voice.

'What do you mean?'

'You were supposed to land at midday.'

'I did land at midday. In the garden. I couldn't just materialise out of nowhere in the middle of a corridor.'

I sighed with relief. Of course.

'So you've missed me then?' he asked with a huge grin.

I kissed him and realised I'd missed him more than I'd ever want to admit.

I looked up at his face, still with my arms wrapped around him. 'It's been a long and winding road waiting for you to get back from across the universe, but I guess all you need is love.'

Scott laughed. 'You've been listening to The Beatles then?'

'Still eight days a week.'

He laughed some more. 'Be honest, how long have you been practising that for?'

He knew me too well. There was no way I could ever string all those song titles together on the spot.

'Only since February,' I shrugged.

'Well, I love it. And I love you.'

'I love you too.' I kissed him again. 'I've booked us a room for the night. I thought it might be nice. We have a lot to catch up on.'

'I suppose we do. Although nothing new has happened

to me in the two minutes since I last saw you.'

'Well I've got tons to share. Does that mean you'll have to listen to me for a change?' I smirked.

'I guess so. I can't wait.'

'Good.'

We kissed again just as a man walked past. He didn't seem impressed with our public display of heavy petting. We both sniggered at his disapproving tut.

'I think that was a hint to get a room,' Scott said.

'It's lucky we've got one then.'

'It seems nonsensical travelling all that way when there's a vacant room right next to us.'

Scott pulled me towards the disabled toilet with a lascivious grin.

'I'm not kissing you in there,' I said.

'Oh Pepps, I don't know whether it's not seeing you for a whole two minutes or whether it's knowing that we're finally going to be together, but I've never wanted you more.'

His lips pressed to mine as he closed the disabled toilet door behind me. With words as sweet as that, who was I to argue.

ABOUT THE AUTHOR

Lindsay is a British author who lives in Warwickshire with her husband and cat. She's had a lifelong passion for writing, starting off as a child when she used to write stories about the Fraggles of Fraggle Rock.

Knowing there was nothing else she'd rather study, she did her degree in writing and has now turned her favourite hobby into a career.

Lindsay is also the author of:

- The *Bird* Trilogy, a supernatural love story full of magical twists and turns.

- *Emmett the Empathy Man*, a comic tale about a superhero who comes to life with disastrous results.

- *In the Blood*, a science fiction love story about two people who could never have possibly met yet know everything about each other.

All of her books are available on Amazon.

9 781999 585532